LIZ MARCH

Owen Marshall has written, or edited, twenty-five books. He has held Fellowships at the universities of Canterbury and Otago, and in Menton, France. In 2000 he received the ONZM for Services to Literature in the New Year Honours, and in the same year his novel *Harlequin Rex* won the Montana New Zealand Book Awards Deutz Medal for Fiction. Marshall is an adjunct professor at the University of Canterbury, which awarded him the honorary degree of Doctor of Letters in 2002.

Owen
Marshall

the
Larnachs

VINTAGE

A VINTAGE BOOK published by Random House New Zealand, 18 Poland Road, Glenfield, Auckland, New Zealand

For more information about our titles go to www.randomhouse.co.nz

A catalogue record for this book is available from the National Library of New Zealand

Random House New Zealand is part of the Random House Group
New York   London   Sydney   Auckland   Delhi   Johannesburg

First published 2011

© 2011 Owen Marshall

The moral rights of the author have been asserted

ISBN 978 1 86979 497 2

Cover design: Carla Sy
Text design: Megan van Staden

Front cover illustration: Trevillion Images Heather Evans Smith
Endpapers: Jan Van Son (Dutch b.1658, d. 1718), 'Roses, Honeysuckle and other flowers in a sculpted vase', oil on canvas, Collection of Christchurch Art Gallery Te Puna o Waiwhetu

Printed in New Zealand by Printlink

For William, Lydia, Sophie and Christian

This is not a biography and not a history.
It is a novel: the imaginative interpretation of
a situation experienced by real people.

Acknowledgements

My chief source of family material was *King of the Castle: A Biography of William Larnach* by Fleur Snedden (David Bateman, 1997), great-great-granddaughter of William Larnach. She in turn acknowledges Hardwicke Knight's *The Ordeal of William Larnach* (Allied Press, 1981).

I am grateful to Michelanne Forster for generously allowing me to read material she gathered in the course of writing her successful play, *Larnach*, and to Joanna Woods for her book *Facing the Music: Charles Baeyertz and the Triad* (Otago University Press, 2008), which contains much concerning the musical tastes of the period.

Other material is taken from the letter books of W.J.M. Larnach 1884–1898, held on microfilm in Dunedin's Hocken Collections, and from contemporary newspaper reports.

I am grateful, too, for the encouragement and support of my editor, Anna Rogers, and publisher, Harriet Allan.

One's real life is often the life that one does not lead.
— Oscar Wilde

The Larnach & de Bathe Brandon Families

William James Mudie Larnach (1833–1898)

married Eliza Jane Guise (1842–1880) in 1859

Donald Guise (1860–1910)

Kate Emily (1862–1891)

Douglas John (1863–1949)

Colleen Shawn (1865–1951)

Alice Jane (1868–1942)

Gladys Beryl (1878–1900)

married Mary Cockburn Alleyne (1849–1887), half-sister to
Eliza Guise, in 1882

married Constance de Bathe Brandon (1856–1942) in 1891

Alfred de Bathe Brandon (1809–1886)

married Constance Mary Anne Brandon (no relation, d. 1841)

in 1840

Henry Eustace (1840–1886)

married Lucy Poole in 1854

Alfred (1854–1938)

Constance (1856–1942)

Charles (1860–1942)

Sarah

Fanny

Annie

Hugh (1868–1923)

Prologue

The *Wellington Post* reports that the nuptials of the Hon. W.J.M. Larnach, C.M.G., and Miss Constance de Bathe Brandon, daughter of the late Hon. Alfred de B. Brandon, M.L.C., was solemnised in St. Paul's Pro-cathedral this afternoon (January 27). The bride was attended by Misses F. and A. Brandon, her sisters, Misses F. and L. Brandon, the bride's nieces, and Misses Doris Johnston and Cecilia Higginson. Dr Cahill acted as the bridegroom's best man, and the bride was given away by her brother, Mr A. de B. Brandon. The ceremony was performed by the Rev. J.C. Andrew, M.A., assisted by the Rev. J. Still. There was a large congregation present, consisting principally of ladies, who naturally took a great interest in the affair. The wedding party, at the conclusion of the ceremony, returned to the residence of the mother of the bride, where a large number of family friends partook of an early afternoon tea. Mr and Mrs Larnach will spend their honeymoon on the West Coast of the North Island.

Otago Witness, *5 February 1891*

*C*onstance de Bathe Brandon married in summer. Curious people, mainly women, gathered in the sunlight and breeze outside the pale wooden walls of St Paul's with its modest slate spire. The lawn was green and freshly mown, the small pohutukawa, still with a few last flowers, stood in close, dark foliage by the picket fence, beyond which carriage horses fidgeted. Thorndon Road dipped down towards Wellington Harbour, and steep, tree-stumped hills overlooked the city.

The interior of the Gothic church was dim because of the dark, native timbers — totara, matai, rimu and kauri — and the buttress arches rose to the high ceiling. As the guests waited, one man complained to his wife that it was like being inside a giant walnut, but the wonderful hues of the stained glass windows, especially the sapphire blue, shimmered in the gloom, and the Reverend Andrew's white surplice and stole were richly tinctured by the colours cast. The guests witnessed Alfred give his sister away, although it was rumoured that he considered she was marrying someone rather beneath the family's position. The bride's voice, however, was clear and definite when she made her vows.

When the bridal party came from the cathedral, both those invited and the gawpers could make inventory of everything external: details of dress, deportment, the abundance of flowers, the quality of jewellery. Feelings were not so unequivocally displayed, although excitement showed on many female faces. Every marriage is a victory for women. It was a large wedding, socially significant, and most guests showed their pleasure in being included by slightly self-conscious poses as they stood around the church front, and slight distraction in their conversations as they watched the wedded pair. Constance's cream satin wedding dress was figured with sprigs of lily of the valley, and her pale jacket had a high collar and puffed sleeves. She wore flowers in her light brown hair, and her posture was very upright, her gaze direct. That she was small, neatly formed, was emphasised by the almost portly figure of the groom, an older man with drooping moustache and balding head, but considerable assurance none the less.

One woman observer, whose natural proportions made unnecessary the considerable bustle of her dress, commented that Dr Thomas Cahill, the best man, would make a more suitable husband for Constance, and also criticised the hairstyle of Cecilia Higginson, one of the bridesmaids, but most present responded to the occasion with affirmation and goodwill. Even more than a baptism, a marriage has a fine sense of optimism, for it is a conscious coming together of two people who consider a partnership better than individual selfishness.

The wind was strengthening across the harbour and up the slope to Thorndon. It stirred the train of the bride's gown, and wafted a scrap of paper that startled a horse harnessed to the carriage waiting by Bishop's Court to take the bridal party to the Brandon home. Two carriages were needed, in fact, for although Constance's father was dead, she had three brothers and three sisters.

Davy Williams, who was to drive one carriage, moved closer to a skittish grey to quieten her, while still watching the people on the front church lawn, and talking with fellow driver Colm, who stood with his own two horses.

'How long then d'you think we'll be waiting here?' asked Colm.

'It'll be a while, you'll see. They'll want to make the most of it.'

'And when we get there we'll be turned away without a decent meal, I dare say. Seems an odd pairing, don't you think? He must have a good few years over her,' said Colm. 'Who the hell is Larnach anyway?'

'That's William Larnach,' said Davy. 'He's a Parliament one just like her father used to be. Comes from way down south in Dunedin where it's all Presbyterians and whisky.'

'Me, I'll have the bloody whisky and leave the Bible walloping.'

'They say he's married twice before and both died on him.'

'Old goat.'

'You're right, but chance would be a fine thing, Colm boy.'

Perhaps some of their betters thought the same, but no indelicacy was expressed then among the guests of both sexes. It was all felicitations and admiration, all sharp observation of people who mattered on the day, especially, of course, Constance and Alfred de Bathe Brandon, and William Larnach, the happy groom. No one paid much attention to twenty-seven-year-old Douglas Larnach, who went forward awkwardly to kiss his stepmother after the ceremony.

The afternoon of 27 January 1891. A day as real and vivid as any other, before absorbed by the deepening mist of the past. A day of sunrise and sunset, of heightened significance for some, and routine boredom for most. A day of high ceremony, of mutton chop and potato dinners, of a specious land deal, the generosity of a patron, a long forgotten boy beaten with a razor strop for soiling his britches, the reconciliation of elderly sisters, a murder on the gumfields, kindness and malice shown in a thousand homes and workplaces. A day, like all others, that held the possibility of advantage and misfortune. The day on which Alfred de Bathe Brandon, in place of his dead father, and displaying a manner that was to serve him well as mayor of Wellington, gave his sister in marriage to William James Mudie Larnach, self-made successful businessman, landowner and politician.

Conny, William and Dougie. There they are: alive, guiltless and smiling in the sunlight and the sea wind, with no shadows of the future cast over them, and choices still to be made. There they are, sharp and three-dimensional on the fabric of the present.

One ~

Not a mistake. When we went back to Wellington from our honeymoon in the north, more than six months ago, I did not think that I had made a mistake, but that it was going to be different from my expectation, and more difficult. But what does difficulty matter if a secure and successful partnership is achieved? Despite what the Reverend Andrew said at the wedding, marriage does not make two people one. Not even death, so much more powerful, can do that. What marriage does is to involve a woman in the life of a man, and its course can be a deepening pleasure for both, or a careful construction of boundaries, measured distances, which permit a civilised relationship. It is not necessarily one or the other, mind, like the choice of seasonal gowns for summer or winter. Some couples move between these situations, or inhabit any of a hundred stages possible between. And the advantages are not always in the one camp — ah, yes. Every marriage is of unique construction because the partnership itself cannot be repeated.

None of my sisters is married, and Annie, closest to me, showed natural curiosity concerning the honeymoon. There was much to satisfy and amuse her, without exaggeration, but considerable experience, too, that I keep even from Annie. Fifty-seven-year-old William without his trousers is not an Adonis, but as a man of the world and twice married before, he at least lacks the gaucheness that would have caused us both more embarrassment than occurred. And although I am twenty-two years his junior, and had not slept with any man before him, I am not ignorant. He is an ardent husband and pays me many compliments. Becoming a wife has not been a physically ecstatic experience, but any such expectation was not a reason for my marriage, and my wedded friends have told me enjoyment, or at least complaisance, comes with time and repetition. Our first night together caused me discomfort no friend had warned me of, but the act is more agreeable now.

Before my marriage I had the normal curiosity regarding love-making, talked about it discreetly with women friends, especially those who were already married, but it is an embarrassing subject to pursue, lest you sound unnaturally eager. From what my mother had said, it could be assumed that the only difference between men and women is that one sex wears dresses and the other trousers, and that all children, like Jesus, are of immaculate conception. As a new bride I was uncertain what I should wear to bed, whether William would find my body attractive, what would be a decent frequency for the union, and what beyond that would seem wanton. I need not have concerned myself. During the honeymoon, and for some months after, William was keen to take me every night and many mornings. Thereafter the act became much less regular and quite within my tolerance.

In any case, I endeavour to be a good deal more than bed partner and mistress of the house for William. I encourage him in his public life, and seek to be close confidante and supporter in all that is private and personal. And I intend to have my own social causes and interests in which I hope he will support me. Marriage to William will enable me to have influence for betterment of others that I could not hope for unwed, or linked with a lesser man.

I pay William this compliment — not once on our honeymoon did he deliberately, or as a slip, mention Eliza or Mary. It was a courtesy I appreciated. As an intelligent and caring man, he must have realised how sensitive I would be to such references until I became accustomed to my role as wife. It is not that I fear those shades, but his consideration is reassurance that he and I both look to the future, and with optimism.

As he had promised at Island Bay when he proposed, our marriage provides the opportunity for us to please ourselves concerning our pursuits, without the intrusion of others. Both of us enjoy society, but equally the chance to concentrate on each other's true nature, and to have time for our individual privacy and particular interests. We talked a great deal, especially in the evenings spent in hotels while we were travelling. William is essentially an active and practical man, but better read than I had realised before our marriage. He has an interest in Australian and Scottish history, both places with Larnach family connections, and his knowledge of plants and animals is greater than mine. On our walks and carriage travels in Taranaki and elsewhere, he identified many trees and smaller plants unknown to me, and pointed out differences between the flora of the two main islands. This inclination to natural history is one of the things he shares with Thomas Cahill, who is even more absorbed, and has provided rare, live birds for Dr Buller. In regard to music and literature William is happy to allow me the advantage.

Part of our honeymoon was spent in Wanganui. We stayed in the wooden hotel overlooking the wide, muddy river. I have never before seen so many Maori people. Some of the young men and women were quite striking specimens, but the older ones had aged badly and the children were uncontrolled. No one of any age seemed to have any work to do. William said that, like the Aborigines of Victoria, they have weak dispositions and many die from diseases less deadly to Europeans. He fears they might cease to exist as a separate race. There are few of the native people in Wellington, and William told me they would be even fewer in Dunedin.

William enjoys what he calls my personality summaries, and in the evenings draws me out concerning the people we have met, or been with. One evening, as we dined together in the Wanganui hotel, he asked me to create a disposition for each of the others present from their appearance alone, and burst out laughing when, after caricaturing a small man with a sore on his face, and his dowdy wife, I said that a boil on a man's chin is more contemptible than his wickedness. Such conversation also served as a distraction from the food, which was uniformly bad in every place we stayed, apart from the private home of the Wallaces. The vegetables were boiled to a slop, the meat served in chunks, and condiments usually nowhere to be seen. In most dining rooms the cutlery was ill matched and the china of oafish thickness. Neither was cleanliness a virtue much in evidence. I shudder to think of the condition of those kitchens we were served from, but unable to see.

We had more serious discussion also. Our marriage should be one of minds as well as bodies. I told William of the political issues my father and I had often discussed, especially those concerning education and advancement for women, and the need for more immigrants with cultivated backgrounds to act as a leaven in the lumpen colonial population. William was surprised, I think, when during our trip back to Wellington on a very wet day, I pressed him for his political manifesto, but in his answer rose to it admirably. Above all he strives for a society in which talent and industry are recognised and rewarded, and not impeded by the outdated conformities and class distinctions of the old country. In essence, I suppose, he wishes for others to have the opportunities of which he has taken full advantage. He is not one for much regulation in commerce, or life, and trusts to character and practical good sense. 'I believe in the power of enterprise and goodwill, and in having a pretty and gifted wife,' he said, and kissed my cheek as the carriage swayed, and rain gusted onto the window. What bride denies such flattery is welcome?

It is quite different in the world when you are married: even more so than I imagined. With a husband I can do things and go to places denied me as a spinster, and I find I am treated in a different way by both tradespeople and society. I am paid attention, partly because William is a man of means, and notable as well. There are more subtle distinctions too. Women expect a shift of conversation once you are wedded, the range of acceptable topics broadens, and the attitude of men also changes. They eye you less, or at least less obviously. A woman who marries to advantage, but retains independence of opinion, is given respect by both sexes.

The evident pride that William takes in introducing me is flattering, but more importantly it is a sign of the value he gives our marriage. I stand well with him, and there is no reason we should not be good for one another and happy together. A woman alone is always at a disadvantage, and usually the subject of unexpressed pity, even if it be her own choice.

I like to amuse him. Because he is so often at the centre of any society, he is apt to miss those spontaneous nuances of behaviour, or expression, that best represent a person's true feelings. In this he and I are typical of our sex, I think. Men seek to impose themselves, and concentrate on their own performance; women have the habit of observation, and are sensitive to the response of others. How often Annie and I exchange glances in company, complicit in some amusing, or poignant, observation to which the men present are quite oblivious.

William tells me that often he sees acquaintances in quite a different light after hearing my opinion of them. Like obsequious Mr Bulte the shipping agent, to whose house we were invited on several occasions. He did his best to entertain and flatter us, arrange the delivery of fine wines, yet he spits on the pavement and speaks to his subdued wife cuttingly when he thinks they are alone. 'You know nothing at all about anything, you stupid woman,' I heard him say while waiting behind the carriage. I made sure there were no more visits. I will not be in the company of a man who talks to his wife, or any woman, in that manner. William was at first taken aback that I should be adamant in excluding a particular person from our house or company. He is accustomed to making those decisions. But when I put forward my reasons, he agreed with me.

'I can see you intend to be the very modern and equal wife,' he said, 'even conscience for us both perhaps, and I love you all the more for it. I too hate cruelty and malice.'

In the main, those first few months in Wellington were both happy and busy. William is gregarious by nature, as a young man sometimes uproariously so according to his friends and family. He doesn't touch liquor now. I think this is because of Mary's bouts of drunkenness, though we do not talk of that, or her. He likes people about him, and to be at the centre of the group. We were much in society in Wellington, and enjoyed the purchase and fitting out of our new house in Molesworth Street. William would have made all the decisions down to the last stool, curtain cord and doily, I think, had I not asserted myself, but he accepted with good grace my right to have opinion on everything within the home, especially once he realised from the comments of others that my taste was appreciated. Had I not taken responsibility for the furnishings, I fear that the rooms would have been stocked with unwieldy leather-buttoned chairs and settees such as he is familiar with from clubs and public sitting rooms — of the best quality admittedly, but not at all what I was after.

In the interviews to find servants, I took the initiative also. Molly decided to come with me from my home, even though I told her she would not be housekeeper. She is a steady young woman, and not one to tittle-tattle about the lives of her betters. I like her, and to have someone familiar to me in the new house has made transition easier. Of the other people we shall see, but Cook has been recommended by my friend Doris Johnston's family, and so far has pleased us all.

William was considerate and attentive to me, despite his obligations as chairman of the royal commission investigating the Public Trust Office, and the continuing concern for his investments as hard times come to the country. His defeat at the elections last year does not appear to bother him and he says that public service has always been to the detriment of his financial dealings. Business is very important to him, but it is the one significant concern he has in which I have little aptitude, and less interest, apart from running an efficient household. In all public issues on the other hand, I ensure I am fully informed, and able to debate them with William, or anybody else, no matter what their station.

When in Wellington we saw many friends, and both the Wards and Seddons are frequent visitors to Molesworth Street: the Seddons, in fact, are our neighbours. Joseph and Richard consider themselves connoisseurs of a dinner and the latter is very fond of euchre. I am expected to play the piano, with the others gathered about me afterwards to sing. Louisa Seddon is Australian born, a strong-looking woman who wears heavily patterned dresses and has given up a waist. She has a deal of perception and awareness of political issues, but has been kept from much involvement and making the most of herself by having a family of six daughters and three sons. I think she imagines I will follow suit. Even without so many children, I doubt if Seddon would encourage her to be active in politics. He is more conservative than William, or my late father, in his view of a wife's role. Ballance, the premier, is not a well man, and William says Seddon is now the driving force.

Joseph Ward is about my own age, and we have a good deal in common. He is very much the coming man. His wife Theresa, who is a decade younger, could pass for the daughter of William or Seddon. I wonder what she makes of them? She is tall, elegant and favours large, splendid hats. Although perfectly correct and agreeable company, she is not yet a confidante for me.

Thomas Cahill remains William's closest companion, and was often with us in Wellington. He is a handsome man with an easy and obliging manner. I like him. He is lively and interesting to talk to, but I see also that there is a certain calculation in his cultivation of William and other people of influence, and he receives significant official appointments. Because of his profession he is often called upon to attend the most bizarre and horrific deaths. This keeps his name in the papers, and also provides the stories on which he dines out. But he is no bore, and takes a sincere interest in the lives of his friends — unlike some who use them only as a sounding board for their own concerns. Thomas is also musical and well read, and has a fund of social gossip from his wide acquaintanceship for which he expects me, as a woman, to be avid. We enjoy our frequent talks, but, I feel, share a slight wariness of each other's intelligence. As he is so close to William, it is important that I have him as my friend.

'Can we be trusting towards each other?' I asked him, when he came to visit soon after the honeymoon. 'Surely we both want all that is best for William. You're his closest companion, and I'm his wife. There's no competition in that for me, and I hope you feel the same.'

'I do indeed,' he said. He appeared a trifle startled by my frankness, but he and I need an understanding, and I think we have begun well enough. He shares his love of poetry with me, and I imagine he writes it also. I will broach that with him when we know each other better.

I hoped that, when we moved to Otago after the commission ended, William's positive spirits would continue, that we could make a place for ourselves in the somewhat watchful community here, and that, more important, we would develop that intimate understanding that would make time together more meaningful than spending it with acquaintances.

All, however, has been thrown into painful disarray by Kate's death. William loves all his children, sometimes too unconditionally, but Kate was his favourite. Plain, sweet Kate, who I had hoped would come with us to Dunedin. Alice and Colleen dislike me not for myself, but because I am not their mother. Donald, a country away, I know feels the same, but perhaps because of fear that I threaten his prospects of inheritance. Well, maybe they dislike me personally as well, although, however amiable I am, it would make no difference to them.

I was coming to share William's love for Kate, and she and I spent much time together in Wellington after the honeymoon, but only a few months later she caught typhoid and died within five weeks. A nurse herself, she was very brave. When I visited her in hospital she would insist she was getting better, talk of what changes should be made at The Camp when her father and I moved down here, or of musical events we could attend in the capital during our stays there. She enjoyed music, though, as for her sisters, too much money has been spent on poor teachers. Rossini was her favourite, which showed her innate taste was sound. One evening while we sat and waited for William to come from a bank meeting, she told me she was happy for us, for the marriage. 'Father needs people to love, and to love him back, but can't seem to say it,' she said.

'He loves you a great deal,' I said.

'And he loves you. He's been lucky and unlucky, hasn't he. Nothing's just ordinary for Father, but a lot of people don't realise all he's been through,' Kate said. 'What happens to him often seems to be on a bigger scale — the good things, but the bad too. He's happier with you than he's been in a long time.'

That was Kate. She could not have known how much it meant to me to have that support, and she gave it while suffering from high fever and stomach pains, and being unable to eat. Even in her own agony, she worried about causing distress to her father, whom she loved above all. Some people recovered from the fever, the doctor said. Would that Kate had been one of them. What purpose is there in such a death?

William suffered enormously, despite an effort to be manly. Sometimes in the evening I would look across and see his tears glistening in the light, though he would be talking of public matters, or I would come into his study, and find him in the darkness with head bowed.

We came down south with the casket on the *Hinemoa*, and I kept close to him for the whole voyage in case he leapt overboard. It sounds absurd, exaggerated, but not so. Once we reached home he was in virtual seclusion at The Camp for three months. All the money worries he has are nothing compared with the loss of his daughter. I know some acquaintances consider him a blustering and vain man, but if they could see him mourn his daughter, they would understand his capacity for feeling. After Kate died he laid flowers on her breast. Her body was placed in a glass coffin, which was displayed in the ballroom before the funeral. It was overly dramatic perhaps, but the emotion was completely sincere.

Most people see him as the big man, with resources and abilities beyond their own, but the risks and the shocks are greater also. Two wives lost through sudden illness, then Kate as well. Her death is a blight on all of life. William never expresses it, but I think he fears it is in some way a punishment for our marriage; for disregarding convention and gossip, for trusting to fortune and the goodwill of others.

'Were we too happy, Conny?' he asked. 'Why to God does happiness demand such a high price?'

'You did everything a father could,' I said. 'You did all possible and Kate loved you for it.'

'I still hear her voice. I hear the footfall that was hers alone.'

'Because you loved her.'

'How she suffered at the end, my poor girl, and there was

nothing I could do,' he said.

In the Molesworth Street house we sleep in the same room. At The Camp William has his own room on the second floor, flanked by bedrooms that had belonged to Eliza and Mary. Does a man ever understand how a new wife feels when brought into the home of her predecessor? The Camp is a mansion laid out like a huge stage set for a company of actors to which I do not belong. And so solid, personal and numerous are the props that they seem to call up the presence of those who have moved among them. Not just the phantom of one wife, of course, but poor Mary too. I say poor Mary because I can never see her memory a threat. Mary, who lived on the margin of her half-sister's life with William, who married him after Eliza's death more from mutual convenience than passion, who had no children, and who followed her sister to the grave within six years. And she occasioned the rumours that give people such pleasure, even as they feign reluctance to credit them, or pass them on. The servants sniggered about the sisters' two rooms, one each side of the master bedroom, and wider and better society discussed the propriety of a man marrying his deceased wife's sister.

People from all stations in life thought to make insinuations in my presence, but I responded sharply. I make clear that casting aspersions on Mary, or Eliza, is not a means to my favour, and I will not collect gossip about William's past. He and I begin life anew. I sent away one silly girl whom I overheard talking of the liquor she found hidden about Mary's bedroom.

We call this great house on the peninsula The Camp. Douglas

tells me the name began as one of William's little eccentricities from the time, in the early seventies, when the place was being built, and during his supervisory visits he roughed it in a cottage close to the workmen in their subsistence accommodation. Despite William's enthusiastic descriptions, I was not fully prepared and found The Camp's scale and sumptuousness indeed impressive, although in a slightly self-conscious way, perhaps, that indicates new money and the self-made man. My own upbringing has been privileged by colonial standards, but Father had neither the resources gathered by William, nor a nature determined that they should be conspicuously displayed. In my opinion, the quality of the inner man is more significant than any outward show.

William originally purchased two thousand acres, much of which has been subdivided into farms and leased to tenants. He has chosen well as to the setting of his mansion, and the vistas are quite magnificent. Dunedin is clearly seen, with almost the full length of the harbour open to view, the small islands within it, the forested hills and, far beyond it all, an expanse of ocean. The gardens and grounds have now largely overcome the initial rawness of the place, so the house is settled into its surroundings. William has made considerable plantings of native trees and species widely gathered from overseas. The estate is almost a hamlet in its own right, with a forge, grooms' quarters, an abattoir, a coach-house, a dairy, farm workers' cottages and a four-roomed residential laundry among the buildings. The Great Stables, so termed, are architecturally designed, and visitors stand to admire their lantern skylight and slate and lead roof. I have joshed William that here horses have at least the same importance as women. There are busy people everywhere and as yet I still do not know the names of all those dependent on us.

The interior of the house is superbly appointed, and in my opinion its proportions are superior to those of the outside, which are rather blockish and abrupt. There are twenty-five rooms, including the recently added ballroom that is thirty yards long, and also subsidiary small buildings around the courtyard. There are two kitchens, an ornate, but overly dark, formal dining room, and tessellated pavements in the entrance halls. William has insisted on the best of materials and workmanship, and so close was his attention and enthusiasm that he stipulated the exact and different colour for each room's bell pull, and that the large double-glazed windows be hung on brass chains, not cords. I am delighted with the spacious music room, which has a fine tiled fireplace and a high wood-lined ceiling. It lends itself well to performance. I spend almost as much time there as I do in the drawing room — which William and Douglas call the ladies' room.

The house is not easy to keep clean, because of so many polished surfaces, and laps and crevices up high, and I have had words with Miss Falloon concerning the cursory efforts of some of the maids, but there is much to admire. I never tire of looking at the marvellously embellished moulded ceilings, the result of years of work by French and Italian artists, and the birds, flowers and butterflies exquisitely carved in dark woods by the Godfrey brothers, whom William encouraged out from England. And the striking spiral staircase of mahogany and oak with not a single nail in all of its construction. Such craftsmanship brings together perfectly both function and beauty. It is little wonder that William has taken such pride in it all, and in happier times squired new guests on a tour of its features.

My goodness, it is a cold place, though, here on the hill, even though the double verandahs have been glassed in since originally built. The height of the setting and closeness to the sea seem to attract a polar fog in winter and the southerly wind is bitter in that season too. Often at night I have pottery bottles in the bed and a fire in the grate. I cannot abide to be cold. The master bedroom has six windows and is marvellously light, but unlike the two flanking rooms has no fireplace, and its two free-standing marble pillars are austere. I am glad not to go to bed there.

I am resolved not to be cut off here on the peninsula, over nine miles from the city, nor confined to domesticity, despite William's understandable wish not to be much in society at present. I have joined the Arts and Musical Society and accepted invitations to play in several private homes, but my chief concern, apart from consoling William, has been to advance the cause of the franchise for women. One of my disappointments is being unable as yet to meet Mrs Kate Sheppard, for our visits to Christchurch are rare. In Wellington, with William's support, I was active in gaining signatures on the parliamentary petition, and even though he was without a seat when we married, for my sake, and in accordance with his own liberal opinions, he wore the white camellia that represents women's political rights.

I am not a convinced abolitionist, but the other of Mrs

Sheppard's beliefs I favour strongly — the rights to contraception, divorce and education, and opposition to constricting clothes for women that prevent their full participation in sports and activities such as cycling. My father was staunch for the rights of women, particularly in regard to education. It is partly in memory of him that I support the cause also. I have paid for additional copies of Mrs Sheppard's pamphlet, Ten Reasons Why the Women of New Zealand Should Vote, and distribute it where I see advantage.

Here in Otago there are many adherents, but it is also the home of Henry Fish, presently in the House, and a chief opponent of the granting of the franchise to us. He is a horrid, crude and vain man, in the pay of the liquor trade, which denigrates women and their supporters. His language is execrable in both grammar and vocabulary. William has in the past had some dealings with him as a fellow politician, but I have stated that I will not have him at The Camp, or attend those homes at which he is welcome. Even Seddon, a much better man, is opposed to us, but John Hall, Robert Stout, Julius Vogel and my William are strong for the necessary change. I find it all quite heady, and feel that success is not far off. What a cause it is, and what change could flow from its success.

William's grief is such that at present everything else is immaterial. He has neglected billiards, which is a great indoor love, and for which he had a room added to the main house, with elongated windows to ensure even light. It is not the time to talk to him about how I feel surrounded by the possessions and practices of his previous wives. Still in their rooms are faint traces of perfumes, heavier than those I would wear myself, the disposition of furniture seems ordained, and the household staff are reluctant to break old habits.

Miss Falloon and I had early differences, but if she thought I was too untried as a mistress to run a household, she was soon disabused. As the eldest daughter of a fatherless family of four daughters and three sons, whose mother was acquiescent, I had taken charge of a considerable household, and told Miss Falloon so. She is a very competent woman of about forty, with unusual long blonde hair that appears almost yellow when freshly washed, and square horsey teeth, yet she is not unattractive. William tells me her family have rather come down in the world because of the loss of the father, and her efficiency is sometimes accompanied by a rather pained air, as if she is slightly demeaned by the necessity to be in service, even as housekeeper in charge here. I feel, however, that she and I will pull together in time. On several occasions when I have been at the piano alone, I have been aware of her listening at some remove, and that interest alone counts well with me. I believe she has had some elementary training herself, and is drawn to music, which is even more important. I have not been rude enough to question her, but I have a sense that she is still unmarried because she feels superior to all those with whom she is ranked, yet has not the opportunity to mix on equal terms with men to whose company she feels entitled. If I am right, then it is indeed a difficult situation for her, and I have sympathy.

Somewhat surprisingly, Douglas is my quiet ally in taking control. He, too, has been resisted in small ways since William gave over the running of The Camp to him, and has faced the same grudging obedience from some staff, and ingratiation from others. Because most of his time is spent outside the house, his knowledge of the trivial rivalries and character traits below stairs is necessarily incomplete. I am resolved to have my finger rather better on the pulse of things.

I don't know my stepsons well — Donald hardly at all, for he is in Melbourne now. Once, in '87, not long after Father died, he came down from Auckland, and William introduced him to me when both our families were attending a luncheon to raise money for the Wellington Girls' School. Donald is a handsome fellow in his way: darker hair than the others, and with the confidence of a first born, and an Oxford education. That Oxford assurance he shares with my brother Alfred, and both have been called to the Bar of the Inner Temple.

Douglas is William's favoured son. If I were to be both unkind and honest, I could say that is because he is more amenable to his father's instruction and draws less attention to himself. He has not his brother's looks, confidence and education, or William's drive and shrewd understanding of the world. I think that is true, but yes, unkind, because it takes no account of the dreadful accident he suffered while a schoolboy in England, and his age when his mother died. He has never spoken much of his injuries, but William said he was thrown from his horse while riding to hounds, and as well as suffering broken bones has become weakened internally.

On our move here from Wellington, it was Douglas I expected to be the most difficult to win over, because he had been placed in charge of The Camp and all the activities of the estate, while

William concentrated on parliamentary duties in the capital, and wider business dealings. A considerable responsibility for a young man then twenty-six and with little training, or experience, in any field at all. Yet I find him pleasant enough in a diffident way. His attempts to play the complete gentleman amuse me at times, but I don't show that. He is seldom without his pipe, which I suspect he assumes gives him an air of masculine maturity. In fact he has a collection of them and is as fastidious in selection as a society woman is with hats. He smokes even on horseback.

There are fewer than eight years between us, and I understand his sensitivity to slight. William had wished him to go to Edinburgh to study medicine after finishing school, but Douglas was resolved to come home and become a farmer. He has done that in part, but still, somewhat unfairly, harbours a grievance that he has not a university education like his brother. Yet he has his own set of friends who encourage him in shallowness, and is much about the town seeking diversion. No doubt he is seen as an excellent catch by local belles and their mothers.

William has relied on him a good deal during this wretched time following Kate's passing, and took solace, too, in having Gladys, the baby of the family, home with us from her Dominican convent school for some weeks. Poor Gladys — a mother, an aunt and now a sister gone, and she is only thirteen, and young even for that age, because she has been made much of by the rest of the family, who are so much older. William tries not to show his desolation when they are together, and she attempts the same in an open way that is entirely moving.

Colleen and Alice remain aloof and disapproving of the marriage. I have gone out of my way to be both civil and hospitable, but they are seldom at The Camp. I hope in time to have a friendship with them both, and to be accepted as their father's wife, and mistress of the house.

William is bewildered and cross with their studied reserve, but I have told him allowances must be made, for a time at least. It is more difficult for a daughter than a son to have a stepmother. Women have more areas of common dispute. Besides, they will marry, no doubt, and become busy with their own families. Alice is seeing much of William Inder, who is a lawyer in Naseby, and Colleen will not wish to lag behind her younger sister.

Coming to William's house here in Otago has not been as I imagined it, or would wish it, and much has had to be set aside because of Kate's death and his grief, but I am not a girl bride with fanciful expectations. My concern is to support William in his loss and then to establish myself with people of some distinction of mind and character who can be our friends. Always I have my music, and that is a boon for us both. William spends much time listening to me play, and though Douglas, like his father, has only a rudimentary knowledge of music, he sometimes sits with us. The grand piano is a fine one, because William has ensured that everything in his house is of the best available quality. There is a certain ostentation in his nature that my brother Alfred mocks, and an element of profligacy as well, but there is also such generosity and genuine goodwill, such shrewd perception of human nature, that his vanity seems only a cheerful expansiveness.

Yesterday afternoon several businessmen came to see William in connection with the international exhibition held in Dunedin last year. The doomsayers claimed it would fail because of the times, but William was an energetic supporter, and not only did hundreds of thousands of people visit over the months, but it was also a financial success. The deputation gave William a book on Scottish history and sought his advice on the best way to thank Richard Twopeny for his support when he was the editor of the *Otago Daily Times*. Although William has not wanted to see people much, he was cheered by the thanks and by the reminder of the exhibition's achievement. When we were alone, he made play with Twopeny's name, recalling other oddities such as a Dr Bigg-Wither, whom he knew while in England with his uncle, and the Goodenough family, with their history of naval valour and rank. A laugh in private at the Twopeny name was certainly not a laugh at the man himself: along with Dr Hocken, Robert Stout and William Hodgkins, he has been a conspicuous leader for art and music in the city.

In the evening William's lighter mood continued. He talked of the building of The Camp, and of the friendship he had with my father. Although Father was much older, they had similar political views and a similar sense of humour. William came often to our house, and we were all free with him in conversation. In our family, sons and daughters alike were accorded a hearing and judged on the perception of their comments rather than their gender.

I remember clearly the first time I became aware of William as a man, and not just a family friend. Father had been appointed to the Legislative Council and he and William had been at an informal recognition of that with friends at Parliament. They came home together for the evening meal. As usual, Mary was not with him. She spent much time in Otago. It was generally known that, after Eliza's death, William had married her half-sister, long resident with them, largely to ensure the care of little Gladys. I met her only once, found her a conventional, obliging woman, closely in the orbit of her forceful husband. Kate had the same high, round forehead, although Mary was not even her full aunt.

I was conscious of being unwed, because I was almost thirty, if not turned, and had only recently declined a offer of marriage from an Anglican vicar who played the organ tolerably, but had little else to recommend him. And I was at once experiencing and resisting the attentions of Josiah, one of Alfred's married legal colleagues. I had talked to Father concerning the offer that was proper, but of course made no mention of that which was not. He would have been pleased, I think, to have seen a daughter happily married. None of us then were, and my sisters are spinsters still, but he fully supported my refusal of the clergyman.

In a glancing, light-hearted way the matter came up in William's presence after the meal and he joined in the banter. Later, though, when he was preparing to leave, and we were a little apart from the others for a moment, he said warmly, 'Who wouldn't envy the man fortunate enough to marry you, Conny.' It was said quite openly, and perhaps others heard it, but accompanied by a steady gaze rather than a smile or laugh. I was conscious for the first time, I think, of William's admiration for me as a woman.

Father died three years afterwards. The 22nd of September

1886 was the saddest day of my life, for he was not only a great man in the colony, but a liberal and loving parent. During one of our last conversations, when he was seriously ill, he said that he had been lucky in life, and that he had found his greatest satisfaction in family. 'There's been so much fun, hasn't there,' he said.

'You carried it with you,' I told him. His skin had become almost yellow and folded on his neck like soft, pale fabric.

'Thank you,' he said, and I knew that was a part of his farewell. Mother has never really recovered, and resigned most of the household direction to me.

Mary Larnach died the next year. I knew, when William continued his visits, that I was the object of them. Alfred, now head of the family, was not warm to the idea, and my sisters brought home whispers of William's past, but such tales are spun around every man of consequence, and embroidered over the teacups with mock solicitation.

I imagine that every woman has a clear recollection of each proposal of marriage made to her, and how the manner of it differs from the depiction in romantic novels. The clergyman was earnest and embarrassed, perhaps almost resigned to refusal even as he made the offer. His pronounced Adam's apple made a distracting appearance above his collar whenever he swallowed. We were acquainted through a musical society, and he was at pains to tell me that he had some financial expectation from an uncle who was a prosperous chandler in Sydney. Every meeting we had after I declined him occasioned a certain awkwardness.

William had a deal more aplomb, but then we had seen more of each other, and an understanding had grown up. I have no patience with the notion that one should get to know a partner after the marriage rather than before. William talked a great deal about himself, but men do, and most of them are bores in the process. William is not: he has seen much of life at all levels of society, from the drunken tents of the Victorian goldfields to this colony's Cabinet table, and has a good ear and a good eye for a story, and the human nature revealed in it.

William's was not a parlour proposal, with Annie, or Fanny, hushed in anticipation behind the door. A group of us, including Thomas Cahill, the Seddons and the Montague sisters, took a carriage to Island Bay and walked there on the beach. There were Shetland fishermen who, despite the stiff swell, rowed some of the party out and around the small crag that gave the bay its name. William and I stood watching. 'If we were married,' he said, 'we could do so many things together without the need for others.'

'Would that increase our happiness?' I said.

'I'm certain it would mine, Conny, and I would do my very best to ensure yours.'

'I'm mostly happy as I am. I don't view marriage as either a necessity or a prize.'

'The prize would be mine, of course,' he said, so triumphantly that I had to laugh.

There is a healthy frankness in William that I admire, and I brought a similar realism to my decision when he went on to offer marriage. Opportunity and greater social freedom were the things I most desired, and by marrying him I have moved from the limitations of spinsterhood in the family home. William loves me and he encourages in me the inclination to be involved in the wider world that was lacking in both Eliza and Mary. I have grown up in a family accustomed to public and political life, and have no doubt I can support and influence William in a good deal more than just domestic matters. Also I will make acquaintances of my own in Dunedin, as well as often having my sisters to visit, I hope, and friends such as Doris and Cecilia. I have no fear of the social rank and involvement expected of me as Mrs Larnach.

I can best encourage William at present by consoling him for Kate's unexpected death and efficiently managing affairs here. It is not how we expected our time together at The Camp to begin, but I am sure better days lie ahead. I have position, opportunity, a home that is the marvel of many and, most importantly, a husband who loves me.

When William talked last night of Father, and of Wellington days before the wedding, I reminded him of the form of his proposal, its lack of ceremony, and he smiled, came to my chair, took my hand and kissed it. 'I do so now,' he said cheerfully, as he went down on one knee. And so we acted out a small charade of romanticism. 'I plight my troth,' he said with a music hall flourish, and took out his fob watch to mark the time. There is something quite special in such play and laughter between husband and wife.

Two

Kate was the best of us. Father recognised that. Kate was most like Mother in her wish for people to be happy, and in her unselfish willingness to achieve that. I remember that, when The Camp was being built, Mother had her own ideas about the furnishings, but even there she cheerfully gave way before Father's organising zeal. He seemed to be able to be everywhere, do everything, with a boisterous enthusiasm that carried all of us along.

Gladys came back from school to be with Father for a time. So much younger than the rest of us, she's always been his pet. Her presence is a consolation for him, and she and Conny get on well together, but Kate was an adult who had shared more of Father's life, and remembered our mother well, whom she so much resembled in spirit. Father's used to decisive action: at times he's almost dictatorial, but his generous love for us has never been in dispute. Well, not by me. Donny says with humour, and perhaps some bitterness, that I'm the favourite son, but Kate was the one in the family who understood Father best, loved him unreservedly and was most loved in return. When Kate died it was like a second death of our mother for him.

He's in a terrible place. 'Slaughtered' is the word he uses. Before the wedding it was financial and political worries that triggered an uncharacteristic despondency, but after the marriage he was almost exultant. I wonder if he thought Conny would refuse him? They bought the house in Molesworth Street after the honeymoon and as a couple were much in Wellington society, despite Father's work on the commission. It was a pleasure to visit them. He was tolerant again of people he'd begun to complain about as petty or uninspired. Conny says he even allowed her to update his clothes somewhat, and smiled when she ribbed him about it in front of others. I remember Mother saying that as a young man he was something of a dandy, wearing colourful velvet jackets and high starched collars and carrying a silver-topped cane. Well, the years have a put a stop to all of that. What a state he was in on his arrival back with Kate's casket. He's a good sailor but he was sick on the boat — sick with grief. Enough to lose two wives to sudden illness, and now Kate taken in a ghastly way. That first evening I went to him in the library, his favourite room, and talked of the property in an effort to distract him. I wanted him to see that I'd been conscientious in all the transactions associated with the place, but he was unable to rouse himself, even when I talked of the successful foaling and the growing demand in Dunedin for everything from the dairy herd. He reminisced a little about our family years in Victoria, the satisfaction Kate had in her Wellington nursing, his indifference to no longer being in Parliament, but it was all forced, so eventually we sat in silence, apart from the regular puffing of his breath through his moustache. From time to time there were small contractions on his face, as if painful thoughts came, and he was attempting to ward them off.

Although the whole house is an expression of himself, it's the library that shows best what manner of man he is. He prefers it even to the billiard room. His large collection of specially leather bound books of Scottish and Australian history, natural history and exploration. The heaped financial papers on the dark expanse of his desk, where also sits a clear bottle containing three gold nuggets. The paintings, oleographs and engravings crowded on the walls, many depicting places he knew. The gun cases, fieldglasses and nautical instruments. The photographs of himself in Wick and California, in Wellington and the wilds of the West Coast. He gravitates to his library when inside alone and loves to gather men friends there after dinner.

Normally he's cheerful with all the evidence of his life about him, but not with Kate gone. I think he'd almost forgotten I was there, and when in an effort to rouse him I began speaking of my recent fishing in the channel, he broke in and said that he wanted Conny to play for him, then stood up, meaning to find her. Kate often played for him, and although her talents were much less than Conny's, Father had loved that too. 'Haven't I had enough?' he said. 'What else could go wrong for me? Thank God for Conny, and you too, of course. Business presses on me, but family blows are far worse.'

'Things will clear.'

'Thank God for my Conny,' he said again.

How he used to enjoy talk of The Camp and his plans for it. In his mind's eye I think he saw himself creating something to rival Great-uncle Donald's Sussex estate of Brambletye. Uncle Donald has been Father's model in most things rather than his own father, whom he claims gave him nothing of practical, or spiritual, value — except a major part in the gift of life itself, as my brother pointed out. Father wasn't amused.

I spend a good deal of time attempting to cheer him, but sadness is never far below the surface. Even his enthusiasm for billiards has diminished, although we play often as a distraction from his unhappiness. He is a sly devil at the game, and in normal spirits gets considerable satisfaction from his skill, crowing boyishly at victories. 'The eye of the marksman, Dougie. That's the thing,' he will say, for he is capable with the gun too, and then he'll squeeze my upper arm.

How different now is the time we have together from that in the autumn of '82, when Kate and I returned home from England. Father was recovering from the awful buggy accident, the most dangerous injury being a broken leg, and I still wasn't fully fit from the fall I took at Uncle Donald's while riding to hounds. For many weeks he was holed up at The Camp, just as he is holed up now, but for a less terrible reason. Father hates forced inaction and loves to be about. He equates movement with progress and is restless to see and do.

Now I see more clearly the parallels, and the differences, between the two times. He had then recently married Aunt Mary, just as he has now recently married Conny, and after each wedding came an unexpected blow that confined him to The Camp. But then he had the pleasure of Kate and me coming home to be with him in convalescence, and now Kate is dead. The leg healed in time and he was gadding about again with his usual optimistic, thrusting frame of mind. Now he has suffered a wound far more serious and difficult to treat, even though I believe he can be happier with Conny Brandon than he ever was with Aunt Mary. All of us recognised that as just a marriage of convenience to make respectable her continued presence in the house, and allow him to protect his assets by legal use of her name.

Then he, Kate and I spent a great deal of time together, in the house and also moving about the grounds and the farm in the buggy, slowly so as not to test his leg. He loves the stock. His dairy herd was the first on the peninsula and the Alderney bulls win prizes and fetch high prices. But he and I set most store by horses and that shared enthusiasm is something we both cherish. What magnificent animals — despite my accident I admire them greatly. We had well over fifty of various breeds then, fewer now: the working Clydesdales, the carriage horses including the six matched greys and six blacks, the hacks, the ponies for the girls. Father and I would go down to the Stars and Stripes field on fine days to spend time with the horses, and often visit the stables, which he had designed with almost as much care and extravagance as the house. When Father first went to Wellington as a member of

Parliament, he caused something of a stir by riding his impressive white mare, Reindeer, about the city streets. It was a way to signal his arrival, I suppose, and also a challenge, as is Father's way.

Nothing of that seems to interest him now, and when I talk to him of the property and my supervision of it, he has an air of impatience and is quick to complain of the small return on everything he's invested in The Camp and its associated properties. I'm not privy to all of his finances, but things aren't as they were. It's the whole colony, of course, not something confined to Father's dealings. Land values are falling and defaults on loans and commissions are common. Father and Basil Sievwright still meet regularly, but there's not the boisterous humour of earlier times and the lawyer seldom stays the night after their business as he often did.

Last Tuesday afternoon they were talking loudly on the lion steps as Sievwright waited for his horse to be brought round, and I heard Father reminding him to sell Kaitangata Coal Company shares and buy more in the Colonial Bank. 'Follow my instructions as promptly as you can,' he said. 'I feel I've trusted too much lately to the advice of others rather than retaining faith in myself. Too many fair-weather sailors are being found out. Damn small-minded and timid people hold everything back.' His voice lacked the tone that formerly showed their long association and friendship, but he made an effort before the lawyer mounted, and shook his hand firmly.

I went out and stood with him as Sievwright rode away. I asked him how serious things were. 'Ready money, that's what it's all about now, Dougie,' he said. 'It's not a time to realise on assets, and everyone's out for ready money. A man's word and best endeavour aren't sufficient any more. I'm being pressed, but by God I'll make it warm for any man who tests me in the courts. And your brother and sisters don't seem to have any appetite for economy, or any ability to provide for themselves. In England and Germany they became accustomed to living well on my money.' I reminded him that he'd wanted us to have the education he was denied. 'Yes, and use it to advantage to make your own way in the world,' he said. 'But Donny has a wife and family now and still he battens on me. At his age I was appointed manager of the bank here and at your age I was chief officer for the Bank of New South Wales on the goldfields.'

I know all his Australian stories from constant retelling and embellishment, although I have little recollection of the country myself. Normally he would have taken the opportunity to revisit those memories again for my instruction and his pleasure, but it was a sign of his condition that he fell silent for a while and remained standing on the steps, looking out to the fir trees that had been planted when the house was still being built, and when he, Donny and myself would often spend weekends with the workmen, staying in the cottage. He put his hand on my arm in the old, affectionate gesture. I asked if he would like to ride to see the Alderney herd, but he said he would go inside and have Conny read to him. 'I must accept what's happened in a philosophical manner,' he said. 'Many people have greater troubles. I'll bear up. Money matters can be dealt with, but Kate is a loss terrible to me. Poor, dear Kate. Only you, Conny and little Gladys make it bearable for me here. We must support each other and come through it all the stronger and closer for the ordeal.'

Many times, when Father was in Wellington, I had occasion to go to Basil Sievwright's office, but he was too much the professional adviser to say any more than was necessary for the transaction between us. He concentrates on Father's wider interests and doesn't seem very concerned in the affairs of the peninsula property and The Camp, except to stress the need to limit expenditure and to suggest further reduction in household staff. In its heyday the place had four cooks and four gardeners, laundry and cleaning women aplenty, an ostler, a personal maid for each family member and numerous others. A butler ruled the servants more absolutely than Miss Falloon does now. Even today many people are needed to keep the place going. One girl spends all and every day tending to the kerosene lamps. I'm diligent about the farm but I can do little about house staff without Father's agreement, and he was reluctant to make decision at a distance.

I hope Conny will take charge of everything inside The Camp now. She has greater resolution to be mistress than Aunt Mary. Miss Falloon and Jane I find inclined to agree with my direction and then disregard it, so I'll watch with interest to see how they fare with Conny. Certainly she began as she intended to go on. Father's low spirits meant he had little interest in introducing her and establishing her position, but she called Miss Falloon to her the very day after her arrival, and the next morning had all the servants assembled in the large music room, where she spoke to them concerning their responsibilities and her resolve that the entire household be happy and well organised. Jane told me that Conny decided to observe the running of the household for three weeks before making what changes she thought best, and she set a time each day for Jane and Miss Falloon to meet with her, as well as stipulating that she is not to be disturbed when at the piano. 'Oh, it's all very military indeed, Mr Douglas,' said Jane, who no doubt makes comparisons with my mother's time, and then Aunt Mary's. Conny's sharp enough, that's for sure. I don't think I'd like to serve under her.

The outside and farm workers seldom give me any cause for complaint, and in the main I enjoy my time with them. In England I was always a mere schoolboy, or a guest on the property of others. Here I'm someone in my own right, entitled to give instruction on our family holdings.

If Sievwright doesn't give much away about the Larnach finances, then Donny doesn't hesitate to give advice from Melbourne. He's a lawyer too, but far more open in his opinions, both within the family and in public. I must admit, however, that there's truth in his assessment of our father's abilities. The Otago papers regularly refer to William Larnach as one of the richest men in the colony, with interests and involvements that go from one end of the country to the other, and overseas. But he is, as Donny says, an expansionist, full of optimism about potential. He possesses an instinct for a good deal, and the banking and business experience to create an enterprise. When things were going well, when finance could be easily obtained, then most things thrived, but money's being called in now, and people like Stout, Vogel, Ward and Father are feeling the squeeze for that ready cash he talks about. Guthrie & Larnach has officially been wound up, but proceedings drag on and he bleeds money because of it.

I know he's drawn Alfred Brandon into land speculation. I assume Conny is aware of her brother's involvement. I hope the association remains without recrimination on either side, for Father can be hasty at times and Alfred was initially cool about the marriage itself. I know for a fact that before the wedding he asked Father what settlement he was prepared to make on Conny, and was dissatisfied with the answer: no settlement, just the pledge of a loving husband to support her and provide for her in his will. The de Bathe Brandon family have an assumption of privilege, but there's no evidence of significant importance in their past. Most in the colony are in the same position, and that's the main reason they're here, I imagine. I've had little opportunity to get to know Alfred. He's nine years older and he patronises me also because I lack the gloss that Oxford has given him.

Donny, Colleen and Alice are even more uneasy, for a contrary reason: the fear that Father will leave everything to Conny, and so our inheritance will be lost, including the money Mother brought to her marriage. I'm prepared to trust Father, and Gladys is too young to understand the matter. He's been generous to us in the past, and has told me several times that he intends The Camp eventually to be mine. I see nothing in Conny that leads me to think she is hostile to the rest of us, and Father has never been one to be led by the nose in anything! Perhaps Conny has yet to learn that.

If Kate were alive, she may have been the one to achieve

family harmony. She saw no reason for people to be at odds, and thought goodwill and toleration would solve everything. We all loved her; Conny liked her. Donny is offhand and scoffs at Father's third marriage. No fool like an old fool, he says openly, though he admits Conny is a fine figure of a woman, and has no particular animosity towards her, or the Brandon family. For Colleen and Alice something more personal seems to be at work, which I don't fully understand. No one expects them to see Conny as their mother, but they also make it clear that they don't recognise her as Father's wife in the way to which she's entitled. Colleen bridles because Conny's less than a decade older than her, and more than twenty years younger than Father. It's embarrassing when they're in society together, Colleen and Alice say. The way Father displays Conny and attempts to play the younger man. It's like a slap in the face for our mother. In some female fashion they seem to find it logical to blame Conny for Father's wish to have her.

For myself, I hope to make a more reasonable, less immediate judgement. And I won't have Gladys prejudiced by her sisters' opinions. At her age she's still essentially of the household and must be allowed the best opportunity to be happy with her father and Conny when she is home from school. Colleen and Alice prefer not to come to The Camp. They have much of their lives elsewhere and make obvious their preference for other company.

I met Conny first in Wellington as the daughter of Father's friend, just one of a rather self-assured and outspoken tribe. The marriage was as much a surprise to me as to the rest of the family, and to Father's wider acquaintance. Of the four de Bathe Brandon daughters she's the eldest and prettiest. Personally I find her figure too slight. She's petite, and my admiration is more aroused by fuller proportions. Also, she persists in wearing her hair tightly drawn back, as if to prove she's a modern woman. She carries herself well, and is free from the simpering confusion or conscious archness that so many women affect, but her shrewd interrogations can be disconcerting.

Her father was a great supporter of education and gave his daughters unusual opportunity for accomplishment. I'm not much interested in music, but Conny is agreed to have special talent there. What I do appreciate is her ability to converse on a wide range of topics, and her confidence to substantiate her opinions. She's formidable in argument, is Conny de Bathe Brandon, and Father delights in that, despite not brooking opposition in others. Men allow good-looking women a latitude they won't give to plain females and fellow males. But Father's accustomed to getting his own way, and when the novelty of Conny's independence wears off, maybe some sparks will fly.

Two nights ago I had another of my dreams. We were dining formally, with Father at the head of the table talking about the newly built ballroom. I think all of the family were there, except Donny's wife, who's unwelcome. Others sat with us, but without place settings, or any food, and their faces were indistinct. Mother, Aunt Mary and Conny sat side by side, and, as is the way in dreams, there seemed nothing untoward in that. Father was calling on each of us in turn to twirl about the room. 'Dance, Kate,' he cried happily, and she got up obediently. Then, 'Dance, Eliza' and 'Dance, Mary, Colleen and Alice', and they did, quite unconcerned and with concentration to perform to their best. 'Dance, Donny and Gladys.' But when Conny was called on she didn't reply, or rise, just kept on with her meal. Father merely laughed and continued to call us up, until all except Conny, even the shadowy, unnamed guests, were dancing in the dining room under the ornately carved ceiling as if that was the accepted practice. Yet I was embarrassed to find that my old injury had returned in full, so that I could move only clumsily and with pain. All other dancers seemed graceful, while I was a fool, and tried to avoid being in Father's sight, or Conny's. My last awareness in the dream was that there were a great many plates of assorted nuts on the table that I hadn't seen before, and the time began to feel like Christmas. Conny remained seated and alone, yet quite composed and looking away from the dancing. What strange visits we pay in our sleep.

Since she's been at The Camp, I've become aware of Conny's considerable estimation of herself, and a certain sharpness, even asperity, in her observations concerning other folk. She can be especially hard on the people she's been introduced to here in Otago, and doesn't seem to care that her witticisms can sometimes give offence. She's a great one for women's advancement, and quite determined to take an active part in pushing for the vote, even arguing the point with parliamentarians she meets socially. I don't doubt her quick mind, but she can be dismissive of those with a lesser intelligence, especially if they're ignorant as well. She doesn't conceal her impatience with silly or shallow people.

Soon after her arrival at The Camp, she offended some of us

in the family by mocking an *Otago Witness* cutting in the family scrapbook, recording musical items my sisters and I had given in Mr Young's barn in aid of the Hooper's Inlet school organ fund. Donny's wife was there too and sang 'Remember me no more' and 'Across the far blue hills, Marie'. Alice played the violin, Colleen Welsh airs on the harp, and I sang 'Goodbye' and 'For ever'. All very bucolic no doubt, and Conny's criticism was of the music chosen rather than individuals, but she was hurtful all the same without intending it. 'No doubt it was all for a good cause,' she said, 'and the organ remains an inspiration for the schoolchildren.' Alice in particular got in a great huff and came to The Camp even less afterwards.

People talk, of course, about the difference in their ages, but when Father's recovered from the loss of Kate, I think they could well be happy. Conny will make him a suitable wife in many ways. She's used to the life of a politician, and she's an accomplished hostess. Father likes having people of his choice around him: lively conversation, music, even gossip and practical jokes. Aunt Mary was never comfortable, or successful, in being equal partner at such gatherings.

I wonder, though, how Conny will find life at The Camp rather than in Wellington. Dunedin is over an hour away, and now that Father is no longer in Parliament they may be here much of the time. Both Mother and Aunt Mary found life here isolated and preferred the Manor Place house in town. Mother never got used to the cold, or to the rawness around her.

I'm selfish enough to be concerned, too, for the way in which their residence at The Camp may affect my own position. When Father regains his interest in affairs, I'm unlikely to retain full control of the day-to-day running of the property, and all the effort I've put into establishing myself, and proving my competence, may be for nothing.

It's also put a damper on having my own friends at The Camp, not just because of Kate's death, but because Father doesn't think much of them, apart from Robert, whose father is a business friend. Robert has come from England and, like me, doesn't completely fit in with the set here. Father finds us too idle, and not resolute enough in forging careers for ourselves. He doesn't reflect that there may be other roads to fulfilment apart from his own self-help and industry. It's just as well he knows nothing of some of the weekends in his absence: Robert, Hugo and others lairing with me outrageously. He accepted the story I gave him regarding the damage to the wishing well, and the disappearance of his peacocks.

Such mobbing times weren't my favourites in any case. Too many of the people came to enjoy hospitality that they hadn't the inclination, or the resources, to return. The Camp and I were used: friends invited friends who brought acquaintances. Donny's nature is inclined to such largesse, but he's seldom with us now. Some fellows regarded the women servants as part of the extended hospitality, and on two occasions the consequences were both embarrassing and costly for me. I've only once given in to a dalliance with one of the maids, a loose-limbed, forward girl who gave me considerable pleasure despite her love bites, but who became increasingly demanding of my attention. Thankfully she didn't conceive and I found an excellent position for her in Oamaru, and gave her five pounds besides.

I've come to prefer having just one or two good friends here, and joining larger groups at the Fernhill Club, or in town. Robert I like best. He can be something of a beast with women, and goes off for days at a time without any warning, or explanation when he returns, and he has black moods as well as more frequent times of high humour. He's a full drinker on his day, but holds it well and becomes neither maudlin nor unpleasant. He has a sense of the possibility in life, and the deficiencies and crudity of much here compared with England. Like me, I think Robert chafes at a father's close instruction and high expectation. More than anything else he'd like to own and train racehorses, but hasn't the means for it, and is restless in the dull grain business in which his father has an interest. He and I sometimes spend a whole day riding on the peninsula, or take a dinghy out from Waverley and fish in the channel. Such times give us greater pleasure than the all-night loo sessions in the card rooms at the club. 'Ride hard, live hard, die hard,' he says.

I'd been on the water the day I received the news of Kate's death in Wellington. It was fine, but cool, with an incoming tide making the dinghy strain at anchor. I was in the boat alone, and I remember that as I looked at the headlands on both sides, the wildness of them, the almost total absence of habitation, I was struck by the contrast with the beach at St Leonard's on Sea, where Jeremy Pointer and I would row back and forth on half-days, happy simply to be beyond the school grounds. There was noise and bustle on the shore, and the huddled buildings, and boats coming and going, and the two of us determined not to think of classrooms, house matches and dormitories, as if hopeful forgetfulness might prevent their return.

So much a contrast to Dunedin's channel, with its currents and sand bars to be avoided and no other vessels to be seen. The cod hadn't troubled my line that day, yet I sat contentedly enough with the anchor rope refracted beneath the water surface, and a light slapping on the clinker sides of the dinghy. Kate was dead, but I still unaware of it, safe with the sounds and colours and smells of everyday life around me. Odd, those small overlaps of time, when we are still happy, yet tragedy has already come.

Father's too restless for fishing. He needs movement and talk and people when he's well. He loves to go to race meetings on the Taieri, and often challenges his friends to better his times into town from The Camp. He's an unorthodox rider, but a skilled one from his rough and ready days on Victorian farms and goldfields. When he visited Uncle Donald in England at Brambletye the local horse and hound people joked about William Lanarch's colonial style, but he was seldom unhorsed, and was invariably in the vanguard of the hunt. In Sussex, to ride well is as important an indication of position as having a suitable tailor. Donny and I learnt there the more correct style, but that means nothing here.

When I came back to the colony, Father was upset by the obvious signs of my injury, yet neither of us blamed the horse and I still love to ride. The effects of the fall are always with me, and a reminder to be cautious, yet what moments of exhilaration I have are almost all when I'm riding. Donny says that's because I lack experience with women. He means just to provoke revelation, as well as suggesting success on his own account — those trips to London with Pembroke College friends he likes to refer to, and the social freedom of Auckland's more bohemian elements. I've my own club and riot stories, but prefer not to share them. Everything a Larnach does in Dunedin tends to be known sooner or later, and we have our enemies. Conny will be subject to that now like the rest of us. Her dress and speech, her deportment, her manner with equals and inferiors, her choice of friends and charities, her influence with my father, even her teeth and jewellery, will be assessed. It's people's nature to look enviously at those above them, rather than be satisfied that so many are worse off than themselves.

Tomorrow I'll go in and visit Ellen Abbott, with whom I've been keeping company on and off. Her family has been to The Camp several times, and I'm in good standing with her parents. Mrs Abbott has perhaps some suspicions of my intentions, but she's a woman keen for social advancement. On Wednesdays she visits her elderly mother, and after I've sat with her and Ellen for morning tea, suffered the conversation while disguising boredom and impatience, she will leave, and Ellen and I will be alone. I will persuade Ellen to come with me where we can hear the door, but not be seen from it, and we will hug and kiss, standing hard against the wall, and I will lift her skirts. If I'm lucky, and their housekeeper is out shopping, I might have her come with me to her bedroom and do the whole thing in a flurry there despite the wad of clothing. Or my persuasion may be unsuccessful. 'Is this all you come for?' she asked me on my last visit, and burst into tears when my answer didn't convince her otherwise. What guilt there is in such accusation, for the truth is that in every other aspect of her company I prefer my male friends. Perhaps that's the way it is between men and women.

Three

I see an end to our established life here in Otago, and surprise myself somewhat by admitting that I am in two minds concerning a return to Wellington, where William will take up parliamentary duties once again and we will live during sessions. The two years here have not been unhappy, despite money matters being still much on William's mind. He has regained some of his optimism and equanimity, takes an interest in the property here and we are often in society. Kate will never be forgotten, but his grief is no longer incapacitating.

Both Richard Seddon, whom William has known since their Victorian days, and Joseph Ward were insistent that William stand for election again. Flattering visits and telegrams overcame William's conviction that politics is an ill-rewarded distraction from his own pressing business affairs. Seddon was determined to have him and has implicitly promised the knighthood that would be the just reward for William's insufficiently recognised service as minister of mines, and the raising of loans in London for which Julius Vogel took credit. For William, a knighthood has become the essential recognition for all that he has achieved for the colony, often at great financial and personal cost. Vogel, also William's acquaintance in Australia in the early days, has received such an accolade for a good deal less, and that galls William. Sir William James Mudie Larnach is a great mouthful, but how hungry he is for it, as I am sure Seddon knows. He deserves it, and I am not averse to its advantages, but there is something just slightly belittling in such undisguised ambition.

William was defeated as a candidate for Wakatipu in the general election at the end of '93 because of the opposition of Catholic voters, and slurs in the local paper, but Seddon would not give up and implored him to stand in the by-election for the Tuapeka electorate only months later.

Few wives here accompany their husbands when campaigning, but then I have become quite accustomed to disconcerting the staid matrons of Dunedin, and for me it is a celebration of the granting of the vote to women at last. What a triumph for us, and a test of eminent men that we women will not soon forget. Hall, Stout, Vogel, Fox and Ballance all for us, and William too, though Richard Seddon, as premier, did his best to undermine everything after Ballance's death. And the wretched Henry Fish here, our great enemy, called the talking fish, and the cuttle fish, lost his seat as soon as women had the vote. Bessie Hocken and I had an open toast to his demise at the choir Christmas party, and I wrote to

Mrs Kate Sheppard to congratulate her and her organisation. In her reply she told me of the premier's unsuccessful manoeuvring to defeat the bill, and then his outwardly generous telegram to her conceding victory. He is a more devious man than his bluff exterior might suggest.

William was delighted to have me with him on the hustings. One of his most endearing attributes is the pleasure he shows in my presence with him in public. I take that as a compliment, and do not reflect too much that his attention then is more welcome than in our private moments.

In those weeks I saw him at his best and admired in him qualities I have perhaps begun to take for granted. His natural bonhomie enables him to engage with people from all walks of life, and both genders. If perhaps there is a slight coarseness in comparison with the most refined people of the colony, it is more than compensated for by achievement and openness, and more than any other person, except Seddon himself, William can reach the hearts of ordinary people. Men in particular see that he has intimate knowledge of the lives they lead, despite the position and wealth he has gained, and they are swayed by the directness and forcefulness of his speech. His command to rowdy hecklers to 'kennel up, you curs' has become almost a legend, shouted by his supporters at any who opposed him during the Tuapeka meetings.

His opponent in the by-election was Mr Scobie Mackenzie, a great landowner and a man of self-regard and condescension. It was a close thing, but William triumphed by less than sixty votes. He and Mackenzie went at it hammer and tongs, to the great delight of the voters who gathered in church and town halls, and sheds, or congregated from their work in open spaces if the weather was fine. Both of them said things improper for women to hear, and both sexes enjoyed the comment all the more for that impropriety. It heartened me to see the number of women there, and I hope my presence with my husband on many of the campaign trips encouraged them to take full advantage of the greater political responsibility they have been granted. They have turned out to vote in excellent numbers, and now must become accustomed to using the power of the franchise to remedy long-standing discrimination against themselves in both law and practice.

Dougie tells me that his father is a man's man, but he has a regard for women that goes beyond the natural admiration the male sex is born with. At a musical evening in Wellington before my marriage, Joseph Ward, another before whom Seddon dangles a knighthood, told me that William supported women's franchise, and he later proved it, though I have not yet persuaded him that we are quite responsible enough to be members of the colony's Parliament. I will come again at him with that question. William allows me liberties in argument that he opposes in others, and that is surely one of the privileges of a wife. He will not be cowed himself, and has no respect for those who allow themselves to be cowed. Dougie sometimes shows impatience at what he sees as his father's old-fashioned views, but William has a strong concern for the common man despite his own elevation. He spoke up for the decent treatment of Chinese miners here when others were hostile, or indifferent, and his employees are treated better than most. Some of the household staff have taken advantage of his goodwill. I have had cause to correct several who had become lax, or presumptuous, when poor Mary was mistress of The Camp, and later when there was no mistress and Dougie was in charge.

Being out on the hustings has made me realise that life is not easy for many of these people in out-of-the-way places. We were given the best public accommodation, and that was often only bearable. The glimpses of everyday life make me aware how fortunate I have been in family and circumstance. Heavens, the smell of many of those in service, and many whose position offers less excuse. And the familiarity of address. Local chairmen of this or that insignificant board who spoke at length and grandly of their contributions and aspirations, while my attention wandered to their grimy collars and fingernails. I have been invited to see rabbits shot, to join a good lady in salting pork and to instruct spinster women in the putting up of their hair. It is hard for women here, and many are coarsened by work and weather. In the city I am active in improving the lot of my sex, but I find it difficult to see how much can be achieved in remote places at present.

William loves to travel, despite the fact it must tire him more than it would a younger person. The long sea voyages, the wearisome steamer trips to Wellington and back, the uncomfortable coaches on ill-formed roads, seem little to him in his consuming interest in new places, people and opportunities. When he was minister of mines he insisted on visiting camps no other politician would contemplate. Even Donald and Dougie, who accompanied him separately on such trips at different times, were left in his wake. He is not a settled man: change and movement are his defence against any gloomy circumstance and there is extra excitement when things go well. Only to Kate's death did he temporarily succumb.

Yet he is an unlucky traveller who has experienced a variety of accidents, not all from riding hard. The family joke with him about this attraction for misfortune, but there is no humour when you are caught up in it, as happened on our return trip from Lawrence after celebrating William's election success. There had been heavy rain, and at one of the worst of the swollen rivers William urged the driver on, despite misgivings on my part. The carriage gave a horrid lurch, swung side on to the current and the whole thing overturned. The swirling water, furious in sound and movement, seemed suddenly to have come to malicious life. I thought I would surely die, if not drowned, then killed by the panicking horses. The weight of sodden clothes in such circumstances places a woman at great disadvantage, and any movement is difficult. For one instant my face was below the water, and I could see the blurring image of my boot against the sky. I believe my life was saved only by hanging onto an iron rail, and by William, who heaved me to the bank, all dignity forgotten.

There we were in the wilderness, bedraggled and shivering on the stones and among the tussock, with the driver and William arguing loudly as to fault. I think William expected me to be angry at his impetuousness, but I was satisfied just to be alive. And I had been determined to accompany him on his electioneering after all. We had to remain chilled and soaking wet for over two hours while the coachman rode one of the horses bareback to the nearest habitation. The people, who were called Driffel, came down with a buggy and took us back to their cramped place, made partly of yellow sod.

My case had been taken from the water before it was saturated so I was able to change into clothes that were only slightly damp. Mrs Driffel remained with me throughout, commenting on the garments effusively. In other circumstances I would have asked to be left alone to dress, but felt under some obligation. I think our misfortune provided her with pleasing variety in a lonely and narrow life. She was born in Waterford, she told me, came out as a servant and had three proposals of marriage before the ship landed, with better ones to follow. Judging by the appearance of her husband, the earlier men must have been markedly unprepossessing. Mrs Driffel was more interested in my travelling clothes, especially the one silk embroidered evening dress, than in the newly elected member for Tuapeka, though William sat down with her husband as if with an equal. Everything I owned she exclaimed over and proclaimed 'fit for bridal wear'.

They have no help in the house, or on the property, and do everything themselves. Mrs Driffel was excessively proud of a cheap oval mirror fixed to their bedroom wall. Her face was brown, her hands roughened with work and her teeth quite wrecked. The winters are exceedingly harsh in these inland places. She knows nothing of Dunedin life, has no society and is a sort of cheerful drudge. She lost one child in birth; the other is a ragged boy of seven or eight without speech who ran about and grinned.

Not all has been melodrama and success, however. In May, we

attended the funeral of the Reverend Dr Stuart of Knox Church, whom we both admired: William because he came of humble Scottish stock and was yet another example of what can be achieved by industry, enterprise and self-help, and I rather because he was generous, open-hearted and liberal. He was a chairman of the boys' and girls' high schools, chancellor of the university and also knocked on the doors of the poor. He was many times at The Camp, and often we talked of books and music, as well as the numerous families dependent on William for their livelihood. He had a particular love of cats. As he sat with us he would put one of the tabbies on his knee and fondle its ears. 'A cat is the best of friends,' he said once. 'It gives affection, but retains independence.'

Two years before his death, almost to the day, he was the minister for Alice's wedding to William Inder at The Camp. None of us have particularly taken to her choice, but that is of no consequence. The wedding was not large, and the weather was cold. Alice and her bridesmaids, Colleen and Gladys, wore dresses of serge trimmed with fur, and stayed in the grounds only long enough for photographs, despite the weeks of preparation by the gardeners. My William was hurt by the lack of gratitude and affection from both of them. Dougie and Gladys apart, the family are a grasping lot.

Dr Stuart's cheerful and obliging manner was instrumental in the occasion passing off well enough. He was a great mingler, and it was difficult not to respond generously in his company. I remember that day he told me that as a young man in the old country he had taught small children to raise the money he needed to pursue his studies. He said with mock seriousness that once you understand children, adults pose little problem. His death has left a gap here in Dunedin, and in our personal society.

But it is Dougie I will miss most on our return to Wellington, even more than Bessie Hocken, and Gladys too, though she is at the convent with her cousin Gretchen, Donald's girl, and when the two of them are at The Camp they are close and mysterious. Gladys perhaps shows more reserve towards me than formerly, but not the antagonism of her sisters. I was initially obliging towards them, and have remained civil, but because I insist on my due as William's wife, they seldom visit us. William takes my side, but I sense a growing sadness at estrangement within his family, and hope that he will not come to see me as the cause of it.

Despite his liking to talk of the good old days, he hardly ever mentions Eliza or Mary. This past Thursday, however, I had an unpleasant brush with one of these predecessors while replacing some of William's journals in the library. From one he had been reading fell an open envelope bearing Eliza's name, and within it were some pale, pressed flowers and a miniature painting signed by her. Executed on a gum leaf, it was a view of a sinuous road through scattered trees and scrub. The intrinsic merit was slight, but that showed the more the sentimental value he attached to it. The incident reminded me that my own father's first wife died soon after they came to the colony, and I have never thought to ask my mother whether she ever felt the presence of the earlier woman in her marriage. Since becoming a wife, I find myself closer to my mother, more understanding of the placating nature that once made me impatient, and I champion her sometimes when Fanny or Sarah complains.

I am not superstitious, or much concerned by shades of the past, and Dougie says his mother disliked The Camp and preferred to spend her time at Manor Place in Dunedin. But it is impossible to live here in William's grand house, with his and Eliza's children, and Mary's existence recent, and not at times feel some oppression from these women, and the extent of his former life so much greater than my own. The Camp can be a lonely place for its mistress, for although there are always people about, of those who live here only William and Dougie are of my own station in life.

I wish my sisters could be with me more often, to bring more of the de Bathe Brandon world into my house, but Wellington is rough seas and a steamer away. Although my brothers are not great correspondents, my sisters support me well. Annie in particular sends me the most full and loving letters, in which parade our family, friends and acquaintances. I miss her especially, but also my friends Doris and Cecilia, both of my bridal party and still close. Just yesterday I had a letter from Cecilia talking of her plans to travel to Sydney, and asking about Charles Baeyertz here of the magazine *Triad*, and his feud with the Reverend Ready. Soon, however, when William takes his seat in Parliament, I will have my own people, my own city, my own life, around me again.

My opinion of Dougie continues to improve. He has been increasingly supportive in my dealings with the staff and his father, and a confidant concerning the Dunedin society we entertain and visit. There is a certain reserve among some of the families, but I feel no necessity to ingratiate myself. It amuses me to find people so complacent in their personal history, and ignorant of a wider one, that they consider Dunedin the capital of the colony in all but title. Many of the women, in particular, have little skill in general conversation, or awareness of their listeners' interests, and bore everyone with triviality. Mrs Oswald Harman, whom I sat beside at a recent party, talked for a full half-hour about her square dinner set, and almost as long concerning the deficiencies of her servants. To dress to advantage and to know appropriate fashion for yourself is important, and I enjoy the choosing and wearing of attractive and well-made clothes, and talking about them when with women friends, but I have little in common with those who are more interested in apparel than attitudes, and who cannot discuss the issues of our time on equal terms with men. No doubt my circumstances and upbringing have made me accustomed to this, but it must become what is usual for educated women if we are to claim our rightful place.

There are, of course, people of justified reputation and accomplishment. Soon after our return from Lawrence, we entertained the Blacks, Hockens and Sumpters, as William wished to celebrate his election success. Mr Sumpter I find to be a businessman only, and his wife capable of little conversation apart from domesticity, although her dress sense is a good deal better than many. James Black is the genial and humorous professor of mineralogy whom William admires for his practical application of science, and for the resolve that saw him succeed from humble Scottish origins. When William was minister of mines, James accompanied him on visits through

Otago and the West Coast. Dougie was on the first trip with them, so knows the professor well, and they enjoy one another's company despite the age disparity. Knowing that Donald is somewhat out of favour with his father, the professor amused the table with tales of the first-born's inappropriate luggage on a later trip. Forgetful of the rigours of travel here, and the uncouth nature of the mining regions, our Oxford-educated, fox-hunting dandy carried dress shirts, a Savile Row suit, eau de Cologne and white gloves.

Of all William's friends whom I have met, I feel drawn most to Thomas and Bessie Hocken. He commands great respect within the city as medical practitioner, lecturer, civic supporter in so many ways, and a great enthusiast for history and the collection of memorabilia, journals, photographs and documents. Among so many people preoccupied with scrabbling for a foothold in the colony, he is one of the few with a sense of the value of the past as well as the needs of the present and the possibilities of the future. Despite being the son of a Methodist minister, he has become a devout Anglican, and in his company I disguise somewhat my religious scepticism. In all other respects I find his company stimulating and congenial. He is very sensitive about his small stature, being not much over five feet, and care must be taken in any reference to people's height, not to give offence. His fondness for me is perhaps partly because I am myself petite yet forthright. I do enjoy his company, and William shares his love of history and artefacts, though more inclined to Scottish and Australian annals.

It is unusual to find a really cultivated and perceptive man with a wife quite his equal, although this must be more a circumstance of convention and upbringing than natural ability. Bessie Hocken I like a great deal and she has become a close friend. She is a Buckland from that wealthy Auckland family and, like me and my sisters, was given opportunity and leisure for a wide education. She takes a full share in her husband's scholarly interests and loves music, which made a bond between us immediately. They also have a daughter named Gladys, though younger than William's girl. Bessie and I confide in each other without reserve. I think that is as much a pleasure for her as it is for me, since neither of us easily gives ourself completely to others. Bessie is sympathetic to my situation, partly because of her somewhat similar experience. Her own husband was married before, to a woman who was an ex-seamstress, a drunkard and a close friend of Eliza Larnach. So many links, so much concealed knowledge, in our small stratified communities that one has to be careful with any comment in society. The statuesque Ethel Morley I find a very pleasant companion also, though not her wealthy, but boorish, husband.

I hope to remain close to Bessie, despite the time we will spend in Wellington. We have talked many times, here, at functions and at her home, and, apart from Dougie, she is the person I shall miss most when I go. I knew when I married and came to Otago that I was leaving my own life behind and was to live in William's. His house, his friends and acquaintances, his business, even his preoccupations and his past, crowd in on me, but I am not daunted, and have kept a life of my own. My music I take with me always and anywhere. It is not only sustaining when I am alone, but a bridge to the friendship with people similarly inclined.

In that evening's company, where he was well known, Dougie was less in William's shadow than other times, and despite being younger he was quite able to talk as an equal on some topics. He spoke of his many visits to his great-uncle's estate in Sussex, sometimes with others of the family, sometimes alone on holiday from his boarding school. He is perceptive in noticing the differences between a colonial and an English upbringing, as he has experienced something of both. And his sense of humour is less obvious and more insightful than his father's.

William recounted at length his expedition years ago to seek out the Larnach family origins in Wick. All of us had heard the story before, and Bessie and I were close enough at the table to be able to continue our own enthusiasm quietly. She shares my opinion that far too much of the musical world's attention is at present given to the operas of Gilbert and Sullivan. I have seen both *Iolanthe* and *The Gondoliers*. Although they are diverting and colourful, it is sad that Arthur Sullivan's superior talents are so constrained by the dictates of his collaborator's jigging lyrics and improbable plots.

I will suggest we invite that same group again soon, with perhaps the Caughtreys, and the young organist Edward Miles, in place of the Sumpters. Thomas and Helen Bracken would be welcome, but he has accepted the job of parliamentary record clerk in Wellington, offered after William's intercession. I have noticed, however, that Dr Hocken is slightly discomforted in the presence of his fellow Thomas, not because of any intellectual incompatibility, but because of Bracken's imposing physical presence. The Brackens will be among the first of our guests in Wellington. I accept that William is pre-eminently a businessman, and then a politician, but I encourage also his natural and intelligent curiosity for the pursuits of the mind.

I feel it was a successful evening. All our guests stayed the night, as is almost a necessity here, and went the next day with palpable reluctance. The day before the dinner I had spent some time with Miss Falloon and Jane and was pleased with the result. The soups and entrées were all good, as was the saddle of mutton and the duck. The turkey was excellent and commented on as such, and we had two puddings as well as jellies and cheese. The wines were champagne, claret, sherry and port. William abstains now, but he provides for others. Although he rather likes his generosity to be noted, it is there, and I benefit from it, even in such difficult times as these. There is no meanness in William. If anything he has indulged his children and certain friends too much, and the comparative stringencies to which he is driven now are a source of embarrassment to him and threaten his self-esteem.

It is interesting to see William's attitude to the Cargills, who are a foremost family here. So many similarities in achievement and involvement both bond them and create rivalry. Edward Cargill has been as closely involved as William in the Colonial Bank and the refrigeration company, is a member of the House of Representatives and a community leader. He, too, built a grand mansion in the seventies — Cargill's Castle, on the cliffs above St Clair. Twenty-one rooms and walls of poured concrete that were a source of amazement to many. The place is famous for its balls and parties, at some of which we have been guests, but I find it colder even than The Camp, and the trees of the drive are permanently sloped because of the wind.

There was a terrible fire at Cargill's following the Otago Anniversary Ball of '92, and although Edward rebuilt, it has not regained its former splendour. He told me that the times were very different and indulgence could not be justified again. Much of considerable beauty was destroyed. William was sympathetic, yet could not repress a sense of smugness that misfortune had passed him by. He called a special gathering of the household staff to warn of the dangers of fire, and laid down that someone be designated last thing at night to check all fireplaces except those of the family bedrooms. Edward has the round, benevolent face of a Mr Cheeryble, but the edge of competition means, I think, that the two families will be public, rather than private, friends. Once, in reference to Cargill, William said with satisfaction that it must be a disappointment to such a successful man to have only daughters. Such a thought would never have occurred to my father.

Marriage to William has disclosed no particularly unpleasant side to his nature, but I admit to some disappointment in the relationship we have in private. His physical expectations I permit rather than enjoy; more disappointing for me has been our failure to fully share an inner life. The fault may be mine also, but apart from the brief entreaties and exclamations of the marriage bed, William talks to me when we are alone much as he does when we are in familiar company. His innermost feelings and aspirations are closed to me, and he shows impatience if I attempt to draw him out. Neither has he much interest now in my own confidences and he seldom asks about my happiness, or the reasons for any despondency, or gaiety, that might mark my mood. He talks of external things with confidence and at length, but is apprehensive of sustained revelation of deep, personal feeling. Annie, Bessie and Ethel are all greater confidantes than my husband. I may well be no different in all of this than most wives, but I had hoped for a soulmate.

In many ways Dougie is more aware and companionable than his father. Although he has had no musical training and is no great reader, we have become quite pals. He is the only one of William's adult children, apart from poor Kate, who has been prepared to accept me for myself and not as a supplanter of a mother's memory, or a threat to expectations. Thrown together here at The Camp, we have found a growing understanding. It is our joke that he is Outside Dougie and I am Inside Conny, for he likes nothing more than to be on horseback, or fishing, or working on the farm, whereas I feel most at home at a piano, or with my sketchpad and books.

In the winter especially I cannot be bothered with the constant change of clothing needed if one is going out and in. Yet in our friendship we are, I think, effecting a change in each other's habits. Dougie, quite as much as William, now likes to hear me play and even has his favourite pieces and some interest in the lives of those who composed them. And I have taken more to walking in the grounds, and rides in the buggy around the property and the peninsula, sometimes with William if he is not occupied with business, sometimes with Gladys and Gretchen as well if they are home, often with Dougie. His manner is more confident when he deals with the estate workers without William's presence, and more relaxed than within the house. I have come to appreciate the somewhat austere beauty of the place, all the more perhaps because I know that Eliza did not. Dougie always sees something different in the countryside, no matter how many times he passes through it: noticing that a field has been worked, a barn roof neglected, the course of a creek changed, bush darkened by the shadow of the clouds, or the tide line altered by a storm.

Boating is something I definitely dislike, and even Dougie's encouragement does not overcome it. The steamer is trial enough and I find no enjoyment in the little craft that men take out for pleasure or fishing. The motion is unsettling, as is the smell, and there is always a slop of foul water in the bottom, and often sticky scales on the surfaces. I cannot imagine it a pleasure to sit for hours in a swaying dinghy, open to sun and wind, cramped and uncomfortable, and have as the uncertain reward a few odorous fish.

William has as little time, or patience, for shopping, but Dougie often will take me into town, go on to the Fernhill Club awhile, then meet me at a tea shop and carry my parcels. He asks for my opinion as to his own clothes and often follows it. Together last week we chose a dinner jacket that had a shawl collar, silk and velvet facings and a single button. During the fitting the plump tailor's digestion was rudely apparent several times, and although all three of us studiously ignored the sound at the time, Dougie and I laughed together afterwards. He is the only man I could possibly share amusement with over such a thing. But life is life after all.

Dougie enjoys it most when the command at The Camp is his alone. He is no scholar, but from what he has told me the Adams

School at St Leonard's on Sea did nothing to awaken his mind and he was miserable there. He resents his father at times because of it, although William made the decision to have the children educated in England and on the continent from the best of motives. Somehow, however, it seems typical of William's generosity: a failure because he did not consider the recipient's wishes when bestowing it.

Dougie and I can talk about such matters and still not feel disloyal. I never criticise William, or enter personal dispute, within earshot of the household staff, or in the society of our friends. Dougie and I have come to trust one another and are free with confidences as close family should be. Both of us are concerned for William and the increasing pressures on him. He is not the man I remember in our Wellington home, laughing and reminiscing with Father, or ribbing my brothers about their dalliances. He is not the man I married. Kate's death, the snide ingratitude of Donald, Colleen and Alice, and the difficulties he is experiencing in business, have altered and reduced him. Now entering his sixties, he expects his life to have a certain ease of accomplishment after his earlier spectacular successes, but finds himself beset by more difficulties than ever, and with his vigour impaired.

'The times have moved against us,' he said yesterday, as he prepared to go into Dunedin on business, 'and I must fight to hold what I have, but sans peur, aye, without fear.' Such is the Larnach motto he has chosen.

'Surely things will swing back your way again,' I told him. 'Property doesn't grow smaller, as Father used to say.'

'Yes, but politics, too, has become a bog, and it threatens to swallow all of us in scandal.'

'Give it up then, if you neither need nor like it. It's knocking the stuffing out of you, and all for other people,' I said.

'I feel I must stand by my old friends,' he replied.

Seddon and Ward should have left him alone and not forced him back to the House to support them. The energy he will loyally expend there should be directed towards his own affairs, and there is no financial gain in parliamentary service. Even his natural optimism and goodwill are wearing thin. His outbursts of impatience have become more frequent, and he alternates between a demand for company he can dominate and an inclination for solitude. As his finances and patronage have diminished, so have the sycophantic followers, and he is increasingly disillusioned about the motives of almost everyone he meets.

Towards me he remains kind enough, but does not put himself out to please as once he did. In a strange way he seems to be ageing more rapidly, as if, having reached sixty, there is a canter downhill. I had hoped that after our marriage the difference in years would become progressively less significant as we became more familiar, but the opposite has occurred. He continues to put on weight but to lose hair, and there is a staidness to his movement. When he is awake his breathing is heavy; when he is asleep his snoring is thunderous.

He still likes to watch me dressing, but there is little exhilaration in our lovemaking, and often his embraces come to nothing. William is a clean man, but his body emanates a slight mustiness that I must steel myself to ignore, and hair grows upon his back as well as his chest. That we have separate rooms here is something for which I am now thankful. All of this is a most private reflection: I say nothing of it to any other, and barely to myself. But it is so. Even to my sisters I would not talk so directly of such things. I have never felt with my husband that unnerving lurch of excitement I experienced with Josiah, that rush of blood, that constriction of the heart and giddy temptation to cast all reserve aside. Men are free to go in search of pleasure and satisfaction; women, who have so much more to lose and fear, yet equal power to feel, must wait for an approach truly based in love.

I have not seen Josiah since the day of my wedding, but being a friend of Alfred's he will be about in the society we frequent in Wellington. I expect to confront him with equanimity, yet we will both be aware of those times when he was very pressing in his attentions. Sometimes I recall us together, alone, and the freedom he took with his hands and lips, despite being married, and my refusal. I think he would be a callous man, although very handsome. I slapped his face in the cloak room of a party for the Speaker of the House and said I would appeal to Alfred if he kissed me again. I am not a parlour maid to be so used. Yet I remember the disconcerting pressure of his lower body against mine, and the assurance with which he described a private entrance to a room in his legal chambers.

So we will go to the capital and spend a good deal of time there during sessions. Alfred is presently mayor of Wellington, which he sees as more advantageous for his legal firm than parliamentary duties. William and I will take our choice of society, and I will be close to many friends of my single years. I think I understand the nature of politics better than most women, and indeed most men, because of my family, my education, and my inclination.

William says little to me about business, but much of the time is unhappily preoccupied with his finances. Basil Sievwright comes often, other men with legal and financial advice at times. The Colonial Bank and its connection with the staggering Bank of New Zealand have become a quagmire from which William struggles to extricate himself. For me, even as explained by Dougie, it is a boring mass of manipulated figures, of claim and counter-claim, but I see clearly enough that William fears it could bring all down.

When we returned from Lawrence and our adventures, it was so good to see Dougie, and he was happy to have me back at The Camp. As I got down from the buggy he came quickly from the lion steps. 'Back at last,' he said, and kissed me impulsively on the mouth. He has never done so before, but it seemed very natural and open, a salutation between close friends and close family. William was present, and if he noticed he saw nothing untoward in it, and neither did I.

He was in good spirits that evening. We had no guests to entertain, and Gladys was at boarding school, so the three of us sat together until late, Dougie giving Dunedin and household news, William and I cropping the best of the Tuapeka experiences. William was pleased to have bested a big man like Scobie Mackenzie, and even the carriage disaster, and the poor food throughout most of the trip, were made a joke.

Harriet Connelly, one of the laundry maids, has provided our household scandal by falling pregnant. Dougie says that even Miss Falloon cannot persuade her to name the father. I can see that my welcome-home task will be to confront her and her family. She is a quiet, obstinate thing, not one I would have picked to give in to the farm men, who like to flatter the girls. I imagine she is little to blame, but unless she names the man and we can have them married promptly, we shall return her to family. I believe firmly that men must accept their responsibility: too often they escape it and the women involved do not insist sufficiently. My guess is that poor Harriet has fallen prey to a married man, who has offered her money to say nothing. It is a sad situation, but a common enough one.

Because William and I have been married only three years, and he is so much older, I must sometimes expect from him conversation about places and people with which I have no connection, and I try to accept that without impatience. I wish, however, that he would stop occasionally to think how little interest there often is for me in such recollections. In Lawrence we stood before the church and post office in the cold, because they had been designed by Robert Lawson, another Scot, the architect of The Camp and also of the mournful miniature of First Church that William commissioned as Eliza's tomb in the Northern Cemetery. The second evening of our return ended with William talking at length about his friendship with Lawson and wife Jessie, whom I have never met and who shifted to Melbourne before our wedding. Dougie sensed my boredom, but was unable to move William on to subjects more interesting to me, so I excused myself and went to my music.

I have become even more appreciative of the compositions of Rossini, especially since the series of concerts last year arranged by musician Charles Baeyertz. He is an amusing and outspoken performer and critic who has gingered up the local artistic community. I intend to invite him here before we leave for Wellington. At one of the concerts we heard him give a humorous recitation called 'A Masher's Story'. William was much taken, but the clog dancing by others and the demonstration of the new phonograph machine were less entertaining. When I talk with Mr Baeyertz I will point out that low vaudeville is well enough catered for here and he should ensure he gives us more Rossini, and Beethoven.

Also I shall challenge him to explain why there are no great women composers, while in literature, singing and art they increasingly assert themselves. I am sure it is not any absence of talent, but the blinkered conviction of male critics, backers and conductors that they are not worthy. I would like to make a serious attempt myself, but am reluctantly realistic enough to realise that I have neither the supreme ability, nor the dedication to the point of sacrifice, necessary to succeed. A paradox, perhaps, that I have had too pleasant a life to focus entirely on the one thing most important to me.

I was able to follow my inclination and determine all the pieces to be played at the ball held here at The Camp early in the year, and to invite individually the five players for an ensemble to accompany the dancing. It was quite the grandest social affair William and I have attempted since our marriage, and one that both of us enjoyed planning and on the night. Although quite imposing and spacious, the ballroom is seldom used for its avowed purpose. The exposed beam ceiling captures sound. I had the three great fireplaces dressed with holly and flowers. The double entrance door from the house has oak leaf and acorn carvings that I love to brush with my hand. They are in such wonderful relief that I almost feel I could pluck them in passing.

More than a hundred and sixty people in a considerable variety of formal dress. All my friends, and a few of my enemies if their families were sufficiently significant. Even Colleen and Alice put aside petulance for the night, and visited to dance with us. Every bedroom in the house was in use, with other rooms pressed into service besides. Often the weather frustrates, or limits, our plans, but this night was almost balmy. William claimed to have achieved it by drinking an alcohol-free toast to his Scots forebears the night before, Dougie by commissioning a Maori chant to the weather gods.

William spoke well, and briefly as I had advised him, and what interjections were made arose from good humour, wine and the high spirits of the occasion. Ethel Morley later told me she knew of two proposals of marriage made after the dancing, one of which was accepted on the spot — perhaps before it could be retracted. I stood up with a number of men apart from William and Dougie, and was paid the usual compliments. Dr Langley, who said my dancing made him acutely aware of his own deficiencies on the floor, also commented that he had never seen the ballroom so resplendent. Mr Guthrie said he knew of no other woman so light on her feet.

There was a moment of farce when Mrs Paisley tripped in a turn and fell on her husband, so injuring his leg that he had to be carried from the dance floor, attended in the house by Dr Langley and then taken home early. Very cross that he had proved such a weakling and denied her the pleasure of a full night at the ball, his wife accompanied him with distinct reluctance. Dr Langley murmured to me with a smile that he feared Paisley might suffer further harm at home.

During a waltz, Dougie told me I should go outside and see how the ball had drawn the farm workers and tenants to catch a glimpse of it all. I did so, keeping some distance in the dark from the building. In the glow from the tall windows of the ballroom, children and adults were clustered to peer in, some whispering excitedly about the goings on inside, others silent, but intent on a life so different from their own. There were carriage men too, watching their employers after a supper at the kitchen door.

Standing in the warm, still night, mistress of it all, but for the moment, like them, an observer on the outside, I had a powerful sense of the privileged existence that was mine. How little I considered that, how much I accepted it as my right, how readily I found limitation and inconvenience in it. How it must seem to ordinary folk: the bedecked private Larnach ballroom, the spilling light and music, the laughter and dancing of important, well-dressed people who all seemed to know each other. How perceptive of Dougie to have noticed these gawpers, and to understand how they would affect me. When I was caught up with the whirl of the ballroom, that seemed everything the world held, and then I was standing in the darkness, on the soft grass, with natural scents of trees and blossom rather than women's perfume, and the realisation that, even in that one place, experiences were quite different. How multifarious life is, and yet we assume our own activities and feelings to be the sum of it.

When I came back into the ballroom, Dougie soon sought me out. 'Did you see them?' he asked. 'Another population on the outside looking in, isn't it? I wonder what they think of us.'

'They want to change places, I suppose.'

'The children,' he said, 'they'll go home and dream of it, I imagine.'

'You and your dreams, Dougie. The real world has enough interest for most of us.'

'But not everybody has our world.'

The ball was a considerable success, and quite repaid my many days of preparation and the money spent by William. For a time he was quite buoyed up by it all and read aloud the numerous cards sent by those who enjoyed our hospitality. Old Mrs Hallan, who still carries smelling salts, wrote that it reminded her of the great private balls in the Edinburgh of her girlhood. Dougie's friend, Robert, told me soon after that he had never before seen so many animated and good-looking women together, and said there should be a Larnach ball every year. To have the event go off so well reassures William of his position socially, even though his business dealings are faltering. I wonder how many of our guests, who so readily accepted the invitation for the night, would support him if he needed it.

The one unfortunate incident, which we didn't discover until the next day, was a fight between two carriage men in the stables where a group had gathered to drink ale. Neither of them was from The Camp, but one had his nose so badly bitten that the bone was showing. Dougie said they had to wash blood from the cobbles, and the police had made an arrest. The best and worst of human behaviour can be so close together.

I was struck by a most appalling cough in the aftermath of the ball. Maybe I had exhausted myself, or perhaps one of the guests had brought the infection and spread it in the close crush of the dancing and dining. Several people complained of similar symptoms. For six days I kept to my bed. The cough was not only painful, but kept me from sleeping at night. Dr Langley gave me a thick, sweet potion and also a camphor ointment for my chest. Dear Annie came from Wellington to nurse me, and to pass the time she read *David Copperfield* to me and brought out all my dresses for scrutiny. A timely sort out: some will be sent to Wellington for my sisters. Annie will have first choice, then Sarah and Fanny. I am now fully recovered and happy again.

Not long after, we had a picnic at Broad Bay, to celebrate good health. A surprise for me that I suspect Dougie instigated. It was one of those most beautiful autumn days: frost early, but not a breath of wind or a cloud in the sky. In the great blue bowl of sky, a full sun that was warm on the skin, but not scorching. William and Dougie must have made a decision early and sent Boylan and Jane down to prepare a spot at the bay, all without my knowledge. Later in the morning, when I was in the music room, Dougie came to me and said he and William wished my company while they looked at a cottage left vacant by one of the tenants, and when we had jolted over the poorly formed road to the bay, there were Boylan and Jane waiting in the very best warm place close to the shore, with horse covers, rugs and cushions set out, and food in the shade beneath their buggy. Jane had gone to considerable trouble and smiled so openly when I complimented her. She is a funny old thing, the closest The Camp has to an 'ancient retainer'. A tall body and a tall, lined face, and almost always she wears a starched apron. But she is devoted to the family and knows every inch and custom of The Camp. I am the third Mrs Larnach she has served, but she has warmed to me and now comes sometimes to confide concerning her occasional differences with Miss Falloon. It is not sneaking: she feels long service carries the right of commentary.

William and I walked by the sea for a time, and talked of the Seddons, who were planning to visit us, while Dougie went off and measured the girth of native trees that he was proposing be sold. When the three of us sat down in the stillness to have our picnic, the sun was so pleasant that I took off my hat to feel the warmth full on my face. Afterwards, William lay down and appeared to sleep while Dougie and I talked of everything and anything — the ball, the leak in the observation room, the merits of the Fernhill Club as compared with the Dunedin Club, the sudden death of the Hockens' cook during a dinner party, the elopement of Millicent Powys with Eustace Apse. Although William lay with his hands folded on his chest and a serviette over his face, he was not asleep, for he would sometimes laugh when we did, sometimes abruptly alone, and sometimes interrupt with a brief comment.

Such times are special, for William is a busy man and much in demand. So often there seems some urgent matter of land, money or investment, and obstacles posed by unscrupulous and grasping people. There at Broad Bay, though, lying happily in the sun with me and his favourite son, he was at his most cheerful, and when William is well disposed all around seems likewise. We stayed there until mid-afternoon when a cool breeze began from the sea, then set Traveller trotting for The Camp, leaving Jane and Boylan to bring things home.

Yesterday, Dougie took me in to the Dunedin Orchestral Society's Meyerbeer concert, where I joined the Hockens, before going on by himself to the club. I enjoyed the buggy rides just as much as the performance between them. Dougie is much closer to my age, and how good it was to feel and act young, to laugh at silly things, to be with someone who knows the same people, but will pass on nothing I say about them.

From the men, especially Patrick Sexton and Boylan, Dougie gets to hear indirectly of goings on within The Camp that I am often unaware of myself. There is less formality outside than within the big house. 'Miss Falloon has an admirer,' he said, and refused to say more until I admitted interest. 'But I know you don't like to engage in idle gossip.'

'Just tell me and stop being smug.'

'Remember our tenant Edwin Tremain, who has a fishing boat as well?'

'Yes, he brings us part of the catch and often won't take payment because of William's long-time support.' When I said this, Dougie raised his eyebrows and pretended an absorption in the surroundings as we trotted along. He likes to tease me in this way as a means of proving I am interested in the trivial, despite my greater concern for what he terms my 'causes'.

'I'll punch you,' I said.

'Well, evidently our Mr Tremain is more concerned for what might be gifted by our housekeeper in the future than anything he's received from Father in the past. At the kitchen he'll release his offerings only to her, and goes as red as a turkey cock. Jane says he asked her to tell Miss Falloon he has been widowed for almost a year. I doubt he mentioned that his wife died quite worn out with child-bearing.'

'Doesn't he have awful mutton-chop whiskers?'

'Maybe they'll tickle Miss Falloon's fancy,' Dougie said. 'She does seem partial to a good piece of fish.' Dougie is fond of such nonsense, but it is fun to be so relaxed with him, to have no need of guarded language, or conventional propriety. Because he lives with me as family, yet is not a son or brother, we have a friendship closer than any other I have experienced with a man not my husband. But proximity is only what has allowed us to know each other well: the real basis of our understanding is a similar view of things despite our very different natures. Beneath his slightly puffed up and uncertain pose, the real Dougie is kind and thoughtful, still searching for his right place in a world dominated by his father.

We arrived back at The Camp quite light-headed, and Dougie pursed his mouth in mock solemnity as we entered the house, which made me smile the more. I feel that he is on my side, against whatever opposition might arise. He has become a special friend, and I will miss him.

Four

Conny and Father will be spending much of their time in Wellington now that he's been re-elected. I have very mixed feelings at the prospect. I'll have greater freedom and authority here, but it means Conny will be absent for many weeks at a time. Her duty and her family are in Wellington, a journey of days away. She's made a great fist of it here, despite knowing very few people at first, and being snubbed by Alice and Colleen. Not only has she established her own presence in the city despite a degree of gossip that was bound to follow the marriage, but she's asserted herself at The Camp.

The passing of the Electoral Act last year made her more excited than I've ever seen her before, and even Father's failure to secure the Wakatipu seat at the election soon after did little to dampen her sense of victory. How wonderful, she said, that in this our small colony has led the world. It's impossible not to be glad with her, though in my experience few women have the common sense and knowledge to use a vote wisely, and she does go on so. Those reservations I keep to myself, of course. On Monday, during the buggy ride into town to meet Father, I enjoyed provoking her by suggesting a whole range of matters most inappropriate for women to express opinions on, yet she had a quick answer almost every time. I like it that she's not prim and proper when we're together.

Conny and Bessie Hocken organised a luncheon to celebrate the granting of the franchise. Thirty-three leading ladies, and no men allowed, not even as waiters. There were toasts and anecdotes from the long battle. I imagine that a good many politicians and civic leaders who had opposed them would have felt their ears redden and wonder why. Conny said it was great fun, and the talking point of the town for days. No doubt Henry Fish and his supporters regard it as the first sign of women's general insurrection.

Conny has found her proper level in Dunedin and is sought for her own company as well as being Mrs Larnach. She is unimpressed by dull, conventional people, whatever their position and influence. Mrs R. McGeadon, a long-standing hostess and patron of the arts, who claims distant kinship with Gladstone, tried to put her down at several starchy gatherings, but came off second best in the joust, and Conny's reference to her as Armageddon is now a favourite witticism in town. The two have engaged in several skirmishes in the campaign for social supremacy since Conny's initial disagreement with Mrs McGeadon's pronouncement that a woman should on no account be seen in public without both hat and gloves. I teased Conny by saying that I'd heard the two of them crossed the street rather than meet, but she said the significant thing was which of them chose to cross.

Conny's friends have talents and progressive views. Bessie Hocken has become her closest ally, but Ethel Morley is often a companion also. I particularly enjoy it when Ethel visits, for she is quite beautiful. A great pity she is married, Robert says, and admits she's the woman he most often imagines naked. I have done so myself when in her company and finding the conversation of others boring. Although Robert lacks deceit and malice, he likes to be louche when with male friends. Women's flesh is heavier than ours, he insists. Most recently he made me laugh by describing his mother and father in pious discussion at Sunday lunch about the vicar's sermon regarding the sanctity of marriage. 'What a lot of cant is talked about it,' he told me. 'A man's vision of marriage is to wake each morning with his wife's hand on his cock. God knows what a woman's is.'

Conny and I have become great friends, and partly to keep her good opinion I've broken off my unofficial engagement to Ellen. Not that Conny ever made an open criticism of her, but I admitted to myself that I'd no intention of marrying, and became increasingly uneasy, for I knew Ellen's hopes. Her family are decent enough folk, although the father mangles the Queen's English, and the mother's a snob. I suspect I'm not Ellen's first lover. There were hints from her mother about the formality of engagement, and it became clear that some declaration had to be made, or the friendship retrenched.

Ellen cried when I told her I didn't wish to marry. I'd rather she'd been angry, though I'd made no promise. She wept and said she'd thought I loved her. The sadness was worse than any accusation. We were standing on the walking track above the sea at St Kilda, with others of our party not far away. I hadn't meant the matter to come up in such circumstances, but she asked me if I wished to come with her family the next weekend to visit relatives at Palmerston, and in declining I found the conversation moved on willy-nilly to our future generally. We reached a point at which I was forced to contemplate an outright lie, or confess I had no intention of marrying her. So we finished standing awkwardly above the pale sand with its tidal patterns, close to dark green lemonwood scrub shaped by the sea wind, with Ellen trying to hold back tears, and me making some foolish comment about the small island just offshore, as the others joined us. I never feel satisfaction in inflicting hurt on anyone, and her white face turned away, and shaky hands, almost overwhelmed me, but I knew that if I comforted her then, the same situation would have to be faced in the future.

Women instinctively close ranks in such times. As we made our way back to the carriages they clustered around Ellen in support, glancing back disapprovingly at we men. It was assumed, I suppose, that I'd been cruel, and perhaps Ellen lessened her unhappiness afterwards by sharing it with her friends. The thing was clumsily done, I know, and I regret that, but it was unpremeditated and I was caught up in the sorry whirl of it. I've not seen her alone since and have spoken only superficially. However, her suffering is apparently over, for she's often in the company of other fellows.

The good thing is that there's no slur, or gossip, attached to her, as far as I know. My fear was that she might become pregnant, despite precautions I disliked, and I'd be compelled to marry. It was almost entirely physical satisfaction that drew me to her. She's attractive, in reasonable society, and prepared to indulge me fully, but I felt more and more uncomfortable about taking advantage of her. To be a cad isn't my nature, and I've never discussed Ellen in a loose way with other men. Unlike some here, I don't see love as some sort of game, and Ellen is the only woman of standing I've been long with. Robert says it's far better not to get involved with girls of respectable family, but my few experiences with women of other backgrounds have generally been both sordid and disappointing. I sometimes go with Robert, Hugo Isaac and others to what used to be the Vauxhall Gardens above Andersons Bay. Women are easy to find there, but there's a soullessness to such liaisons and I'm always in danger of being recognised wherever I take them. It's usually only after rioting with the others that the need for a woman overcomes me, and I drink less, and less often, now. A man's needs are best satisfied with a woman he loves, surely, yet those needs can be urgent.

I feel The Camp is truly home for me, and although Father still talks occasionally of my taking up some profession — making something of myself, he says — this is where I belong. Melbourne's just a few hazy vignettes of infancy; the good times were here as a boy with the building of The Camp and all of us happy. Then there seemed nothing Father couldn't do, and all was on the up. The later trip across America and on to England and Uncle Donald's was high excitement, though it ended for me in a sort of muted misery.

All photographs have an element of sadness because their time is over, and some are doubly sad because of feelings they evoke. Recently I came across one of Tolden House, Adams School — ranks of us with keen faces and arms folded, all united in an apparent camaraderie. At the end of 1879, Father and Mother returned to the colony with little Gladys, and the rest of us were divided and left. Donny went grandly to Oxford, my sisters remained with Miss Visick their tutor, and I was stuck in the Adams boarding school at St Leonard's on Sea. The only times we children reunited were at uncle Donald's.

My boarding school life is recalled like a time of sickness: an illness from which I could see no recovery. There are certain foods I can't eat, smells that disgust, and sounds that deaden my spirit, and all because through them my school days rise up again. Even bells bring only the memory of rigid servitude and loneliness. Is there any institution more unbendingly conventional than an English boarding school, more driven by nonsensical conformity? I've dreams still in which I revisit that unhappiness: the dreary life in which there was no-one who loved me.

Not one other boy came from New Zealand, or Australia, and I was marked and ridiculed from the first as an outsider. There were quite a few Raj boys whose parents were in the military, or the Indian bureaucracy. Some others had been despatched to board there by guardians, and even more by fathers who wanted their sons to have a public school education, but neither their pockets, nor their influence, stretched to Rugby, Winchester, or Harrow. St Leonard's on Sea I suppose was no worse than most second rate schools, and thankfully out of term time I wasn't forced to attend the dingy exam-crammers that were a feature of the town, and staffed largely by the same grey teachers of the school.

The rote lessons seemed to have no connection with my past, or future, and the teachers fawned on boys whose parents were of the slightest consequence. They would have been amazed to see The Camp, the many thousands of Larnach acres in Central Otago. At the height of its success, the firm of Guthrie & Larnach had more than a thousand workers and owned fourteen ships, I could say nothing of that, or else be fiendishly ragged as a skite. The stupid boy whose father owned three apothecary shops was more important. I was just a colonial brat as far as the masters there were concerned. At least in class I was safe from the theatre of cruelty that existed so often on the playing fields and within the dorms. How I envied the day boys, who could leave the place behind and go home to family.

My companions were oddities like myself, and we drew together not by attraction, but because of exclusion by the mob. I made only one staunch friend. Jeremy Pointer, my Housemaster's son, and shunned by most because his father was detested. I detested him too, but recognised from my own unhappiness the injustice of Jeremy being blamed for his father's ridiculousness. Pig Pointer was disdained even by his fellow teachers, but Jeremy had a blind loyalty that caused him to rise to every insult made. I admired that loyalty even though I saw the persecution he suffered because of it.

Jeremy was in another House, but often on half days we would go down to the shore, and for a few hours imagine our lives different. We would buy beer at the old Horse and Groom pub, and drink it by the stone steps while we watched the shop girls. We would take a dinghy out, or walk up to the common used by the school for the annual cross country run, and sit amongst the cover to smoke our pipes, and light fires that in the summer came near to disaster. We would talk about everything except the school, and yet that hung over us, was always the inevitable return.

I've happily forgotten the other boys I knew at St Leonard's, even those I then claimed as friends, and those known as enemies, but I wonder sometimes what's happened to Jeremy Pointer, and imagine what relief he must have found it to leave school and go into a world where his father was unknown, and no longer an encumbrance. No matter how much of a ragging he got, he always stood up for his useless father, perhaps because his mother was dead, but more I think from stubborn allegiance. And he and I never talked about his persecution, as if ignoring it denied its existence. I wish just once I'd told him I admired his unflinching and misplaced fealty.

He was mad on conjuring and tricks of magic, bought books on it, and practised with cards and small, false bottomed caskets purchased from advertisements. In every school concert he came on to universal derision, the only applause when inevitably something went wrong. What strange courage he had. In war I imagine he'd be marked out by some great feat of heroism, and die in the execution of it. When we left the school, he and I pledged to remain friends, and he wrote a few letters to which I made no reply, not because I didn't value him, but that his comradeship was borne down by my greater resolve to leave everything of St Leonard's behind me. In his last letter he said he intended to become an artist, and that he'd met a girl whose father was a museum curator with a famous collection of butterflies.

The single person I see fondly in recollections of St Leonard's is Jeremy Pointer. His long face and flat, dark hair: his failures as a magician, and his absolute loyalty as a son, and friend to me. All that's long gone, but memory is beyond conscious control. We can't choose our past, or ever quite bury it.

I received the news of my own mother's death while still at school. It was a wretched winter day, and I was in sick bay because of a flare up after my riding accident. Pig Pointer came, and in front of the only other boy there, a junior I despised called Davidson, told me he'd had a cablegram with the news. 'Letters will follow, lad,' he said, standing as usual with his legs well apart and his great flaccid, downy cheeks catching the dim light. 'I'm sorry to be the bearer of such bad tidings. I'll tell matron you'll be better in here for the night,' and then he went. I turned away from the other boy so he couldn't see my face. The beds were of thin, knobbed iron, the bare wooden walls pale and scratched like a zoo pen, and the sky as grey as the blanket under which I lay.

I was determined not to cry in the presence of the other boy, and lay in a quaking misery waiting for darkness. I could hear boys shouting and laughing on High Field as if nothing in the world had changed, and later matron brought in shepherd's pie and a dark custard stuff we called Mississippi mud. I couldn't stomach either, and Davidson had the cheek to ask if he could have the tray. 'I'm fair starved,' he said, having hogged everything of his own.

So little of my time at St Leonard's gave me pleasure, or even placid monotony, yet I know Father thought he was doing well by me. His welcome letters would come addressed to 'My Darling Son' and in typical schoolboy fashion, in return I would only hint at unhappiness. He thought everyone like himself, possessed of presence and the ability to impose on any situation. He never understood how much out of place I felt, though after Mother's death I spoke strongly about wishing to return. Donny's extravagance and hasty marriage may have influenced Father's final agreement, so in that at least I have some reason to thank my brother.

Brambletye was my refuge while in England. Uncle Donald and aunt Jane were ever hospitable, and the cousins carefree companions. William, the eldest son, was sixteen years older than me, yet he too was supportive and generous. I was saddened when he died suddenly at only thirty four. James, next in line, was the horseman Donny and I aspired to be. Sydney and Herbert were closer to my age, and although still senior were both friendly. In that family existed an amiable cheerfulness and encouragement quite lacking in my school life.

Father would like The Camp to be a sort of colonial Brambletye, but it doesn't fit as comfortably in its surroundings, or in the minds of Dunedin people. The Sussex estate wasn't quite a heaven, but certainly a haven, and St Leonard's almost a hell. At Brambletye no-one quizzed me, or mocked my speech. People there didn't take pleasure in the humiliation of others.

My Sussex cousins were a champion, outdoors band, seeming to show no reflection of their quiet and polite parents. Privilege and indulgence were their right. The house is not more than twenty-five years old or so, and famed for its frescoed ceilings, wall papers and furniture. Uncle Donald has a magnificent conservatory for his collection of rare plants, and it's the custom for all visitors to scratch their names on the large glass door. My signature is there among all the others, and I hope some day to return to underscore it, and relive the pleasure I received there. The family also owned a fine home in London's Palace Gardens.

Odd misfortune then that it was at Brambletye I had the fall from the hunter, Mercury, that almost killed me. I suffer from the effects still, and yet the moment of it is hidden from me. The mind's way to protect itself perhaps. I remember a long chase across a flat past a spinney, being shouldered by another horse at a low hedge, and then lying on my back, a clear sky above and a damnable pain in my leg. And the smell of sweat not my own, for someone had put a jacket under my head. Concussion that reoccurred for many months, fractured cheek bone, broken bones in the left arm and leg. Even the convalescence from all of that could not save me from the return to boarding school at last. I would've chosen a second tumble if it could have kept me permanently at Brambletye.

I have vivid memories of the place, some inconsequential, but almost all happy. Once, coming back from swimming in the bridge pool, Herbert and I found spawning frogs in a warm pond. Dozens of pairs on the weedy surface, each male clamped on the back of its mate with forelegs tight about her throat. So strong was their urge that they took no notice of us, and we scooped up many into our towels, just because we could. What variety of slick green they had, from the faintest glass blush to deepest emerald.

Another time he and I were part of the search party for the local idiot who had become drunk on cider and begun beating sheep and cows with a paling. We found him asleep in the big meadow with straw in his boots, blood on his hands and no trousers. His cock was small, but it was my first realisation of how hairy are a full adult's genitals. When he was woken, he laughed and sang in front of us all. His old mother came and took him away like a child. How different he must have found the world.

Although Father put me at the school, I never doubted he felt it for the best. I received many letters from him while I was recovering from the accident, and he welcomed me warmly on my return to New Zealand, despite our differences. Some years later, when I had to have further corrective surgery in Dunedin, he came all the way from Wellington to be with me. When Basil Sievwright, Henry Driver and others came with business they said was urgent, Father turned them away and sat with me for hours, talking of Mother, Aunt Mary and the days he, Donny and I spent on the peninsula while The Camp was being built. Soon after, he made a sortie to Australia in an attempt to bolster his businesses, but that was another financial disaster for him, and he narrowly avoided being dragged down by Melbourne swindlers. He was very low when he returned and, with Mary not long dead, he found The Camp the sad place it remained for him until Conny made it home again.

Father isn't a confessional man: he believes in fortitude, trusting that energy and hard work will enable him to succeed. But yesterday, on what may well turn out to be the last trip to town before he and Conny leave for Wellington, he spoke more openly about his feelings than he has for a long time. The day was blustery, and he complained of the new horse as we passed his failed Dandy Dinmont hotel at Waverley, which I knew better than to refer to.

'Fat and out of condition,' he said. 'I'll talk with Boylan. Just a nag compared with Stockings, or Traveller.'

'Horses don't last for ever,' I said. Father had a tartan blanket for his knees and wore a tam-o'-shanter. I knew some in Dunedin laughed behind his back at his devotion to Scottish custom and dress, but he had a vision of himself as laird, despite, or perhaps because of, those relatively humble Larnachs of Wick from whom he came.

'I've no great stomach for more of Parliament, Dougie, but Seddon and Ward have been very pressing and the affairs of both the Bank of New Zealand and the Colonial Bank are dire. The government will have to intervene or all will be brought down. Ward's heading for bankruptcy. Seddon doesn't understand money and says he relies on my advice. But it'll be no picnic for any of us.'

'Surely the government will have to support the banks? Otherwise the colony will be just a shambles.'

'But everyone wants to call in their money,' he said. 'People want it under their beds so they can sleep soundly on it. No one wants to lend.'

'But there's the ultimate value of property, isn't there?' I said. 'You can't gainsay that. You can touch it and walk over it, build on it and, if the worst comes to the worst, you can eat off it.'

'Damn rabbits, though, and poor prices.' He urged the horse to a brisk trot. 'The money for development has dried up. Everything's ready cash, and I'm as stretched as the next man. Confidence is going, and that's what drives business and growth. It's a mean hoarder's world at the moment. No one's safe. It's look to yourself and damn the next fellow.'

Father would rather spend all his time in Otago. He's joining Richard Seddon not just from a sense of duty but because he hopes for the elusive knighthood. As his financial difficulties increase, so does his vanity.

Robert says it's the same story with everyone: businesses are finding everyone slow to pay. 'It's squirm time,' he says. When he spent two nights with us last week we took the guns out twice and walked a long way, shooting gulls and even an albatross, for fun, and pigeons for the pot. Our game bags were a good load on our way back to The Camp. We also rode and raced along the bay tracks and clambered over the boat wreck at Portobello. He's a carefree friend and we can have a grand blowout together, yet in the house he plays the gentleman for Father and Conny, while privately keeping the maids atwitter. As the two of us drank together until late, he told me of a governess he has conquered in Belleknowes. An absolute succubus, he told me with delight, who names his body parts in three languages. He finds life alternately a great lark and a bitter constriction. His company is a relief from the routines of The Camp, but strangely I now find more satisfaction in talking with Conny.

Perhaps it seems ridiculous that, as a man in the prime of life, my favourite woman companion is my father's wife. But it's so, and why should I be ashamed of it? Conny and I find so much in each other's company, and Father likes the three of us being together: he's buoyed up by our talk. She would have me educated in music, and as keen a reader as herself of Austen, Eliot, Oliphant and Dickens, whereas my natural inclination is for Conan Doyle and Scott. And more than any reading, I enjoy being out and about.

For my part, I persuade her to walk more, to enjoy the natural world. She'll never make a farmer, but she's increasingly interested in the grounds of The Camp and the wilderness of the peninsula. She encouraged Father to extend the glasshouses and to plant colourful flowers on the lower garden rather than native shrubs.

The growth of understanding isn't just on my side. Tuesday was hot and cloudless, and after working with others to repair stalls in the stables, I walked out to the front gardens with my shirt loose and the sleeves rolled up. I was standing by the wishing well to catch the breeze from the sea when Conny and one of the gardeners came past with their baskets of cut flowers. She complained of the heat. 'Of course you're hot, being all togged up,' I said. 'You've no idea of the pleasure there is in the cooling feel of the wind on your skin. Watch sometime as a lathered horse turns into it for relief.'

'The comparison isn't a compliment,' she said, with a quick smile.

'I mean that you haven't had the simple and natural satisfaction of the wind on your body when you work.'

'I suppose you're right,' she said. 'It's a funny thing, but I've never thought of it before. I do believe that women must be allowed garments that give freedom to play sport, cycle or climb if they wish.'

Conny has made me aware of a society of modern women

unknown to me before. She, and her friends such as Bessie and Ethel, have a quality of understanding and conversation that is the equal of any man's. What a gulf between her enlightenment and accomplishments, and poor Ellen Abbott, whose prattle is difficult to concentrate on once she's been bedded.

When Father and Conny leave I will be sole master here again. I've had good discussions with Father about my plans for the estate. Now that his investments are returning less, he's particularly concerned that the peninsula property more than pays its way, and from the profits will come my return for overall supervision.

In the grand times a great many staff were employed to maintain enterprises that were appropriate for a manor house but contributed little to funds: rather the reverse. The vineries, hothouses and fernery are largely indulgence, yet popular, but I see no need for peacocks and guinea fowl to roam the grounds. We've also dispensed with the cock-fighting pit, the llamas and monkeys of my childhood, and a boy whose occupation was to individually wrap coal pieces in tissue for the bedroom fires. There are far too many dogs. The Newfoundland is Father's favourite breed, but he has reluctantly agreed to a reduction in the pack. I hope to sell a good number: like almost all of our animals, they are true bloodstock.

We need to concentrate on the excellent Alderney herd that's been built up, and the potatoes and oats that do well here. As Dunedin grows so will the demand for dairy products, vegetables and meat. Despite present conditions I agree with Father that the success of refrigerated cargoes opens excellent prospects for the colony. He was the managing director of the refrigeration company that sent the first frozen lamb to England, and still takes pleasure in telling how he stood at the high observation window of The Camp to watch the *Dunedin* sail from Port Chalmers. His vigour and enterprise have benefited so many, yet those gains tend to be forgotten in the present criticism many make of him. The ingratitude is, I think, one reason his interest and enthusiasm for further innovation are waning.

I'm all for clearing more of the land, and wire-fencing paddocks rather than building stone walls, though I'm pleased that we have these on all the boundaries of our property. Before Father's marriage to Conny, there was a large fire on an adjacent property, which did a good deal of damage to ours, and Father's relationship with the neighbour has been frosty since.

I believe there are too many people employed for the household and not enough on the farms. What need have I for a full complement of inside servants when I'm the only family member here most of the time? There are plenty of local men and women who can do part-time work when required. I've had all this out with Father and he sees the sense of it. I've started to use the stratagem with him that I notice Conny employs successfully — introduce proposals in such a way that he comes to see them as of his own devising. Patrick Sexton is a sound overseer and we work well together. I've a plan that will ensure progress while still maintaining the visible lifestyle so essential to William Larnach.

It's what I've looked forward to, yet now I think I would rather play second fiddle, as ever, to Father and still have Conny at The Camp. At first I thought her rather too sharp in her judgements to be ideal company, and too fine in proportions to be admirable as a woman, but my opinion has changed on both counts.

She and her family have had little to do with open country and farming, but she shows a comradely interest in what is done here on the properties and what Father and I hope to achieve. On Tuesday there was a blue vellum sky and hardly a breeze. Conny came out with me to see the Clydesdales sledging timber from the cut below Fork Ridge. She marvelled at their size and strength, but wasn't fearful, going right up to stroke them, and wasn't repulsed by the froth of sweat they'd worked up. She was interested when I explained how calm and affectionate they are, and that size and strength in an animal don't necessarily mean an aggressive disposition. 'The runts in species are often worst,' I told her. 'I've been bitten and kicked more by damn ponies than any larger breed, and lap dogs have the temperament of frustrated spinsters.'

'You want an argument, I know,' she said, 'but I'll not rise to it', and she smiled. 'The horse is a fine animal.' She bent down to stir the feathering on a hoof. And when she was standing by its head again, she touched the great, flat jaw, the white blaze and tousled forelock, and said, 'What beautiful eyes it has.' That perception pleased me, for indeed horses have beautiful eyes.

One of the men was cheeky enough to ask her if she wanted to get on its back, but she said she wasn't dressed for that. When the horses and men were back to work, Conny and I sat on the stone stile and talked. She said she'd been told by a tradesman that both Father and I were known to get hot at any cruelty to animals, which she regarded as a compliment to us both. She wore a large-brimmed sunhat, so sometimes her face was lost to me. She has the ability to draw people out, does Conny, and I found somehow the conversation came round to my school days at St Leonard's and my deep unhappiness there. Never before have I spoken honestly about those years, but Conny was sympathetic and interested, her own education having been so different. When I told her of the desolation and loneliness I felt when Mother died, she took my hand and we sat there for a time without speaking, watching the great horses come down the gully, and admiring the skill with which men and Clydesdales managed the logs that constantly threatened to crush them.

When we are together she is perceptive, as well as quick, in conversation, and encouraging of my opinions. We allow few barriers of gender in our talks; we are just as two people, equal and attentive. Yet, yet, I'm increasingly aware of the swell of her breast, the pale base of her smooth neck, the brown hair glossy above her ears, the fragrance that is part perfume and part herself — and sometimes, when we're alone, there seems to pass a sort of frisson between us, so that everything I see has a momentary shimmer. Conny, I feel, is equally aware of it, but neither of us makes acknowledgement. Just to be in her company is pleasure, and there's no awkwardness in any silence that we share. Somehow when she's with me everything seems complete.

Often I think of the spontaneous kiss I gave her at the lion steps on her return from Lawrence, the jolt it gave me, the look that passed between us, although we've not referred to it again. We're the closest of friends, without guilt. We're family, after all.

Five

This Christmas and the seeing in of 1896 have been a low point indeed for William, and threatened so for me. We were not long back to The Camp from Wellington at the beginning of December when William's bad luck struck again. Horse transport bedevils the Larnachs. The three of us were travelling into Dunedin mid-morning when the axle of the buggy broke just as we came into Anderson's Bay. Dougie and I were shaken, but uninjured, except for a bloody graze on the palm of his left hand. William was flung onto the hard summer road, breaking ribs and dislocating his shoulder. Rather than railing against yet another blow, he took it with an uncharacteristic and sad fatalism that has become one of the moods we see in him now. Thank God Dougie suffered nothing serious. I don't think his constitution would stand another serious reverse. The shock of it, however, made him swear in a foul way I have never heard from him before, and for which he apologised later. There were the three of us, and a spooked horse, on the road quite bare of any other traffic or immediate help: William lying dazed in his suffering, Dougie swearing like a trooper, me close to tears, with my silk and cotton town dress, worn only once before, quite ruined and torn.

Dougie was about to walk to the nearest dwelling when a timber dray came up the road from town. The driver turned around, helped push the buggy from the road and took us, jolting and uncomfortable, to the Lefroys' home, from which Dr Langley was sent for. Despite his pain, William remarked with satisfaction that Traveller, walking tethered behind the dray, seemed unhurt. Mrs Lefroy was doing her own cooking, but broke off to make us comfortable in her front room, which cannot have been open to the air for many days. It held a fine old sea chest. She quite put herself out to be kind, but such occasions create the awkward obligation to afterwards acknowledge the benefactor when in public. Two days later one of the Crimmond boys brought back Dougie's black bowler hat, discovered in the grass, and stood his ground until I sent him to the kitchen to get a pudding as reward.

For two weeks after the hospital attention, William could do little else except lie in an armchair, claiming he was more comfortable there than in bed. His stoicism has been replaced with irritability, not so much from pain as from the confinement and the mounting and almost despairing worry he experiences because of the state of the Colonial Bank and the Bank of New Zealand. Ward's excessive borrowings, and the political cover-up with Seddon's connivance, add greatly to his concern. Their Banking Act, and the consequent merger of the two banks, will cost William personally more than sixty thousand pounds. The ins and outs are gibberish to me, but his financial fortunes, and those of the colony, seem to be unravelling. I am glad for even the small amount of money I have from Father.

Colleen came home for a time, saying she wished to comfort her father, but in truth she was, as always, on a spying mission. She spends most of the year with Alice and travels about during the other months. Her sojourn was even less of a success than usual. She invited a Christchurch friend, which rather defeated the stated purpose of her visit. To me she is barely civil, and she pays attention to William mainly to ask for money. Although well aware of the hours I prefer for myself at the piano, several times she and her companion set up camp in the music room at just that time. Had they talent, or even serious intention, I would not have cared, but it was all chatter, laughter and mismatched instruments. Each morning when we were together at breakfast, she made an obvious appraisal of my dress and hair, and I think she went into my room on occasions when I was in town, for the jewellery in my drawer had been disturbed. How distasteful to think of her rummaging there, making a catalogue perhaps for Alice.

Also she presumed to give direction to Miss Falloon and others, sometimes in contradiction to my own wishes. The Camp can have only one mistress, and I had it out with her. She knew better than to appeal to William, or Dougie, and brought forward her departure. 'You make me very aware that I'm of no account in the home and family that I've belonged to for many more years than you,' she said. 'Alice calls you The Cuckoo. Did you know that?'

There is no point in arguing with such entrenched dislike, and I think her sister, although younger, has a powerful influence over her. Perhaps marriage would ease Colleen's dissatisfaction with almost everything, but she is no beauty.

So there was little festivity in our Christmas and New Year at The Camp. Only Dougie and Gladys show any real affection for their father, and his varying moods of withdrawal and irascibility increasingly alienate even them. My playing no longer takes him from his troubles as it used to. Gathering misfortune is a severe test of his assurance and ability. He is not the man I remember from my father's house; not the man I married five years ago. In that time I can say surely that I have been a supportive wife. Whether I can be a loving one, whether I have ever been, in a sense newly revealed to me, is a question I must confront.

In past years we have had large gatherings for both Christmas and the New Year, with fireworks for the latter, which family and household staff would watch from the tower, several carrying kerosene lanterns. This year true celebration was lacking, and even the full meal and entertainments on the 23rd for all who worked for him, in which William usually takes such genuine delight, seemed more a duty for him. Tables were set out in the ballroom and I had Jane and the gardeners create profusions of flowers and greenery in the fireplaces. Even the antlers of the stags' heads were festooned with colourful Christmas decorations. But William made little effort to join in. He went to his study before it was all over, saying he was sore, and complaining of the slovenly dress of some of the men, despite them having been invited inside his house.

I notice that many of our people lose their natural manner and confidence when their accustomed roles are altered: some become clumsy and gauche within The Camp, some quieter and ill at ease, a few loud with false familiarity.

Yet William is still able to recognise that others have been equally buffeted by misfortune. At an evening at the Hockens', soon after New Year, we met Charles and Bella Baeyertz again, and although he in particular was in good form, about both music and the slipshod pronunciation of colonials, we were reminded by Bella's reserve that little more than a year ago their infant daughter fell into a well at their home and drowned. William remarked on it as we returned to The Camp the next day, and I knew he was thinking of Kate, although nothing was said directly. I think to lose an infant, and in circumstances that might imply some negligence, must be even more crushing than to experience the death of an adult child from disease. Earlier in our marriage, William and I may well have ventured upon the subject, but now we have lost that closeness and confine ourselves largely to the commonplace.

Thomas Cahill came for a brief visit, which lifted our spirits. He said it would be unprofessional of him to make any judgement, or interference, concerning Dr Langley's treatment of William, but he made an informal examination, and William was the better just for his company. Thomas regaled us with a scandal that arose from the Wellington Guards' Ball in July and with an account of a walking tour in the Marlborough Sounds. He accompanied Dougie and me to a soirée at the Hockens', and all three of us to a dinner party at the Sargoods'. And he encouraged William to be out and about with him and talk about his plans for grounds and farms. But he was soon north again, and William gloomy.

With all of this I should be cast down. I am not. I float and dance within myself, for Dougie has said he is absolutely in love with me, and I find I cannot refuse him. My God, what a declaration: at once the most unexpected, and yet the most natural, outcome of a true and deepening friendship. Everything has an added sparkle and significance that even William's moroseness cannot destroy.

Tuesday began in an ordinary enough way with the ordering of linen and a discussion about laundry. In the afternoon Dr Langley came to make a routine examination of William and I stood at the steps to farewell him as he waited for his horse to be brought. 'Please go inside, Mrs Larnach,' he said. It was not cold, but a fine drizzle came in from the sea, hazing the fruit trees planted beyond the glasshouses. The slight dampness was drawn into my throat as I breathed, and there was the smell of pine resin and the newly cut grass.

'He's started riding again,' I said.

'He says it gives his ribs no pain, unless he trots.'

'So you don't advise against it?' I said.

'Pain is the body's message, but your husband has always pushed himself. Better that he use the buggy or carriage. I've told him so.'

'You know William. He won't be told.'

'That's true, but I'm sure you have influence and will persuade him to take greater care of himself. He's not young any more, yet makes the same demands on himself.' And when Boylan came with his roan, the doctor swung up and said goodbye. William had taken to him after the recommendation of Dr Hocken. A straight talker, William said, and a keen rugby man. Personally I find him rather too fond of himself, and entrenched in his opinions of social development, which are not progressive.

I went back in to the library where father and son were talking in tones of mutual impatience. William was seated close to the window, Dougie standing with his hands in his pockets as is his way when nettled. They were arguing about the financial returns from the property. William's own resources are diminishing, but he is still free with advice and criticism concerning Dougie's management. William arranged for a telephone office to be set up at The Camp last year to serve the peninsula and Dougie is expected to be the telephonist, being paid threepence by the post office for each message he receives. He hates it because it is such a tie, and even more because of its menial nature. 'This is what I've become,' he said to William, 'a bloody clerk.'

'And who's to blame for that? After all the opportunity I've given you, still you can't make something of yourself.'

'You kept saying you wanted me to look after things here, didn't you?'

'What else were you going to do?' said William harshly.

'What would you know about my ambitions, and what would you care!'

They stopped their argument when I joined them but the tension remained. Their feelings towards each other have soured, as has so much else in William's life. It saddens me. What an unhappy house it has become, with even Gladys and Gretchen preferring the homes of their friends.

When we talked a little of Dr Langley's visit, William said he was physically recovered, but found it almost impossible to sleep. He began again with his complaints about Ward and Seddon, how his political contribution went unappreciated while at the same time preventing him from concentrating on his business interests. 'I'll resign within the month,' he said, as he has so many times before, but he will not, of course, as long as Seddon continues to flatter and use him — and dangle the promised knighthood before him.

I left them, went upstairs and was about to enter my room, when I realised Dougie had followed. 'The old man's become almost unbearable,' he said, trying for light-heartedness. He came closer. 'You've got quite wet,' putting his hand on my shoulder to test the dampness.

'I was outside with Dr Langley,' I said. 'I'll change before the meal.'

Dougie said nothing, but his hand remained on my shoulder and he gave slight pressure. 'I don't think I can stay here much longer,' he said, 'not the way things are. It's become unbearable. I so need to talk to you. I'm going to the vinery now. Come and meet me there.' And he put his other hand on my other shoulder, leant forward and kissed me full on the mouth, as he'd done well over a year ago when William and I returned from Lawrence after the by-election. Yet this kiss was more than a welcome back and an expression of friendship. It was a long, ardent kiss with his breath held and his hands steadying me against the door jamb. William's kisses have become abrupt, almost cursory: Dougie's was both declaration and proposition. I could feel the insistent movement of his lips, taste the saltiness of spit and smell the slight tobacco mustiness of his wide moustache. None of them was at all unpleasant. Within me was the giddy instinct I had felt when pressed against Josiah at the Wellington party before my marriage, but Dougie was someone I trusted and liked so much more.

'Please come and talk, Conny,' Dougie said. Knowing that the maids could be anywhere about the house, he stood back, and when I made no answer he went down the staircase with just one hurried glance behind him, a look of vulnerable entreaty on a face so disturbingly a youthful version of his father's. I made no promise, or reply, gave no commitment. Had I rebuffed him then, who knows the outcome? Maybe we could have carried on as the close confidants and supporters we had become, knowing that a boundary had been drawn; maybe our closeness and our trust would have ebbed away. A Tuesday of drizzle, a doctor's visit and an admonition to surly laundry staff came to a moment right then that formed a clear crossroads in my life, and in those of others.

I changed into a dry dress, pretending to myself I was deciding whether to go and meet Dougie, but I knew I would go. I knew without any rational toting up of pros and cons that I needed Dougie in a life becoming more unhappy and lonely day by day, and I felt almost an exultation that he had felt the same so strongly. For the first time, there in my room, with the mist silently clustering on the window like insistent, liquid insects, looking at myself in the mirror, I felt all the world except us recede a step, and Dougie and I come forward, magnified and in brighter light.

With an umbrella, but wearing only house shoes, I went out through the little courtyard with its servants' rooms and across to the vinery. Dougie was standing at the far end, his face slightly upturned in his typical way. 'I was about to go,' he said.

'I'm not coming in,' I told him. 'Let's not be ashamed of anything we have to talk about. I don't want to start by hiding away out here. Come back to the drawing room and let's be together,' and I turned from the door and returned to the house.

I knew William would be in his library until the meal, and if he should come into the room, what of that? How often Dougie and I sat and talked together, walked in the grounds, took the buggy into town. Our conversations were sometimes flippant, but also often confiding. Why should we feel guilt?

Dougie came in not long after me and we sat in the high-backed chairs close to the unlit fireplace, where he'd told me Mary used to spend much of her time. For a house little more than twenty years old, what a deal has happened within it; what vain dreams and aspirations have gathered, and how little affection it created in its first two mistresses. 'I'm not angry that you kissed me,' I said. 'I take it as a true and natural expression of our feeling for each other — our closeness and trust.'

'I need to be with you. It's as simple as that,' said Dougie. 'I realised it when you went back to Wellington, and we no longer had so much time together. Although I was free of Father's interference, nothing seemed to matter here afterwards. No one could replace you, and everything seemed flat and humdrum. I couldn't even write to you as I wished. You must know how I feel.'

'There's love and love, Dougie,' I said.

'No one else means as much to me. I miss you so much. When we can't talk often, life gets out of kilter somehow. So much of our lives is connected now, so much understood is between us. I need you. We need each other.' His face was pale and his eyes insistent.

'We couldn't be closer friends,' I said. Our life had been busy in Wellington, and the trips back had been few and hectic, but I had missed Dougie's company, and his declaration made me realise how much it meant to me.

'But we could,' he said. 'We could be closer, and we should.' And he reached out, took my hand in both of his and kissed it.

People who do not know him well would form a completely wrong assessment of Dougie's nature from his appearance and manner in society. He is not as handsome as Donald — has his father's less regular features. Unlike William, however, Dougie has a fine head of hair. To be honest, he looks more than his thirty-two years. The lasting effects of his injuries have no doubt contributed, but there is also a striving for dignity that disguises uncertainty. Uncertainty arising from his experience at his English school, an awareness sometimes of alienation here, and living in the blaze of his father's personality and achievement. Colleen told me once, with considerable satisfaction, that her friends think him pompous and ordinary. If that is so, and not merely an expression of her malice, it shows how little of the real Dougie they understand. The true man revealed sat before me. We looked into each other's face and admitted how much we valued each other, how significant was the understanding we shared. 'It's a damned predicament, isn't it,' he said with an uneven laugh, 'but I had to tell you. I'm not ashamed of it. I refuse to be.'

'Why should you be? Love's always a tribute. It comes from admiration and respect.'

'Damned if I know where it comes from, but I feel it,' he said. 'I hope you do too.'

So there it was, his statement of love for me, and my welcome of it as a natural thing with no guilt attached. After all, we are family, and only seven years separate us. We are united by circumstance, by the need for support, by enjoyment in each other's company. Nothing was said then of what the kiss at the top of the stairs conveyed, the pressure of Dougie's hands on my shoulders, the closeness of his body. Nothing was said, but a possibility was clear to both of us, and it vibrated so in the quiet room that when Jane came in with a question from Miss Falloon, I half expected her to become aware of it. 'Tell her I will come myself presently,' I said.

'You must have known,' said Dougie when she had gone.

'You've been the only real friend to me in the family. The only one who gave thought to what it meant for me to marry William, to have regard for my feelings, not just your own.'

'But it's my own feelings I'm talking about now.'

'We have to be so careful, though, in everything we do. Careful not to deceive William, but still share what we're entitled to.'

I believed that when I said it. I believed it as we sat at the table later, just the three of us, and Dougie was in high spirits, joshing me about the Brandon family pretension in passing on the eldest son's name. My brother bore our father's name and passed it to his own son — Alfred de Bathe Brandon. Even William seemed enlivened despite the earlier argument, and joined the banter, seeing no irony in laughing at the vanity of my family, while sitting in his great house some derided as a castle, and having commissioned a family sepulchre. William and Alfred presently have disagreements about mutual investments. This no doubt inclines William to welcome Dougie's fun.

When a man has declared love that is not repugnant, he seems quite different afterwards, seen and judged with emotions not extended to other men. The feelings may change, or ebb away, but he will never be seen in the same way again. For a woman, there is a transformation, and to be honest, part of that is a sense of power.

I think of Josiah's intent face so close to mine in the cloakroom, and another time beneath the dim archway of Mulvey's carriage cover, as he urged me to come to him secretly, of the bobbing Adam's apple of the vicar with aspirations beyond his station, and of William's somewhat contrived naturalness on the beach at Island Bay as he suggested marriage. What woman is without a sense of theatre at such times, of an intense focus on herself from which everything else fades for the moment. And all immensely gratifying to one's self-estimation. That Tuesday, so ordinary in its start, became for Dougie and me the beginning of something greater than any friendship. It proved the sea change that altered the direction of our lives.

We have not dared yet to talk much of it together, for then complication and evasion, expectation and justification begin. When in this little village of The Camp, I have had only two consistent companions of my own station in life — William and Dougie. Both are unrelated to me by blood, and Dougie is closer to my age and less preoccupied with public matters. After seeing the best and worst of both men, I have come to enjoy the trust and companionship of Dougie even more than what I share with his father. How difficult it is to admit that even to myself, but it is the truth, and if I evade it I betray my character. I see, too, that I have been in danger of confining the inner me to my music. Dougie's avowal is an illumination that makes me realise how false my life had become, how tied to the material and mundane.

When I think back, perhaps there was an earlier clear sign of Dougie's feeling for me. There was the evening he told me he was no longer considering an engagement to Ellen Abbott. Dougie had made it plain to me that he was no longer serious about that match, or any other. At the time I thought he intended me to feel complimented that he would share such personal decisions with me; now I see that the intention was to show I was his choice.

The bond I have with Dougie makes most of the time spent with William barren in comparison. Less and less does William enquire about and support my life and needs; more and more he is concerned with maintaining his position as a man of influence and wealth. He takes less interest in his Central Otago land, and even in his peninsula properties, except for the profits and rentals to be gained, which are below his expectations, and spends much of his time in the study writing his long letters to Seddon and parliamentary colleagues, or disagreeing with Basil Sievwright and business associates concerning what can be saved from his affairs. Everything seems to be about the banks, and Ward's indebtedness, which threatens to bring the government down. William has been a man of friends, yet now he talks mainly of enemies, and has found a new one in Mr Justice Williams, who is attempting to bar him from continuing as one of the liquidators of the Colonial Bank. It is all sad, selfish and boring. He and I now share few of the light-hearted and confiding moments we enjoyed immediately before our marriage and for some time afterwards.

Sometimes I think the buggy has become the centre of my true life: riding with Dougie about the properties, or back and forth to town, a drive of more than an hour. Then we can talk and laugh quite openly, showing the affection always consciously muted at The Camp and in society. We can sit close, and Dougie will lean across for a kiss so long that it becomes both a risk we will be observed, and a defiance of that very thing. The horse walks or trots on. Were it heading for a precipice, Dougie wouldn't care, and I must push him away for safety, although his ardour stirs powerful feelings within me. Even when William is with us, if Dougie isn't driving he will often seek my hand beneath the rug, or move his knee against my own. And he will call our attention to particular nooks and stopping places, praising them in an apparently innocent way while knowing that I recognise them, that there we have kissed, held each other, shared confidences. I am sure that Dougie does this not in any triumph over William, but to remind me of our love.

All of that has led in the end to us making love physically, as we knew would follow. It was a night when William was in Timaru on business. We took him in to the train on a lovely, bright day with the green sweep of the peninsula bush in contrast to the gentle, blue-green undulation of the calm harbour. Even William felt his mood lifted and was amused when Dougie advised him to eat nothing in Timaru, because of the scandalous Tom Hall poisoning case there. William claimed that after the foods he had survived while on the goldfields and in mining camps, he wasn't shy of a dose of antimony, and told us a good deal about the poisonings passed on to him by Professor Black, who had been consulted as an expert witness, and Robert Stout, who led the prosecution. What a cause célèbre it all was, because of the connection to Sir John Hall, and the monstrous betrayal of the wife. 'There are always people so much worse off than yourself,' William said, as we passed through the bay and on into the town. He was roused by the prospect of his trip, Dougie and I by the thought of his absence for the night.

Dougie and I came back to The Camp almost as if we owned it: came back with a sense of closeness so special to lovers, as if, apart from the strangely distanced and impersonal world, existed a place of brightness and warmth for us alone. Dougie told me how he loved to stand by the piano when I played, and that no matter who else was there, it was my perfume he was aware of, my voice among the singers, my hands moving on the keys. When no one else was in the room, he would come to the piano, he said, and be aware of my fragrance there. He joked about my feet, saying that he had never seen them, and that perhaps my toes were webbed. I told him I had never seen his, and that if they resembled his father's they were not at all aesthetically pleasing. How close and safe and correct we appeared there in the buggy, returning home from delivering William to his train. Mrs Constance Larnach and her stepson, with a civil nod or wave to the few who passed us, and no way for them to know that our hands were clasped beneath the rug, and our hearts close also.

As we went up the hill towards The Camp, wood pigeons flew so near that the whoosh of noisy flight startled the horse, which reared in the traces. 'I'll take a gun and bag some,' said Dougie when things were calm again.

'You should,' I said. Pigeons made good eating and one of the cooks has a pie recipe from her whaler father that William especially enjoys. Such an ordinary topic, and one we had no real interest in, yet perhaps it helped us to keep some grip on the everyday. He gave me a last kiss before we turned into the gates.

For everyone else at the house it was an evening much like any other, perhaps rather more relaxed because of William's absence. There is no doubt that he has become more tetchy, even with old friends and acquaintances. Dr Langley believes he has a stomach ulcer, but I think disappointment and worry are more the cause. Although I must perhaps take some blame for the disappointment, more should be laid at the door of Donald, Alice and Colleen. All he has done for them, and they have been ungrateful, demanding and vexatious in return.

As there were no guests we had an early meal. Before it, Dougie and I had claret in the drawing room. Nothing out of the ordinary to cause comment among the staff. William stopped drinking before our marriage and preaches temperance to Dougie, who resents it because of William's own indulgence when younger. We had a nice beef, and fish that amorous Mr Tremain had brought to the house as a gift. Perhaps he still hopes to soften Miss Falloon's heart. My only cause for small complaint was that several pieces of cutlery were dull rather than gleaming.

Afterwards I played for Dougie as darkness deepened outside and we sang 'The Kerry Dance' together:

Oh, to think of it

Oh, to dream of it

Fills my heart with tears.

His voice is true, but unremarkable. At least he doesn't sway, or bellow, as Richard Seddon does at our Molesworth Street evenings. For my sake, Dougie has made a considerable effort to extend his knowledge of music. He can play no instrument, but we talk together about the nature of music and the merits of the best composers and performers, and he attends Dunedin events with William and me, and in Wellington when he visits. It is a game with the two of us that I play a piece with the music hidden from him, and he must guess the composer. That night I played light pieces from Sullivan, who is one of Dougie's favourites, and will surely stand the test of time.

When I said goodnight, he told me he was going to work in the library for a while, then said quietly, 'I'll come tonight to make sure you're all right.' Only if I wished to refuse him was there any need to reply. I am not a girl, and had been aware all day, and beforehand, what the night of such an opportunity would bring. We had allowed our feelings for each other to become so intense, so complementary, that only lovemaking could make us feel complete.

A wind was getting up in the darkness, and I knew it was from the south because of the particular noise it made in the turret and chimney stacks. The mournful calls of a morepork were clear, but I was far from sad. As I lay in my bed, and my eyes grew accustomed to the dim moonlight from the windows, I could see the softened outlines of the furniture and the low wainscoting, still much as Eliza would have seen them from this bed over fifteen years ago. There was very little risk in Dougie coming to me late once his father was absent. The servants sleep far from this part of the house, perhaps with their own assignations in their own quarters to satisfy gossip. Here was a small, quiet world for Dougie and me.

How differently from his father did Dougie enter my bedroom. He slipped in, concentrating for a long moment on closing the door without noise. He came close to the bed, smiled, held one hand up in a strange, small greeting, and when I turned back the bedclothes came quickly and easily in and immediately put his arms around me and kissed me. There was a care and eagerness that I had never before experienced — not in the insistent maleness of Josiah, not even in William's mature energy of the honeymoon. But this was not about William or Josiah: it was about Dougie and me.

I do not think we talked. If we did I cannot remember. We had talked when we wanted to make love, so we could do without talk when at last love was decided on and the opportunity was there. That night awakened me to the supreme experience between man and woman: insistent, continual and surging pleasure so that I took the sheets between my teeth to muffle my cries. Now I know what is possible between us, I am enthralled and joyous. I never knew such physical height of pleasure existed, but something in my heart has always yearned for it.

I believe my real life began there, close to Dougie, our quickened breathing and caressing hands, the sound of the wind in the chimneys and the morepork in the pines, and the soft light of a dim moon through the window. A better, more intense life, shared with someone who loves me more than I have been loved before.

Six

I find myself at a strange point in my life, at once experiencing moments of the greatest happiness and long periods of galling frustration. Conny has at last accepted me as a lover in all respects, and the fierce and utter satisfaction of that is greater than anything I've ever known before — even in drunkenness, or sex. But she insists that Father mustn't be harmed, and all proper appearances kept up. Nothing I can say changes her mind. I urge her that the manly and honest thing is for me to tell Father and then she and I can leave to make a life elsewhere, in Australia, or perhaps South America, where I have a business contact. She won't have it. I know Conny. She won't throw away all that her family and mine entitle her to in society, but there's also that strong duty she feels to my father. So much of his achievement is in jeopardy and Conny is determined that she won't be responsible for bringing everything down.

It's sensible, perhaps, but it provides no proper future for us. Because Father spends more time in the house than in earlier years, the pretence Conny and I have to keep up is almost unbearable. I feel trapped in an unnatural way of life, increasingly unable to suffer Father and Conny as a couple. Nights are the worst, when Conny goes up to her room and then Father follows heavily after time in the library. Conny and I never talk of them together, but often I lie in my own bed and endeavour to repress the thought of him padding from his room to join her as husband.

How wretched was this last Christmas and the start of '96. Alice and her husband came with reluctance from Naseby, and Colleen too. Donny's disapproval, and mockery of Father's marriage, are conveyed by his sisters. All this spitefulness doesn't deter any of them from constant requests for money. Even Gladys is being infected and has become less open and happy with Father and Conny. He had perhaps hoped to find another Kate in her, but she hasn't grown up in the same secure surroundings and now shows a different disposition.

We're an awkward family, and Father has had a part in making us so. He used to be able to sweep us all along in his progress, but we aren't children any more, and his dominating benevolence will no longer do. Injury, both physical and financial, has made him impatient and irascible; he feels all the world has turned on him. Conny is caught up in all of this and suffers through her determination to be treated as she deserves. God knows why she married the old man, but having done so she's entitled to respect from all of us.

It was the sour failure of the New Year's Eve party, I think, that decided Conny and me that happiness would be found only between ourselves. Hogmanay at The Camp has always been an event of boisterous celebration, giving me some of my best memories as a boy before my time in England. Father delighted in fireworks for the occasion, and family and close staff would gather on the tower to sing, laugh and toast the New Year, as the rockets flared in violent colours across the plush sky.

This year only Gladys, and Donny's Gretchen, seemed happy, and that only from their companionship and irrepressible youth. Even the staff were subdued, knowing well the undercurrents within the family, especially my sisters' animosity towards Conny. Alice is usually discontent. I hardly recognise her as the sister I once knew well. She lost her baby boy and finds William Inder a disappointing husband. A pushy man, but with little substance. I suspect the marriage will founder. I hope Colleen doesn't find herself in a similar situation, for she too is eager to find a home of her own. They combine to harangue Father for money and snipe at Conny, who is hurt, but determined not to show it.

Father was as loud and managing as ever at Hogmanay, but there was an emptiness to his forced bonhomie, a watchful division within us as we gathered on the tower at midnight, gave our champagne toasts for long life and good fortune, saw the rockets shoot, flare and die. Conny and I were the last to go down the narrow curve of the cramped stone steps, and as we waited by the parapet, I lightly tapped her empty glass with mine, and raised the lantern I held so I could see her face.

'Don't worry about them,' I said.

'Happy new year, Dougie,' she said, with a smile.

'Let's hope for a better one than last.'

'I wish we could determine that by our own actions,' Conny said, 'but there's too much at work beyond our control.'

At least she knows now that I have sufficient love for her to outweigh all the deficiencies in others. In the drabness of the New Year celebrations, the falseness of our toasts and gifts, she and I gave each other true support. I admire her strength and poise while feeling sympathy for her isolation here in the south, so far from her own family and friends. Even in the buggy accident at Anderson's Bay before Christmas, she didn't cry, and was more concerned for Father and me than for her own welfare. She isn't the most patient of women, but she showed considerable tolerance of Father's temper during the time he was laid up.

In those weeks we spent more time together than ever before. I had to carry out Father's business tasks in Dunedin so Conny took the opportunities to visit Bessie Hocken, Ethel Morley and other friends. Twice we stayed at the Hockens' to attend recitals, once with the Cargills, and Conny likes to get relief from The Camp by accompanying me about the peninsula properties. She even pretends some interest in the piffling mechanism of the telephone office so that we have the chance sometimes to sit and talk, free of any chance of being overheard. For some considerable time our friendship has been a sort of alliance against boredom and misunderstanding, as well as the expression of the pleasure we find in each other's company. There was nothing deliberate in it to threaten Father, or Conny, but all that's changed now.

These things happen gradually, naturally, moving forward until you find yourself at a point of decision almost impossible to step back from, and inescapable in consequence. Any man would fall in love with Conny. She's a stunner, with the figure of a girl, but without any giggling foolishness. In conversation she can hold her own with any man, even Stout, and the premier, who can't bluff her as he does most people. Father at first found her spiritedness admirable, but now often takes offence at any disagreement. She won't be put down, Conny, just for being a female. I've never known a woman so adamant about her right to be treated as an equal, and I admire her for it. And it means that when she does agree to submission, what special and urgent pleasure there is.

When you share so much, however, you want to share everything — well, I do. I became so conscious of Conny's presence that even the traces of her scent in a room were a difficult distraction, and when we were in society I had to remind myself to address other people and not just her, to look at other women and not entirely at her. At The Camp I found myself often willing Father to go and leave us alone together. Nothing he has to say weighs in the balance against time alone with Conny.

When he went to Timaru several weeks ago Conny let me come to her. I knew she would because of the freedom with which she leant against me on the drive back from the Dunedin station. Even when Traveller shied at the overhang corner coming up to the gates, she didn't care, allowed me a long kiss and for the first time didn't forestall me when I felt with my hand for her thigh, the material of her skirt sliding beneath my hand. 'I trust you,' she said.

It was a long evening. Conny seemed able to be her normal self, and even went off after dinner to talk to Miss Falloon about housekeeping matters while I fretted in the library. Then she played for me in the music room, and even that seemed just a way of whittling time before bed. I watched her small, pale hands, the curve of her breast beneath the closely buttoned dress, the sheen of her brown hair accentuated by the light from the chandeliers. Her hair is usually worn up in the manner of modern women, but often I imagine it long and free. Until Conny, music was never vital to me, but it's so much a part of her life that now I feel her presence in the music she loves, and it's grown important to me also. Her playing is not just an indifferently demonstrated accomplishment but an expression of feelings and awareness quite beyond me. She plays alone often during the day, so that the notes steal through the hallways and rooms of the big house and drift into the grounds, and when we have guests there is always a call for her to entertain.

Conny takes great pleasure when artists of distinction come to the colony, and loves to make up a party to attend a concert or recital. The company she prefers at The Camp is that of musical and artistic people, but these gatherings are not at all stiff: she's opposed to the separation of men and women at social occasions.

That night it seemed to me she played with particular emotion, and the pieces were among those she knew I most enjoyed. We sang some Irish laments together, although we were far from feeling sad. I'd sing anything with Conny. Any other time that would have been enough, but my mind was fixed on the later rendezvous neither of us had acknowledged in words. When she went up, I told her that I would ensure later she was safe and she lightly pressed my hand. When in my own room, I stood at the window and watched the dark outlines of trees swaying slightly against the night sky. I thought of Conny playing the grand piano, and all around The Camp the barely touched roughness of the peninsula shrouded with drifting cloud. And then Conny waiting for me to join her.

Midnight had almost come when I went to her room. We had been close for so long that there was little awkwardness, no need for talk. She turned back the covers and we lay for a while in a full embrace. How often had I imagined it: Conny and I lying together. I didn't give a damn that it was my mother's bed, and my father's wife. It was Conny and me, that's all that mattered: nothing to do with anybody else. I have greater physical satisfaction with her than any other woman I've been with. She's totally giving and open, and in her own way insistent, which powerfully excites me, but beyond all of that, perhaps the cause of it, is that we love each other.

I have never before felt such love for anyone, or experienced such affection in return. How different from Ellen's amused, sometimes anxious, tolerance. Different, too, from the hurried scrabble with shop girls, or the weary familiarity of the Maclaggan Street women. Conny has known no man before my father, and we awoke in each other a physical longing equalled only by the complete joy of its satisfaction. In our abandon we marked each other's skin, and I handled her so closely and fervently that our bodies were slick and smooth to the eager touch. How wonderful is the smooth flesh of her inner thighs, and how her dark nipples rose under my tongue. Often I relive that first magical grapple, and am quickened in both body and spirit.

Nothing has been the same since that night. Conny has become the touchstone of my life, and all that concerns her is of heightened significance to me. This must be kept hidden from the world, of course: Conny is absolutely determined that my father not be hurt by direct disclosure or by knowing gossip of society. I'll agree to any compromise she insists on, but already I wonder how I will bear her absence. How natural Conny was at breakfast after our night together, showing only by a smile that nothing had been forgotten or regretted. 'Now we are truly friends,' she said when we were alone. 'Each of us is in the power of the other.'

That morning a Mr Pettigrew was coming out to talk about armless chairs in the ballroom, but she said she'd like to come in with me in the afternoon to pick up Father from the train. I saddled Tarquin and, after checking on Walter in the telephone office, rode out to inspect the property. Such was my mood that I took the high gate leading down to the Stars and Stripes paddock at a canter. He's not a big horse, at less than sixteen hands, but he doesn't lack mettle and has a soft mouth. I had him trot and then at the gallop. And all the time I knew the real source of my delight was that Conny loved me.

It was as well that I was out and about, because by the east boundary I came across three young coves trespassing on our land. They were a surly trio, who obviously gave me false names. One of them I recognised as a labourer who had injured his hand when the carriage-house roof was being repaired. They said they were cutting through our property to reach the shore and shellfish, but I suspect they were on the lookout for a sheep to slaughter, or maybe even a cattle beast. We've lost animals in the back paddocks, seen the remains, and Patrick Sexton has a man ride the property most days. There's an element in the colony who see law only as an impediment to their advantage, and who hate those who have built up property and resources through industry and foresight. All three of them needed a damn good bath, and when I sent them on their way, they said, 'Yes, Mr Larnach. Yes, Mr Larnach,' with an exaggerated deference that was yet an insult.

In all respects but one — that it must end — the trip into Dunedin with Conny was the perfect ride. The sun, the sea, the opportunity for us to talk with complete openness and, for the first time, the relaxation that comes from having enjoyed each other utterly. As the buggy took us around the hills, and the gulls swooped and bickered in the bright light of the shore, I thought of Conny in the warm bed, allowing me in the darkness to slip the nightdress from her shoulder. How much greater was the satisfaction because of the many months of anticipation preceding it. Conny and I have embarked on a difficult course, but there's no other way. We're entitled to love: everyone is entitled to such fulfilment, if and when they are fortunate enough to find it. I'm determined to regret nothing and seize what happiness I can.

'Outwardly everything must remain just the same, Dougie,' she said. 'I must trust you in that. We can't do just as we like — everything could so easily come to ruin. People will never understand how we need each other's love and support. They'll see only sordidness and deceit, and get enjoyment from it, because their own lives are so narrow.'

'I'd like to publish an account of last night in the paper,' I said, 'and dine out on every man's envy.'

'Be serious.' She reached out and gently squeezed the lobe of my ear.

'I can't. Not enough blood has returned to my head.'

'Oh, stop being such a proud boy.'

'And lucky — how lucky.'

'If we can trust each other, then we're both lucky.'

Before the drive ended I did become serious, and tried to persuade her that the best thing was a clean break, for the two of us to get out of the colony and be together in a new place and life, but she was adamant. 'You promised me,' she said, and I had.

Father wasn't in a good mood. His business had gone poorly and he had a cold. His short temper made it easier for me to pretend nothing had changed. And what had changed for him? He was as ever master of The Camp, and Conny too loyal, and too aware of the consequences, to give any hint of what existed between us. So we three came back out along the road of the peninsula, just as we had so often in the past, with the glinting sea and the gulls, with the bush and few roughly cleared slopes, with the occasional dray driver or horseman raising his whip to Father. He blaring his nose into a handkerchief and complaining all the way about the recalcitrance of the Timaru harbourmaster; Conny working to cheer him by talking of the newly arrived conservatory plants sent out from Brambletye by ailing Uncle Donald and the additional furniture for the ballroom. What she and I share is something quite set apart from other people, and the ordinary round. Something few are lucky enough to experience, and none is fit to judge.

Now that Conny and I are lovers, I have no sexual escapades elsewhere. We haven't talked of it, but I know she expects me to be faithful, even in the strange circumstances in which we find ourselves. I manage it easily enough, for I truly love her in all respects. The most difficult thing has been to accustom Robert and Hugo to my changed ways without being able to explain myself. It's not that I've ever been a determined, or successful, seducer. Since Ellen I've had no serious interest in any woman apart from Conny, and there will be no more nights like the one last year that followed Mark Twain's address at the town hall.

Robert, Ted Reid and I were part of that large and disappointed audience. The American's humour was less in evidence than we expected, and there was too much of the 'great moral sermon' that he promised he would one day write. I gather he had come this far from the United States to recoup his finances after business failure at home. Robert said he did at least have a damn good moustache and head of hair. I don't think we were the only unenthusiastic listeners. I read later that Twain was heckled in Timaru, and that in Wanganui he was accosted by a madman who claimed the author was to be assassinated. People expected an endless string of jokes, I suppose. He did meet the Hockens privately, however, and both of them were impressed. They said he wasn't well during his tour, which surely affected his public performances.

As we left the hall, Robert met a woman who worked in a shipping office in his building. Clara Fairburn, who was tall and thin, laughed and talked easily. Robert told me later that she was of some significance in the firm and had bookkeeping skills unusual in a woman. Her companion was better looking, with a nipped-in waist and blonde hair in a bun, but I've forgotten her name. Afterwards the five of us went to the Piccadilly Rooms. Everywhere I go in this town, I'm likely recognised by someone, but at the Piccadilly there's more privacy than in most places, and more latitude too.

We had drinks together in the Bower Room, talked of Twain and his comments about the stingy Scots. He must have someone doing a little homework about the different places on his itinerary. While Robert and Ted competed for the attentions of the fair-haired girl, Clara talked to me. She had seen Conny at meetings and at the Dunedin Orchestral Society and admired her support for women's rights. She asked me what it was like inside The Camp, whether Conny had made many changes since becoming mistress. I had a feeling she was angling for an invitation to visit. She and her widowed mother, with whom she lived, liked to imagine the interiors of the big houses. Everything I said caused her to laugh: maybe it was a habit formed from a wish to be obliging, but I found it offputting. Had she been pretty my response may well have been different. Conny has pointed out to me how susceptible men are to appearances, and I have responded that, for women, wealth and social position in a man are almost as strong an attraction.

Robert and Ted, still in a friendly and animated rivalry, escorted Clara's pretty friend home. I haven't their quick conversational flow and easy graces. I took Clara to her house in a cab drawn by a half-lame horse; that led to an exchange with the driver that I would have persisted in had I been alone. The place was close to The Exchange, easy walking distance for a man, and afterwards I did indeed walk back to the club. Clara and I stood under a small overhang at the back door of the cottage. 'You could come in, but Mother mightn't be in bed,' Clara said. We stood close, in a half embrace, but hadn't even kissed when she said, 'You can hug me if you like.' Even now, recalling it, I experience a little start at the unexpected directness. And I did feel her, more because the opportunity was there, than from any special attraction. She was thin, and through those thick, tight clothes there was little yielding to my touch. It was difficult to see her face, but I felt she knew her body was a disappointment — to herself, perhaps, as well as to a man — and that was an embarrassment for both of us. I thought of her mother sitting in the kitchen, or lying in a flannel nightdress in her bed, as we pushed against one another at the door.

'I have to go,' I said.

'Maybe we can see each other again,' she said. 'It was fun, wasn't it, at the Piccadilly.' She had an uncertain, almost desperate, forwardness, and hadn't laughed once since we'd reached her home. I had no intention of seeing her again: already I was regretting having come so close. How sudden the change had been from the talkative and laughing companion, to a thin, longing woman in the dark asking to be felt. It was sad somehow, strangely disturbing, and I knew I'd taken advantage of her.

Like so much of my experience with women before Conny, it

had as much discomfort and unease as it had pleasure. What a relief and satisfaction it is to be at one with Conny — in conversation, in lovemaking, in companionable silence. Explanation is rarely required. Nothing is taboo between us. She has even asked me about sexual attraction between men, wondering if it were true, and I told her frankly what I knew, including the name of a man she saw often and admired. 'How strange and difficult to imagine,' she said, 'but it doesn't change the things I like about him.' I told her that some women, too, preferred their own sex — for sex, but she didn't believe it, and said that supposition has been made by men because women are closer and more demonstrative in their intimate friendships.

Conny looks out for me, in a way no woman has since Mother. When we're apart, I often think of her, imagine her in her pursuits for a morning, or an afternoon, hope that things go well and that she will have pleasure in telling me of them. I see her writing her elegant invitations to our dinner guests, deciding with Miss Falloon on the courses for such occasions, going out each morning with a gardener to decide what flowers will be cut, laying out her dresses and instructing the seamstress concerning their alteration. Above all in my mind's eye I see her at the grand piano, and hear the music drifting, or briskly pacing, through the rooms of The Camp and escaping outside.

I know I live in her thoughts, too, because I have constant proofs, small in themselves, but telling in accumulation. There was heavy rain on Friday, as is often the Dunedin way. Rain is money for farmers, but unpleasant to be working in, and usually the cold comes with it. Conny must have been watching for me from one of the windows, because when I came back from the stables after midday, she was waiting with a thick half-towel and dried my hair and the back of my neck. She had told one of the girls to get me a mug of hot, sweet tea. 'Don't go out this afternoon,' she said. 'Stay inside with us, or work in the telephone office.'

And when we're in company she catches my eye in pleasant complicity, draws off the most persistent of buttonholing bores, enlivens the occasion with her private asides, all without people having the slightest idea that our relationship is anything other than as presented. Afterwards, alone, we revisit the most diverting impressions, as if turning the pages of a photograph album. Remember when Mrs ——, and, what about the slip from Mr ——, she'll say, and bring it all to life again.

Everything is complete between us — except that she is married to someone else.

Seven

The last year has not been an easy one, but Dougie's love has been unwavering. Despite his obligations at The Camp, he came up several times to Wellington during the months William and I were there. He would have come more, regardless of the cost and wearisome travel, except for my remonstrance that it might occasion general gossip, and arouse suspicion in William. And the visits provide so little time for us to be alone. We did, on his last trip, have a wonderful meal at the Trocadero restaurant, which I consider Wellington's best. William was to be with us, but had stomach pains, so Dougie and I went together. What talk and laughter we had, while maintaining a family appearance and showing nothing of our true feelings to the world.

Also we went together to a chamber concert presented by Maughan Barnett, not so long ago appointed organist at St John's.

Wellington is crowded with music teachers, and the newspapers full of their solicitations and extravagant claims. Unfortunately, most are both poor practitioners and inadequate teachers, yet they gather in coteries to flatter and support each other and their students. Many are little more than housewives looking to make pin money from the ever-present demand as every socially aspiring family scrapes together the funds to ensure their daughters have the right genteel accomplishments to bring to the marriage market.

Barnett, although he cannot be much more than thirty, is one of the few with true talents as a player, composer and teacher, and he has formed an excellent musical society here. I adore his piano playing, and if my life was more tranquil would myself seek lessons from him, for I am never satisfied with my own performances. He is originally from England, where he was briefly appointed to St Mary Magdalen at St Leonard's on Sea. What wry delight Dougie took in that, especially as Barnett's health collapsed while he was there: the reason he is with us now. 'You see what sort of a place it is,' Dougie exclaimed. 'Only broken men escape St Leonard's.' The composer played some of his own pieces — 'Serenade', 'Chanson Sans Paroles', 'Valse' and 'Albumblatt'. The first was especially affecting, and as we listened, Dougie and I clasped hands beneath his street coat, which lay between us.

There are few opportunities for lovemaking in Wellington: the house is so much smaller, the servants are always about, the neighbours are close. Callers are frequent, and even when William is away little can be ventured. To have proximity without release goads Dougie into a strange tension, although he tries to restrain himself for my sake, and says just to be with me, even in company, is pleasure for him.

At the end of the parliamentary session, Dougie also joined us for several days in Christchurch: William and I were travelling south and Dougie was up on estate business. We were the guests of William's acquaintance, Joseph Palmer, at Woodford House. Mr Palmer was once the chief officer of the Union Bank and he and William have had many dealings over the years. William says he is a very clever man, and one who sails close to the wind. His wife, Emily, is the daughter of Sir James Fisher of South Australia. Woodford House, which has forty rooms and stands in extensive, well-kept grounds, is very much at the centre of Christchurch society, and during our five days there we enjoyed a garden party, tennis games, a musical afternoon with pipers and even a pony race in which several women, including me, took part.

The chief subject among the women seemed to be the scandal surrounding a certain Arthur Worthington and his Temple of Truth. I gather that he was an American, a religious charlatan and multiple bigamist, who had built up a substantial following, and personal fortune, by promoting promiscuity under the guise of universal love. Emily said that last year he entered yet another illegal marriage, with a girl of fifteen, fell into debt and final disrepute, and just a few months ago fled Christchurch to Australia. The fierce interest that respectable women take in such sexual imbroglios makes me wonder if the cause is a lack of physical satisfaction in their own lives.

I like Emily, and there was a novelty to mixing with an almost entirely fresh set of people in Christchurch, but a greater pleasure was having some time with Dougie among folk who saw nothing at all unusual in the three of us together, or Dougie and I without his father. The Palmers put a gig at our disposal and we went into the city. How regular and even Christchurch is, and what foresight the city fathers have shown in the provision of that fine Hagley Park. Donald attended Christ's College, but Dougie and William neither know the city well nor have much affection for it. As we came back to Woodford, Dougie drove down a track behind a disused brickworks and halted the horse there. We sat close and kissed and marvelled at how much flat land stretched away before the mountains in the distance. Canterbury's landscape is so entirely unlike that of Otago and Wellington. Dougie would have done more, but it was too dangerous, and too undignified.

At such times I think any risk and sacrifice would be worthwhile if it enabled us to be together, but perhaps our feelings would then subside into the humdrum practice of couples accustomed to each other's company. How much of the intensity Dougie and I experience arises from the brief focus of time we have alone?

I was at least able to come south nearly four months ago for Dougie's birthday on August 27th. I made no pretence to William that there was any pressing reason for a return to The Camp other than to ensure Dougie had family with him on his special day. William would have travelled himself had parliamentary duties permitted, but of the others only Gladys bothered to be present for her brother's celebration. The weather during the steamer trip was foul, and I was quite unsteady for a day afterwards, yet all was worth it to see dear Dougie's face when I arrived. During the long buggy ride home we seldom stopped talking and laughing, despite the cold, and any silences welled with unspoken pleasure in our being together.

During the ride I gave Dougie his gift: oblong silver cufflinks set with bright blue stones the jeweller told me came from northern India. Dougie said they were the finest he had ever seen, that he would never wear any others, and kissed me. All was as it should be when lovers come together once again after being parted.

He wore the cufflinks the next night at the dinner to mark his birthday, happy among his own friends such as Robert, Hugo and Ted, and some we held in common such as the Hockens and Morleys. And afterwards, instead of the men going into the library, or the billiard room, we all went to the large music room that I had ensured was warm and welcoming. Robert had prevailed on Jane to create a surprise: he called her in to tell tales of Dougie's childhood in order to embarrass him and entertain us. Standing there in her apron, she spoke with considerable seriousness and seemed surprised by the laughter created by almost everything she said.

When she was released, Dougie wanted me to play, and I did, all of us joining in to sing, first to wish him a happy birthday, and then on to other songs with great volume, but little melody.

Dougie stood close to me, resting his hand on my shoulder until he caught my eye. But much later I denied him nothing when he came to me, despite the full house, quietly opening the bedroom door and slipping in beside me with a sigh of satisfaction. It was a birthday night as I knew he wished it, and so did I. Hail rattled on the windows, the wind swirled among the jutting chimneys and around the small turret above the tower, and Dougie and I lay in each other's arms, warm and loved. He had brought the blue ribbon that had tied his birthday present, and he looped it about my neck, saying I was the gift he valued above all. When I woke he was gone as I knew he would be, creeping back before dawn to his own room, but the silk ribbon was still around my neck, and his soft words still with me. 'Nothing else matters, thank God,' he whispered. 'Nothing in the world matters except us.'

When William first returned to Parliament, I looked forward to the sessions — my city, my friends and family around me, the political life quite familiar. The cultural life is more various, too, and visiting performers are common. At The Camp I am in the Larnach world, and have felt sometimes almost under siege by William's daughters in the flesh, and by the shades of his former wives. Although Colleen and Alice seldom visit, they have their spies at The Camp and in town.

Dougie has changed my feelings towards Otago. We are so happy when we are together, and Dunedin and the peninsula are the only places where it is fully natural for that to be so. Even my sister Annie's long and special affection does not compensate for Dougie's absence, and now I cannot share with her what has become the central part of my life. So with inner eagerness I came back with William as he prepared for the December election campaign, and we planned another Christmas and the festivities of the '97 New Year.

This time I spent little of the campaign on the hustings with William. His manner at the meetings has become increasingly aggressive and dismissive, and there is not the pleasure in the visits to Naseby and Lawrence that I felt over two years ago. His absences provide the opportunity for Dougie and me to share our lives: not just the matching of our bodies, but the talks and walks, the buggy rides and entertainment of friends. I know Dougie would go all out and make a break with family and society so that we could be always together, but he fails to realise the full consequence of that: the terrible blow it would be to William and my family, the smirking satisfaction of Donald and his sisters, the loss of position and resources that would undermine our love in the end, and lead to rancour and disappointment.

There is a sort of dangerous blindness in Dougie's love that I admire for its completeness, and fear for its unworldliness. What is love? I am unsure if Dougie's dedication is the sign of utter selfishness, or the reverse. To have a man want you is a flattering, but commonplace, experience; to have a man truly care for you is indeed special. I tell him that we must fit our affection within the lives we have, bearing with the compromises that permit its continuation. After all, so much of what we share is quite open and legitimate as family and friends. The other is of concern only to ourselves. For Dougie, love seems an all or nothing thing.

William was re-elected for Tuapeka, but even that gives him little joy. He became involved in a war of words with the editor of the *Tuapeka Times* over the coarseness of his language, and to a considerable degree was in the wrong, whatever the provocation.

Bitterness now seems to seep into everything for him, replacing the generosity and goodwill that attracted me when I first met him. Money matters continue to plague him, and his investments are increasingly difficult to realise in cash. Seddon still demands support and advice, but holds off on the knighthood that is justly due. William is also becoming more and more accident-prone, almost as if he defiantly offers himself to the fates. In the middle of the year he scalded his hand so badly that Thomas Cahill made him spend time in the hospital, and not long after, while briefly back at The Camp, he was laid up from a kick on the knee by a cattle beast. Dougie said had it been a shod horse he would have been lame for life. At times, both of them seem walking exemplars of past misfortunes.

This year, too, William's uncle Donald died. He had been hospitable and helpful when William was in England many years ago as colonial treasurer, and was equally supportive of the children after William and Eliza returned to the colony. It is a disagreeable surprise to see how little William mourns his uncle, how scant the sympathy he expresses for his Aunt Jane. Although he has never quite said as much, I think he is disappointed he received nothing of substance in the will.

In adversity some men show to advantage, while others retreat from the best principles they once held. I try to continue to be a good wife to William, but things are not as they were. The change is as much in him as me, and I confess to myself that I no longer love him, not in the way I thought I once did. I think that would have happened whether or not Dougie and I became close. In a strange way, perhaps what Dougie and I have enables me to be a more stoical and sympathetic companion for his father. I no longer expect, or need, William to be the close confidant I sought in marriage.

Our disagreements grow, often concerning things apparently unconnected with our feelings for each other, yet reflecting in some way what has gone wrong. Last week we had a party for William's Dunedin political supporters — all male, and mainly crass people seeking some advantage from the association. I was pleased not to spend much time in their company, and happy to stand with William at the lion steps to see them leave. On such a sunny afternoon the grounds were an attractive prospect as the buggies, gigs and carriages wheeled away. The trees and shrubs planted over twenty years ago now give The Camp a settled, attractive appearance, in contrast to the stark, raw wilderness of the first photographs. In another twenty years it will be quite as it should, whether I am here to enjoy it or not.

It was warm and pleasant standing there, but watching the businessmen go reminded me of the times guests had scurried down the steps in rain, wind or hail. The Camp lacks a carriage cover, such as the best private homes provide, that would allow women in particular to come and go with comfort and dignity — and the weather is often unfavourable. On dark, inhospitable days, when I stand on the foreshortened steps and look up at the lowering sky, it seems the great stone mass of The Camp is about to come down in turmoil upon me.

I mentioned it again to William, not as any reflection on his planning of the place, but his reply was impatient and unpleasantly sharp. It would spoil the appearance of the front, he said, and would be ridiculously expensive beside. 'A minute in the rain isn't too much to ask even of pampered women in society,' he said. 'You won't melt, you know.' So we went up the steps and inside — William to his library, I to the drawing room — and nothing more was said.

How passing and inconsequential such a brush of different opinions might seem, but every exchange in a marriage is a signal of its underlying strength, or fragility, of positions taken and grievances maintained. The dismissal in his tone stayed with me, and we barely spoke to each other during the evening.

On another occasion he rebuked me for not wishing to accept an invitation to a soirée at the McGeadons. Mrs McGeadon is a Dunedin woman of considerable wealth, but little understanding or talent, who has taken it upon herself to be a leading hostess in the community. Her gatherings are staid and the attendance, predictably, confined to families of influence. Bessie, Ethel and I have to some extent set up in competition to her and several others of like ilk, and I believe we have brought a breath of fresh air to social and musical gatherings. Earlier in our marriage, William would have been supportive of my decision, for he, too, is easily bored, but he complained that a refusal would give needless offence. 'You need to consider our position, Conny,' he said, 'and not merely your own preference for variety. Many of these people are my business associates in one way or another, or political supporters. I wish you'd realise that the choice of our company can't be solely your estimation of people's wit and talent.'

'By all means go yourself then. We're not joined at the hip.'

'But we are joined by marriage,' he said, 'and each of us is judged partly by the attitude and behaviour of the other.'

There are more subtle indications that we have grown apart. We no longer ensure that each knows what is important in the other's life. When we were first married, almost everything of import that William spoke of in company had been shared with me beforehand, but increasingly my knowledge of his feelings and doings comes from what he says in the presence of others, and I suspect that if they were not there I would not be told at all. William does not do it deliberately, I am sure, but it is painful to be relegated in this way. His thoughtlessness makes it the more telling and distressful, and I find myself in turn reserving all that is important of my inner life for Dougie alone.

So William and I have reached the tolerated and baffled partnership that always has appalled me when I recognise it in others: a fortitude of composure lest expression of real feelings release pent-up disappointments. Ethel Morley shares this with me, I know. When they were last with us, Lowell contradicted her brusquely at the table concerning some matter of their proposed trip to Sydney and she gave way graciously. When I mentioned it afterwards, she seemed resigned. 'Oh, we rub along together. That's the way of it for most women in their marriage, I suppose.'

William seldom comes to my bed now, and though I have rarely refused him, I am glad of that. When he does come, he begins with a sort of desperate urgency that has no satisfying outcome for either of us, and afterwards he will mumble something and return to his own room rather than lie with me and talk as once we did. And how predictable he is always in lovemaking, with none of his son's exhilarating and impulsive ingenuity. William seems quite suddenly to have become an old man, and to be both aware and resentful of it. Small things, such as the hairs growing in his ears, the cracking of his knuckles, the sleep residue at the corner of his eyes, and his open-mouthed breathing and puffing moustache, irk me now. The tolerance of such things, which is part of love, has gone.

I endeavour to encourage him in most things, but not in coupling. Dougie is the only man I welcome in that way, though the situation holds special penalties for me. The most dismay and self-reproach I have experienced since accepting him has been in those times when, after some fervent tryst with him, carefully organised within The Camp, or the town, his father has come to me in the night, and I have taken the weight of a husband after that of his son has barely lifted. I have wept when by myself after such encounters, and made pledges to tell Dougie all is over, but they are never kept. He said one night that if I conceived a child, it would not matter who in appearance it favoured, because of his similarity to his father. He meant it as humour, but I felt only pain and anger, and told him so.

There are, though, wonderful and open times with Dougie that require no subterfuge and make all difficulties worthwhile. Yesterday afternoon we sat in the cane chairs on the northern verandah, which looks out to the great stable and the glasshouses. The sun was warm through the glass and the sky powder blue. This is one of my favourite parts of the house. High up are slim panels of green, blue, red and yellow Italian glass, which were made jewels in the bright light. William was with us for a time, talking of Ward's bankruptcy and Justice Williams's part in forcing it. Expressing bitterness and hostility has become one of the few remaining ways in which he gets satisfaction. But then he went and Dougie and I were left to talk together. 'He's stirred up,' said Dougie. 'He'll off to the den and write to Seddon, telling him how the finances of the colony should be managed while failing in his own affairs, and asking for his knighthood.'

'Yes, but let's talk about us,' I said. William occupies enough of our lives as of right, without being the subject of the time we have together. 'What dreams have you had that we can puzzle out an explanation for?'

'I can't believe you don't dream. You have them, but won't share them, or you wake too slowly and they drain away before they're fixed in your memory.'

'I never seem to dream. I do sometimes have a sense of their experience fading, like colours walking off in the distance.'

'I don't always dream,' said Dougie. He feels, I think, there is something childish in the nature of dreams; in the discussion of such things that are not practical. He reveals them to no one but me. William never talks about his dreams, and I don't ask.

'No, but tell me your last one,' I said. Dougie has full cheeks like his father, and a full moustache also. His skin has a slight, attractive burnish from the sun. The light caught his strong hands resting on his lap, a curved pipe in one. I felt a passing frisson at his obvious delight in our being together there: our sharing, the trust we have in each other. We are a lucky couple, here, now, despite our odd situation, of which, I hope, the world knows nothing.

'It was St Leonard's again. I was standing in the cold shadow of the chapel,' said Dougie, 'and I could see Roper, the classics master, in a singlet and long, soft trousers, doing exercises in the quad. He was a sort of muscular Christian who believed strongly in original sin and he had a fat wife who hardly ever appeared outdoors. No one saw her. Anything that was very rare, we used to call a Roper's wife. Anyway, in the dream he was doing these exercises, clapping his hands above his head and jumping astride at the same moment, then bringing his legs together and hands down again. And he was calling out, "I see you, boy. Come here at once, boy", but moving his head about as if blind.'

'Did you hate him?'

'Not really. Almost all the teachers seemed in some way preposterous.'

'And that was all the dream?' I asked.

'Well, it got dark suddenly, as if there was an eclipse, and even colder. I couldn't see him any more, but I could hear his hands clapping above his head, and his voice calling out to me, "I see you, boy."'

'You're free of all that now. You have a life among people to whom you matter.'

'I suppose he's dead now and left a fat widow in hiding.' Dougie waved a hand as if brushing aside unpleasant memories, diminishing their power.

So we sat in the warmth and security of The Camp verandah and talked of Dougie's cold dream of unhappy school days. How altered the Dougie I know now from the diffident yet inwardly sensitive person I first met. Then he was on the periphery of my concern, now he is essential to it. Gradually his life is revealed for me in his confidences, his behaviour, his lovemaking, the places dear to him. Our affection has given us another sense with which to understand each other, and now we cannot live without it.

'I've been reading of Phaedra,' I said.

'Never heard of it.'

'Her. Another sign of the deficiencies of your Mr Roper.'

'In what way?' Dougie had a hand up as a sun visor so that he could read my expression.

'Phaedra was the wife of Theseus, King of Athens, and she fell in love with her stepson, Hippolytus.'

'And they had a damn good time of it, I imagine,' Dougie said.

'They both died.'

'Everybody dies,' said Dougie. 'Just tell me that they loved.' He lay well back in his chair, relaxed, happy and vulnerable.

'You'll have to find out for yourself,' I said, but I knew he was unlikely to bother. Dougie is not much of reader, certainly not the classics. He might dream of Mr Roper, but he developed no enthusiasm for the subject he taught.

'Tell me about it tonight,' he said with purpose. William was to be in town.

Now that we are lovers in all respects, there is a change in Dougie. He laughs more often, is more optimistic, seems younger.

I am reassured and gladdened to see how happy my affection makes him. He likes to create small secrets and signs between us, code words only we two know. He has christened one of the young Newfoundland dogs Potf, and likes to have it with us when we walk in the grounds. 'What?' said William on first hearing it. 'What sort of a name is that for dog? No meaning and unpronounceable as well.'

'It's Egyptian,' said Dougie. He and I know that it stands for the pleasures of the flesh, so important to him that he burns to seize me at every opportunity. Potf is a silly joke between us, but there is a childishness to love that speaks of trust and spontaneous happiness.

In our case, however, there is apprehension too. The bond Dougie and I share has become the focus of my life, but a price of anxiety must be paid for it. In moments of despondency I envy those women who have given up expectation of a close understanding with a man and reveal their true selves only to women friends. They are free from the scrutiny of connection between the sexes that society delights in, and the emotional dependence, painful rebuffs and misunderstandings. It must, though, mean the loss of the most fulfilling and natural relationship of which we are capable.

Not long ago, when Dougie and I were walking by the raised Italian garden, he told me that only when with me did he feel a complete man. What a lovely, flattering paradox, and all about me seemed the brighter, fresher, for it: the sun, the colours, the fragrances. A single seabird, high in the sky, was wheeling freely, as if from some natural joy of flight. I would have kissed Dougie had we been in private. 'Pick me some flowers,' I said.

'Anything but foxgloves,' he replied, for they are William's favourite.

On the 17th of December Dougie and I attended a pre-Christmas entertainment in the Choral Hall, put on by the Dunedin Shakespeare Club. Several times over the last few years, its president, a Mr Wilson, has invited me to join, and once to be its patron, but besides being too busy, I have heard reports that the club consists almost totally of middle-aged women more interested in the social cachet of membership than in study of the great man. The evening proved to be rather like George du Maurier's curate's egg. Professor William Salmond, small, thin and yet another Scots-man, gave an excellent lecture on the uses of poetry, but the readings from *King John* were a trial to sit through and the musical selections mediocre. Dougie said I could have played Grieg's 'Auf den Bergen' so much better myself, and although love makes him partial, it is true.

On the way back with the Morleys, with whom we stayed the night in their Forbury Road home, Dougie amused us by talking of ordinary things in an outrageously theatrical voice, and would have attempted to come late to my room had I not made it obvious, in a brief moment apart from the others, that the risk was too great. He consoled himself by drinking excessively with Lowell at a late hour and had a heavy head on our ride back to The Camp the following day. I had little sympathy. Not only is drunkenness unappealing, but who knows what Dougie in his cups might say about us. The trip home lacked its customary pleasure.

I visited Ethel again just a few days afterwards. The Morley shipping money has provided one of the finest houses in the town, but it is Ethel's taste that sets it off to advantage. She is one of those women nature has fashioned to a man's inclination: tall, olive-skinned and full of figure. It is no surprise that eligible Lowell Morley chose her from among her rivals. Her more enduring asset is intelligence. Appearances would suggest she has everything, but her marriage offers little apart from position and security. While we were walking in her garden, Lowell came out briefly to say he was leaving for the club and to remind her of an evening engagement. Wealth dresses him notably, but it cannot give him presence, or sensibility. Already balding, he has a mole-like, protuberant face and a humourless laugh. He is all physicality, lacking the perceptive response to life and his fellows that would bestow character.

'I am married to a silly man,' Ethel said when he had left us. It was not said with malice, or particular disappointment, but with candid resignation. She had weighed up the advantages and drawbacks of the life he offered, and made her choice. She stood with me in the lovely garden before her fine house, dressed in a manner admired and imitated by other women, and admitted she was tied, of her own will, to an inferior person. William is admirable by contrast, yet I also find myself in a trap of my own choosing. My advantage is that I have someone to love, my dilemma that it is forbidden.

Ethel and I walked through to the gazebo, wreathed with dark red and yellow roses, and sat on the shady side. Her gardener was working close by, but had the sense to take his sack and tools and move out of earshot. He is a Lefroy from the Anderson's Bay family that assisted us following the buggy accident. He himself sustained an injury years before, Ethel said: assaulted while working as a prison officer in Christchurch. Ethel wanted to confide in me concerning her grandmother's decline. Some collapse of reasoning and memory seems to be taking place, even an alteration of character. She cannot recall whether she has had her dinner ten minutes after eating it, and roams anxiously, seeking the small children she loved more than fifty years ago and does not recognise in the adults they have become. All I can offer is a sympathetic ear.

Sometimes I wonder what it would be like to have a child. I married William with no great need, intention or expectation of having children, but there are times when I glimpse a powerful affection and fulfilment that seems to belong to motherhood alone. One afternoon when I was visitor there, Mary Sanford brought her small son to her aunt's house. The fair-haired child could barely walk, but plunged about the drawing room with chortles of delight. In all our conversation there was nothing that could distract Mary from loving attention to her child, and her love for him gave her the radiance of a Madonna. I experienced an odd yearning that was almost jealousy.

Many women of my age and more are in the midst of producing families, often so large that domestic responsibility has taken over their lives and their independence. I have seen it in my own friends, even when there were ample means for nursemaids and governesses, and the drag of constant child-bearing ages a woman and spoils her figure. More than any of that, I would fear for the happiness of any child born into the tightrope world that is mine at present. Containment is the great necessity, I tell Dougie. The world will not understand us.

'How much advantage you and I have,' said Ethel, 'and Bessie, too. Unlike so many we don't have any day-to-day struggle, spend much of our time in chat, or vanity, or telling others how to do tasks we don't wish to do ourselves. Yet I'm not sure we're any happier for it. We take all we have for granted, don't we, and what's denied becomes the thing we most urgently desire.'

'And what's that for you?' I asked, but Ethel just raised her eyebrows and smiled. To ridicule her husband any more served no purpose, except to question her own decisions. What would she have said I wonder, if I had told her Dougie and I loved each other, and expressed it fully? What might that confession have released of the innermost secrets of her own life?

I have also had the pleasure of Annie's visits. Of all my brothers and sisters she is most dear to me. We have a special closeness, and although over the years there have been disagreements, they have never involved malice, and have never disturbed our love for each other. William pays her little attention, but Dougie puts himself out to squire us about the town, and accompany us to functions and family homes. His courtesy and attention are mainly on my account, I know, but he and Annie find themselves easy companions. He likes to tease me by asking Annie to reveal harmless family secrets about my nature and doings as a girl. Also he flatters and amuses her by claiming that several eligible bachelors of his acquaintance are eager to know more of this new arrival on the Dunedin scene.

Annie is willing to play along, but is sensible at heart, and marriage is not everything to her, despite a natural impulse to find a suitable husband. She has a great fondness for gardens, and considerable knowledge too, and is trying to persuade Alfred to help her establish a superior florist shop. He in his conventional way sees the prospect as beneath the dignity of the family, rather than considering what pleasure and usefulness it could provide for Annie.

Annie likes to be here, I think, and is impressed with the Larnach world. When on the last occasion Dougie and I were farewelling her at the steamer, and William had sent in the carriage and four because of her cases, she said, 'How grand you've become, Conny. I'm sure the rest of us must seem quite quaint to you now.'

'You know better than that.'

'Of course I do. You're still the same sister, but I can't help feeling sometimes you've left the rest of us behind, no matter what Alfred says. Everything seems at a gallop at The Camp — so many comings and goings, as if some big event is always in preparation.'

'Yes, but I'm just the same,' I said.

Even with Annie, however, there is a difference now. She is still unwed and at home, while I am married, in love with Dougie, in charge of a very considerable household and in the van of society, both here and in Wellington. When she earnestly tells me of the trivial comments, glances and situations into which she reads flirtation, the joys of her reading and music, or the round of her family life as a spinster, I realise how far I have come emotionally since leaving home: how much greater is my understanding of the real forces between men and women. I have two lives now, one quite public and conventional, one in which only Dougie and I exist. So even Bessie, Ethel and Annie are denied a true comprehension of what it is to be Conny Larnach.

Christmas and New Year are almost here. I look forward to neither, except that Dougie and I will be close. This warring family of Larnachs will gather again: Dougie and I will be under malicious scrutiny; William, subject to demands and ingratitude, will respond with alternating high-handedness and sullenness. Alice and Colleen are particularly petulant at present, and I have long given up the hope of amicable relations with them. When Colleen is here she is a constant obstacle to happiness for Dougie and me, and I am glad she prefers to stay in Naseby. One of the few pleasures of unhappy and bitter people is to damage the lives of others.

So close are they, that Colleen recently wished to marry Alice's brother-in-law, Alfred Inder, which occasioned another shouting match with her father. One would think that the nature of her sister's marriage would be a warning against such folly, but then Colleen is a plain woman and having her younger sister married before her must be discomforting. Naseby is not a town of universal reputation, but I hardly think it deserves two such pairs as the Inders and Larnachs. Putting my own welfare first, however, I was for once on Colleen's side in her dispute with her father. Even this unnatural alliance has not been successful.

I have already talked several times with Miss Falloon regarding the meals for ourselves and our guests, and the Christmas party dinner for all The Camp staff and farm workers the day before. William insists on keeping up appearances despite grumbling at the cost. Because whole families will come I have decided the ballroom is again the most convenient place. The weather here cannot be relied on for an outside feast and I do not want some last minute difficulty with arrangements. When fed, the ordinary people can enjoy themselves on the lawns if they wish.

My first Christmas at The Camp, some of the men raced horses through the grounds and around the cottages, and, despite damage to the lawns and gardens, William cheered and gave bottles of claret to the winners. There will be none of that this year. We will invite fewer friends for Christmas Day than formerly. There will be the Larnach family gifts, the protracted meal, the formal toasts and studied good wishes, but there will be little real joy — apart from the secret happiness Dougie and I share. Nothing much else is important to me now, except ensuring other people do not pay the cost. And at New Year we will gather on the tower again to watch the fireworks, and each of us, I imagine, will have apprehensions, even as we profess to have seen the very best of auguries.

I suppose the Larnach Christmas has always been one of outward show as well as family concern. How different was Christmas in my own family home when Father was alive. He had a busy and successful public life, but took special delight in our birthdays, holidays together and at Christmas. He used to call me the second mother, because I was the eldest of his daughters, and long before I was old enough to be of any practical use, he would solemnly ask my opinion on arrangements for festivities: what games, decorations and table treats did I suggest. And no matter what strangeness I offered, he would consider it with judicious approval and ensure that something of it appeared on the occasion. Where did he learn that affirmation is so valuable for a child? He rarely spoke of his own parents, or his early life in London. I miss him still, for there are attributes in a loving father that even a husband, or a lover, cannot possess.

I see him at the Christmas tree when I was small, pretending not to be able to make out my name on those parcels meant for me, and professing surprise at their contents, his eyebrows lifting. In later life he was like one of those ever-kindly benefactors in a book by Dickens, with a shock of pure white hair extending to full sideburns, and then up to a bushy moustache, only his chin clean-shaven. Unlike some adults, who are bored and impatient in the company of children, he loved to witness the joy with which we greeted small treats and minor happenings. Maybe such simple and open emotions were a counter to the complex machinations and cynicism he dealt with in his legal and parliamentary work. What a wonderful kite he could make from sticks, paper and string, and how deliciously terrifying was his voice for the Goldilocks bears. Mother said he spoilt us, especially the girls, but even as a child I was aware that the pleasure he took in this indulgence was quite equal to our own. Only as an adult have I come to realise that happiness is not the condition of every family.

This morning when I woke, there were bright bars of sunlight in the room that should have pleased me, but I lay and wondered how my life has come to this — how small decisions and great ones, some mine, some made by others; how accidents, luck and coincidence, had all contributed to bring me here to The

Camp, my husband in one room and my lover, his son, in another. Nothing can be turned back. Even God cannot change the past, Agathon said.

How different my life was in Wellington before I married. I would sit with my sisters and we would talk of the novels we read, and even the most extreme and shocking of their implausible plots were less fraught than the life I have now. It would take a Brontë to tell of my situation, and only Emily's imagination, surely, could encompass it, yet once I thought her creations overwrought. A true love, though, is the most important possession in the world: the things of greatest value are beyond our ability to purchase, and are gifts of sacrifice. Without love we are just a great mass of people walking through life to our deaths.

However, whatever one's actual situation, no matter what the perils, or rewards, it is of necessity accompanied by the usual and the everyday: the plod of things of no lasting significance yet impossible to ignore. The choosing of the new season's clothes, the search for satisfactory servants, the supervision of Miss Falloon's supervision, the shaping of nails and the brushing of one's hair, the leaving and receiving of calling cards, the choosing of curtain lengths, the instruction of the tradesmen. Today I will go with Gladys to buy further Christmas presents, try to enter her open enjoyment of it, yet always at the back of my mind will be the sense of a double life, and the absolute need to keep them apart.

Disunity is an attitude that has a natural inclination to spread, and the lack of common purpose between William and me seems to have infected the servants. I have had many talks with Miss

Falloon about the petty squabbles and feuds among the women in particular. The garden staff are seldom at fault, but the laundry women and maids rarely seem to have their minds on work, and there is persistent pilfering in the kitchens. Jane came to me in private and gave an opinion that Miss Falloon plays favourites, and that too many we employ inside come from the same local homes. In the past this was because of William's loyalty to those families associated with the building of The Camp, but it has led to assumptions of preference, and even to indolence. My own observation supports Jane, so I went through all the household names with Miss Falloon and consequently sent away the Murray sisters and Becky Lefroy. All three are flirts and chatterboxes. Becky burst into tears before me, but when I wouldn't relent flounced out, quite the lady. Young women these days think much is due to them no matter what their station in life.

It has been more difficult to detect disloyalty among the kitchen staff, but we know that some have been stealing tinned goods for their families and even perhaps selling them to acquaintances. At my instruction, Miss Falloon and Jane made an inspection of the servants' rooms, and a quantity of stuff was found, along with a fine pair of London boots that William has never worn, and embroidered cushion covers that were gifts to Eliza Larnach from a Dunedin supplier to The Camp. As a consequence of all this tiresome and unpleasant investigation, another woman, and Morton de Joux from the stables, have been sent packing without any testimonial, and there is a certain sullenness among some of the remaining staff. William complains of waste and expense but has done not much to diminish them, and shows little interest now when I talk to him of household matters. Dougie, in contrast, is entirely sympathetic.

I find to be in love is a sentence on all other friends, and that is especially so because of the secrecy Dougie and I must maintain. I recognise in myself some drawing back from those who were closest to me here, Bessie Hocken especially. It is not just a matter of with whom I wish to spend time, or even a lesser need for other confidants now that Dougie and I are so close in all things. It is also, I must confess, a fear that I might reveal too much, and a guilt that my life now would be repugnant to them if they knew it fully. But they could not, of course, know it fully. Only Dougie and I understand where we stand and why. Only we can judge what is justifiable for love.

Whether it is my sensitive conscience, or a reality, I have a feeling that Bessie has some inkling of how things now are with Dougie and me, and, if so, where else has an undertow of gossip and aspersion been sapping? The gradual withdrawal may not be all on my own side. Bessie has not made any open reference, or enquiry, but things are not the same between us. Twice she has found reason, or excuse, not to come to The Camp. I am not invited to her house as often as before and when we do meet there seems some slight measure of reserve.

At the recitations and musical evening held at Oaklands, when we were talking of the praise given to Frances Hodgkins in the *Triad* magazine, Bessie told me of the continuing gossip concerning Grace Joel, another very promising young painter whose father owned the Red Lion Brewery. 'She has given herself to Girolamo Nerli,' Bessie said. 'It's common knowledge and it will be the ruin of her career and acceptance in society.' Both of us were acquainted with Nerli, who established the Otago Art Academy. He is an unconventional, talented man not long among us from his own country, whom I could quite see taking advantage of a young woman, but I didn't say that.

'Maybe it's all just envy and speculation,' I said. 'Assumptions made because she has painted and exhibited the female nude figure. People are so easily shocked at any move to give women artists a greater share of the freedoms permitted their male counterparts.'

'A woman is allowed less latitude in her actions, Conny. You know that. It must be recognised even as we fight against it.' It was not so much what Bessie said, but that she put her hand on my wrist and gave it a brief squeeze. I passed off the moment with some general comment about unfairness, but assumed some personal criticism and warning all the same.

I hope I have guessed wrongly in all of this: when you have something to hide it is easy to imagine others have secrets also. Bessie here, and Annie in Wellington, have been the closest to me, but friendship and kinship are never the equal of love. Those who cannot understand the imperative of love have surely never truly experienced it.

Eight

Conny's back at The Camp, thank God. How I miss her when she's not here. The place sinks back into monotony and trivial malaise. My life now is marked out not by birthdays, or business appointments, not seasons, or nights and days, but by the times I have Conny in my arms, and they are fewer than I wish. Almost fewer than I can tolerate. It's damnably difficult to get her alone in Wellington when I do manage to have reason to be there, and even when all three of us were guests of the Palmers in Christchurch, opportunities for the greatest of pleasures were few.

On one evening, when Father was with our host in the city, and Conny had gone early to her room, I took the risk of going to her, with the pretence, had I been asked, of enquiring if she had any message she wished included in a letter to Gladys. She was reluctant to let me in, but only because we were within a family home. She knew my fervour and need. We made love on a multi-coloured rug rather than the bed in case the springs betrayed us, although the rooms on either side were unoccupied. The rug smelled of camphor, and was rough on my elbows and knees. Conny made me go soon after, and I stooped at the door before opening it, listening for anyone moving in the passage. Love often means a strange, almost comic, loss of dignity, but what the hell.

I went out onto the verandah later with a fellow guest who was a judge from Auckland, and we drank good whisky and talked. He was an amusing companion and keen on racing, but it was all anti-climax after being in Conny's room. Each time I lifted my glass to my mouth I could smell her on my hands, and the faint fragrance of camphor as well. No erudition, or goodwill, on the part of the judge could compensate, though we stayed talking for some time, with heavy moths swirling into the dim light from the window and through our pipe smoke. I'd be surprised by how many opium dens there were in Auckland, he told me.

There was only one other chance. Conny and I had taken a gig to the town, enjoyed the opportunity to talk and laugh, and because we were together even the shops of dresses and ornaments were places I was happy to linger in. On the way back I drove behind a derelict brickworks, half covered with undulating, blue-flowered creeper, and halted there in privacy. While the horse grazed in harness, tugging the gig this way and that, Conny and I held each other and kissed. She wouldn't allow me more, but to put against that disappointment was the joy we always have in just being alone together. I told her I intended to take rooms with a private street entrance in a business block close to First Church, so that we could meet there and spend time without anybody knowing. 'It won't do, I'm afraid,' she said, shaking her head firmly. 'Too many sharp eyes to notice and malicious minds to wonder why Mrs Larnach goes there often.'

'Of course we wouldn't come or go together,' I said.

'It wouldn't matter. No, it won't do, and you know it in your heart. Everything must fit with the outward life.'

'We've taken risks in the past, haven't we?'

'Too many perhaps. You know how much I want to be with you, but we mustn't let down our guard for a minute. Everything could tumble so quickly, so utterly. We make the most of what we have, and that's so much more than most people can even contemplate.' And she tilted her face up to be kissed, the lips cool in the insistent breeze, and her hand on the back of my head. 'Tell me again when you began to love me,' she said, and I did. Such repetition is all pleasure when there are only two of you in the world.

The old man, of course, is back here too, and that I could do without. He goes through the books and claims they are in a muddle. With his own affairs in decline, he expects me to run things here quite free of the forces gripping the whole colony. There's no reasoning with him. And I've never had the training of a clerk, or wanted to be one. The outside work with the stock and the men is what I enjoy, and the direct contact with businesspeople in their offices or at the club. Father doesn't take into consideration the tie of the wretched telephone office, or accept my right to some independent life. He promised The Camp would be left to me in recompense for all that's been spent on Donny, but there's little talk of that now, and I know from comments Basil Sievwright made that he has considered selling both the peninsula properties and those in Central Otago. However, there are few buyers about, only hard scavengers.

One of the few things here during the year that pleased Father was the outcome of the Magistrate's Court hearing concerning one of our properties, an old, unoccupied house in Broad Bay. It was destroyed by fire and some local people insinuated that we'd instigated it in order to collect the insurance. A Mrs Walquest who lives nearby thought she recognised me at the scene the night the place went up, and when it proved I was outside Otago, she switched her suspicions to Patrick Sexton. Amazing what a proffered reward of twenty pounds will enable people to remember. I imagine that swaggers, or rabbiters, set fire to the place, but whatever the cause, the verdict was that no one could be held responsible and the insurance will stand. The newspapers made a big thing of it all, naturally, and Conny was quick to point out to me another example of the underlying envy and resentment some have towards our family.

Father finds it difficult to accept his children are now adult, with views and ambitions of their own. He still wants to make decisions for us, and resents it when we resist them. The role of paterfamilias is so much a part of his dignity that it mustn't be questioned. The past is the only place now in which Father and I feel comfortable — the time when Mother was with us and he going from strength to strength. In my memory he's a different man. Donny, who was with him on his first visits to the site of The Camp, said he clambered up a tree to exult in the view and his possession of the place. After the bush was felled, and the hilltop blasted and levelled, it was our playground for many months while the big house was being built. Donny and I came to know the workmen well, including the French and Italian artists who painstakingly created the moulded ornamental ceilings, the carvers and stonemasons who created the Oamaru limestone sculptures and intricate wooden wonders Father's so proud of.

It's François I remember most clearly. He was at The Camp for several years, and taught Donny, Kate and me to sing French songs. Originally from the south of France, he loved to spend time riding because he had grown up familiar with the horses of the Camargue. In our presence he was cheerful, and got on well with Father and the others, but there must have been times of incongruity for him: the man from Arles spending his days on internal scaffolding like Michelangelo, and cantering about the rough country of this peninsula so far from France. As a child I gave no thought to the sort of dislocation such a life brings, but I was to feel something of it myself in England, and on my return here.

Where's François now, I wonder, and how much of a dream does his time on the other side of the world seem to him? He was fascinated by the generator Father installed that provided gas from the long drops for lights in The Camp. He could sit absolutely still and silent for a long time, which in the whirlwind of boyhood, seemed very strange to me. Vegetables were important to him: he would often go to the kitchens and cook them to his own taste. He would sometimes get drunk in Dunedin, but the police knew him well and would hold him in the cells until someone came to fetch him. He carved wooden birds for us children, and wore a belt so broad that Donny said it had belonged to pirates. François is long gone, but his ceilings at The Camp exist as a reminder to those of us who knew him, and other examples of artistry evoke different craftsmen who were part of our lives then.

When the last stone blocks were being placed on the turret, Father called all the family to see. There was a wet mist so Mother and the girls went inside again almost at once, but Donny and I stayed to watch Father put two sovereigns under the last block laid of the castellated wall and say grandly that they'd be there as long as the stones stood. After we'd all gone down and the mist had become steady rain, Donny and I crept back. From the top of the steep stone steps spiralling to the tower we saw that Drew, the youngest of the stonemasons, had returned too, to lift the last block and take the sovereigns from the fresh mortar before replacing it. As he stepped dangerously down from the wall, he noticed us, and stopped, cocksure and large. 'What you two gawping at? You seen nought, understand me?' He thrust his face close, and I remember how his long, fair hair was plastered over his forehead by the rain. As he demanded, Donny and I said nothing in reply, and nothing to anyone else. We weren't afraid so much as astonished that anyone employed by Father could treat him with such contempt.

So many people have come to The Camp over the years as guests, friends, tradespeople and servants, some ascending the lion steps and being welcomed by the family, some allowed only at back entrances, some doing their trivial business at a doorway without entering at all. Each has a story of the house, I suppose, from the premier to a scullery maid sent away for thieving, from touring Viennese violinists to the one-eyed man who used to buy the hides of dead horses.

When I first returned from England, there was a Gaelic-speaking hermit whom Father let live in the stables for a time. Each day he would collect the eggs and take them to the kitchen. He talked to himself in his own language, but to nobody else, and one frosty morning he was found dead on his blanket. His only possession of worth was a basket-hilted claymore, which Father took for his library, announcing that it had almost certainly been used against the English at Culloden.

It wasn't just people that Father gathered from afar for his great enterprise, but materials too: heart kauri from the Far North, fire bricks from Glasgow, Belgian marble tiles, flagstones from Edinburgh, Marseilles cobblestones for the stables, Welsh slate, Arabian rugs, Italian marble baths and Venetian glass. So much of the very finest of European civilisation brought to adorn his great achievement built on a lonely, colonial hill. Everything had to be punted across the harbour from Port Chalmers, then carted by ox-drawn dray up the steep hill. The bullocky would sometimes let Donny and me sit up with him and raise the whip and shout, pretending we were in control. The workmen would laugh and wave as we came around the levelled sweep before The Camp. Like young princes, we accepted it all as our entitlement.

Such recollections often come to me now, perhaps because of

the realisation, at last, of the choice before me. There's no way I can have The Camp and Conny too. To live with the woman I love, I will have to give up the place most dear to me.

He seldom spoke of it, but Father felt a keen rivalry with the great Otago runholder Robert Campbell. Both were of Scottish descent, ambitious and determined to display their talent and achievement. Campbell's stone mansion at Otekaieke, in the Waitaki Valley, completed at much the same time as The Camp, has thirty rooms and electric bells that astonished everyone. Father sent a man up to photograph it secretly, rather than go himself. 'It's stuck there like a sore thumb,' he told me, 'among those bare hills. I've chosen better by far, and I'll outlast him.'

As a boy I took it all for granted. Only later did I see Father's extravagant confidence for what it was — a challenge to the fates. Too much, too soon, has become the truth for him and many of his friends at the colony's highest level as fortunes founder. Hubris, old Roper would say, weighing a cane in his hand as a possible remedy for it. Father has found it a chastening experience to adjust to difficult times and to realise that so many people he accepted at face value are fair-weather friends. He blames them, of course, and the universal drying up of capital, rather than admitting he has bitten off more than he can chew.

The difficult times have sapped the goodwill of many we come into contact with, and there are people who take pleasure in seeing their betters aren't immune from misfortune. Even Conny is subject to gossip and envy because of her forthright views and position. Last Thursday, after a meal at the club and business in

Stuart Street, Robert, Hugo and I went to the Piccadilly Rooms before parting. Behind us, at tables, was a group of reasonably dressed young men, none of whom I recognised, and despite the amount of noise in the room I clearly heard a voice say, 'Constance Larnach needs to be ploughed.'

I turned and challenged them, but they just laughed, asked me to repeat what it was I claimed to have heard and denied any mention of Conny. I couldn't be particular, and they enjoyed my hurt and fury. I've never been more angry. 'Not so high and mighty now,' one said.

'You need to keep it in your britches, Larnach,' said another amid the barracking. I forced my way to him and took him by the throat, close, so that I had a whiff of his beery breath, but he kept laughing even as we grappled and others intervened to separate us. 'The Highlander's blood is up. I'm quaking in me boots,' my adversary said while his friends whistled and clapped.

As we left, Hugo told me their sort weren't worth confronting. It was a most damnable experience, bad enough if meant to ridicule Conny and Father, worse if it shows a general assumption concerning Conny and me. I've said nothing to her. I hate the thought of these inferior and ignorant people talking about her at all. She says she's not concerned about opinion, but reputation is everything with a woman of her consequence, and I know she's suffered slights recently. Not things said, so much as invitations not extended, and those she's made declined, or not responded to. I hope she'll come to see there's only one way out of our predicament, and that's to go away — start afresh in a new country where we're able to live openly together.

Only days later I met Ellen near the city centre. By odd coincidence, a few minutes before I recognised Harriet Connelly on the street. She'd been in service at The Camp, and become pregnant. She had no child with her. Neatly enough dressed, she was walking with another young woman. My conscience was clear, and I would have addressed her, but she averted her head and talked more rapidly to her companion. She's making a new life, I suppose. Who could blame her for not wanting to be reminded of the way things ended for her at The Camp. I remember once passing the laundry and glimpsing her blowing her nose on a sheet. Harmless, and human enough, I suppose.

Meeting Ellen almost immediately afterwards was a good deal less easy. She'd been shopping and stopped on the corner by the Octagon tearooms when she saw me, swinging her bag slightly back and forth. Both of us were somewhat embarrassed, as happens when people who once were intimate, and have retreated from that closeness, meet again. We talked a little of our common acquaintances, and of the fire that had destroyed a lodging house close to her home, and in which an old miner died. I know the man she's to marry, but neither of us said anything of him, or that. As we talked it occurred to me that, but for Conny, Ellen and I might have already married. There was nothing I would change, but it made me sad somehow, chatting idly with her, and remembering when we'd been important to each other. Maybe her thoughts were similar, for her voice became more hesitant and she said she must go and meet her mother. 'How are your father and mother?'

I asked, and she replied with platitudes. 'Remember there's plenty of cut firewood at The Camp, and they're welcome to come for a load as they used to.'

'We have ample at the moment, thanks very much,' she said, and put her hand to her hat in a small nervous gesture I knew well.

So we stood apart and talked of firewood and acquaintances, when not so long ago I had slapped her thighs, held her breasts to my mouth, had her quick breathing at my face and her wrists held tightly in my hands. Her hair is long, dark and clean, always something I admired. I've disappointed her, hurt her by not proposing marriage, and although she has recovered from that, I wish I'd extricated myself in some way less abrupt and painful for her. What's done is done, however, and I believe for the best.

Conny's the woman I live for. God, how much I wish she was single like Ellen, and we could marry and be easy in the world.

Father's often on at me to show more resolution, and now I've shown sufficient to be sleeping with his wife, but nothing that Conny and I've done is meant to hurt him. In all honesty I don't think Father would find things much altered if the marriage ended, provided scandal was avoided. Money and position are his life, and the accumulation of public dignity brought by success in those pursuits. Whatever he achieves merely brings new ambitions into view. The CMG, being minister of mines, estates, grand friends, merely make him hungrier — especially for the knighthood. Conny says he'd wear the insignia on his pyjamas.

William Hodgkins stayed the night with us yesterday. He's the driving force behind most of Dunedin's artistic endeavours:

he founded the art gallery and promotes music and education. Conny's fond of him and in her he finds a great supporter. He was bankrupted a few years ago, despite his legal practice, and that gives Father a slight feeling of superiority, as he's managed at least to avoid that. Rather than William H. lacking industry, or talent, it was his generous community service, I think, that led to temporary ruin. Conny said to me afterwards that he didn't look a well man, but he wasn't called upon at table to take much of a lead in conversation. Father held forth once more about his visit to Wick, half a life away.

'You can't begin as a family much further north than Wick,' he said, 'and you can't end much further south than Dunedin.' Conny caught my eye. How often we've heard that opening, and indeed what was to follow. While in England Father had taken the long and inconvenient journey north to visit the town, and the thatched stone cottage where his father was born on the farm of Achingall in the Strath of Watten. 'The valley was wide and rich, and Larnachs still plentiful,' Father said. He walked for miles in the countryside and searched the scattered graveyards for family inscriptions. In a pub in Wick he met a Larnach who was a stonemason and poet, and who told him that Larnachs were descendants of the Vikings, not the Irish who moved into most of the rest of Scotland hundreds of years ago. This notion was attractive to Father.

Despite the appalling weather, he had watched the herring boats leave and sat on the river wall looking downstream to the old stone-arch bridge and the spire beyond it. Without the need for our guest's polite encouragement, he elaborated on the pride his stay-at-home Wick relatives had showed in his achievements, once he'd enlightened them. He hinted, as always, that the Larnachs in the distant past had been of considerable consequence, lairds there as he sees himself here.

Father is happy when he talks of such things. Although Donny, my sisters and I grew up with his stories of the Scots nation and our family affiliation, none of us found inspiration in them, or much connection. Uncle Donald's life in Sussex was a good deal more to my taste. He has been dead less than a year, and little mourned by Father, but I remember him with gratitude. A quiet-living man, despite his wealth and possessions, he was never demonstrative, but he and Aunt Jane always made us feel welcome. The sense of clan was inbred.

They made one visit to the colony, not long after Mother's death, and shortly before my return. Uncle Donald was impressed with The Camp, but too shrewd to invest substantially in the agricultural company that Father was promoting strongly. 'I don't like to be so far from my money,' he said, and Aunt Jane termed much of what she saw in Otago, the wilderness. There's tremendous opportunity when a new country is opening up, but great uncertainty as well. Fortunes rise and fall abruptly, or veer off in unexpected directions.

Cousin James will take over Brambletye in an accepted and secure way that should be my path here at The Camp. It was Father's promise to me, but everything has grown rickety, and Donny and the girls are full of jealousy despite all they've been given, and their desertion of the place. If Conny and I could be together here, life would be as complete as one could expect in an imperfect world, but that won't happen, and she remains adamant in her refusal to leave with me and live elsewhere.

Father has built here with such permanence and quality, such optimistic commitment. He dreams of Larnachs in residence at The Camp generations hence, when the colony has regained its equilibrium, when the houses and cleared farms stretch uninterrupted from peninsula to city, when the knighthood he has fought so hard for is worn easily by a descendant. He's an odd mixture, my father. I think if he knew that vision was secure he would willingly put up with all that's happening to him now.

I have Conny, but I'm trapped as far as resources go to get us away together, even if she could be persuaded. The Camp is my livelihood, yet the very thing we must leave if we're to have a natural life together. I've no other source of money, no substantial savings, no immediately profitable skills. Even my ability to obtain credit relies on the name of William Larnach, which means little other than here in the colony. I've wracked my brains to find ways of raising the capital that would persuade Conny we could leave and establish ourselves elsewhere. Robert's business connections in Argentina have again said I would have no difficulty in obtaining a position as manager of an extensive farming property there, but we know nothing of the location, or the conditions — nothing about the society in which we would be placed.

In other circumstances I'm sure James would find something for me to do in connection with horses, but it would be too much for even his liberal sentiments if I came to Brambletye with my father's wife. How much better and more naturally everything would have turned out if the old man had resigned himself to widowhood, and I'd met and married Conny myself.

I can't be with Conny at The Camp as often as I'd like, and if I can't be with her then I'm happier outside the house, and away from the damned telephone office. I like to be about the farm. I ride Tarquin on the roads and tracks of the peninsula, usually alone, since I can't share with my friends what's most important to me now. Life is at once fuller, yet narrowed down to Conny and me.

Yesterday I took the gun out for pigeons, walking from The Camp to the bush ridges. The New Zealand bird is heavier and easier to shoot than the English one: it's slower in flight, and even when disturbed doesn't go far before settling again. I imagine the Maoris made the most of them. I've no trained dog, and lost some birds in the undergrowth, but it was easy enough to get as full a bag as I wished to carry home.

The bush is cool and dark, even in summer, and I enjoyed the secrecy of it. Every part of England has been stood on, I imagine, but here, even at walking distance from roads and the partly cleared farms, you feel you may be the first man on a particular spot: the first to lean in rest on a tree trunk, to piss on a fern, or to fire a gun into the branches. Why that should increase the pleasure I experience I'm not sure, but it does. The bush here is very different to the open forest of England: the foliage uniformly darker, the undercover close and thick, with brown, furred fronds like monkey tails, and beneath your feet the damp give of rotting vegetation.

The shooting startled all the birds, not just the quarry, but when I had enough pigeons, I turned back down towards the sea and the smaller birds came back on song. I walked the roughly cleared edge down to Barrett's mill so that I would be in the afternoon sun. In time, I suppose, most of the bush of the peninsula will be felled and good farms will cover it. They were working at the mill, four men loading drays, and they waved and called out when I held up the leather game bag. Father complains sometimes at the damage the drays do to the roads, and of the smoke from the burn-offs that follow logging, but farmland is being won from the bush for better use.

I didn't mention to Father that I'd been shooting. Perhaps he'll make some comment when the birds appear upon the table. I left the bag at the kitchens and went directly to the telephone office to relieve Walter. He's an odd boy, recommended by Professor Black because of his quick wits and lack of a father. He has hopes of going to university and has his books with him at the office so he can study them between calls. Conny says I should take more interest in him, but I'm too distracted by my own concerns.

Conny and I make our fun and seek our satisfaction when we can, and it's more to me than anything else in the world. How shrewd she is, how attuned to the undercurrents around us. She said we must have an argument apparent to the staff, as a counter to any gossip and spying that might be going on among them. It would concern my failure to collect articles from dress shops in Dunedin, she decided, and she enjoyed setting up the little play beforehand. So we seemed by chance to pause unseen outside the room where Jane and a maid were changing linen, and have a sharp exchange while trying not to smile. Later in the day we met, touched and laughed together. How close we are against the rest of the world. And how accustomed now to deception.

Conny has far more imagination than I have: a marvellous sensitivity, which may be the same thing, but strangely she doesn't dream much, while I, ever since childhood, have had the best and worst of dreams. At St Leonard's they were a form of escape from the misery I often endured there, even the nightmares providing at least a variety in unhappiness. The happy dreams were a great solace, though I spoke of them to no one, not even Jeremy. Often they took me to Brambletye, especially the brick and slate stables and the long Park meadow, or the old nursery room that James and his brothers had made a den in which to smoke and drink; Aunt Jane knew to keep away. What a stink it had — of pipe tobacco, port, horsehair furniture and our indolent bodies.

Some of the happy dreams were of us all at The Camp before Mother died, some of the expedition to England across America. Only nights ago I dreamt of Kate, first and best of my sisters. We were in a train, travelling across the continent from San Francisco, and all was as I experienced it as a fourteen-year-old — the jogging motion and clatter over the tracks, the landscape streaming past, which became, as days went by, as accustomed as a life settled in one place. How plush those carriages were compared with trains here, and how well appointed and serviced: velvet backings, ornate mirrors, polished wood and brass cuspidors, yet all with the finest grit on every surface that's the mark of coal and steam.

Kate, only a year older than me, was always a close companion, and in my dream we sat together and she told me she wanted to be a nurse. I saw again her homely face with its high brow, and her hair tightly pulled back. She said that no doubt she'd marry a very poor man and have to depend on me to support their numerous children. The idea set her laughing, and that's the best part of the dream. Kate's long, open-mouthed face tipped back in laughter, and behind her a country strange to us in apparent motion. Only in the no-man's-land between dream and memory can I meet dear Kate now, and see her still laughing.

I have such dreams still, but more special now are the visions I have of happiness for Conny and me. I dream of us meeting and she is unmarried; I dream of us having begun a new life in a foreign, but welcoming, place; I dream even of Father having died, and so freed us to be together.

~Nine~

I have never been happier than I am now, and don't expect to be so in the future. William, Dougie and I are in Queensland in consequence of William being appointed by Seddon as the colony's commissioner to the Brisbane Exhibition. My happiness has nothing to do with the exhibition, or the people. Here Dougie and I are released from the constant scrutiny we bear in New Zealand, the ever-present need to maintain the appearance of a conventional relationship between stepmother and stepson. In this place being a Larnach is of little concern to anybody, and we have a freedom that is heady indeed. So liberating, in fact, that I remind Dougie we must not relax entirely and be discovered.

We have three months here. William is less pleased: he sees the position as a sop and remains put out that, despite his letters to Seddon before he went to London for the Queen's diamond jubilee, no knighthood has eventuated. William and Richard Seddon are in many ways alike. They have known each other a long time, and there is competition as well as companionship in their friendship. They are both what the papers call 'big men' in the colony, but it is Seddon who holds the ascendancy now, and William chafes at that, while still valuing the bond. Both have the common touch, both are ambitious and with a natural instinct to dominate, both are talented and had great energy in their prime. And it must be admitted they share a certain coarseness and blustering conviction that they know best what should be done in the lives of others as well as their own.

The premier has been a frequent visitor to 45 Molesworth Street, often part of the group singing around our piano. He unbends among society he trusts, and I have seen tears in his eyes when singing popular songs of pathos, and also when telling his sentimental tales of the ordinary people he had much to do with as a younger man. As well he loves to laugh, and like William, and as my father used to, takes delight in practical jokes. He knows all the words to 'Daisy Bell' and 'After the Ball' and sings them with greater gusto than tunefulness. He likes to drink too, and thinks rather less of William for having put that aside. I hear rumour of his other manly interests, but gossip surrounds every person of note and is often exaggerated, or unfounded. In my company he is no more than tolerably suggestive. Had he had the opportunity for a university education, I'm sure he would have taken great advantage of it, for he has a quick and original mind.

Once, when we were travelling by carriage to an evening civic function with my brother, a group of larrikins in Lambton Quay shouted at Seddon, calling him a fat bastard. One man with a great moustache, but no hair on his head, even jumped onto the carriage and held the door for a time, then spat a great gob inside that barely missed my dress. As he fell back, laughing, a few stained and broken teeth showed in his open mouth. No doubt he was drunk. I expected Seddon to be loud and angry, but he apologised to me. 'Unhappy people endeavour to make others unhappy too,' he said. 'What they really hate is their predicament.'

'So what must be done for them?'

'Decent jobs, Conny,' he said. 'Work gives self-respect.'

Like William, he has, beneath his personal ambition and vanity, a sincere wish to improve the lot of the colony's most ordinary people. The incident reminded me also that he has a natural and shrewd perception concerning human nature. I did notice, however, that he had balled his hand and seemed tempted to strike out at the spitter. Had I not been with him, his response might have been different, for it is said that during his time on the Coast he often settled disputes, even debts, with his fists.

William complains about the heat here, the lack of clean water, and having to spend his own money on the trip. He is not impressed with the city and its convict origins. The exhibition itself interests him in parts. He was delighted to see that the stand of our own Mosgiel Woollen Company was awarded two gold medals, and the bush house fernery took his fancy. He returned to it several times and Dougie and I accompanied him on one occasion, escorted by William Soutter, who is responsible for the display. More than three thousand staghorn, bird's-nest and elkhorn ferns, and untold numbers of palms, orchids and potted plants. It was quite lovely, and our favourite of all the exhibits, but as we stood in the shade house among the greenery and listened to the curator's recital of plants, it was Dougie's discreet and passing hand pressure on my back I was most aware of, and which gave the greatest pleasure.

He accompanied me also to the hall display of needlework samplers and silk embroidered memorials. Such painstaking and time-consuming work, that I wonder if it is the best use of women's days, but there were some quite beautiful pieces, especially a series on classical themes from the French city of Lille. The colours are breathtaking, and the pride the custodian madame took in their charge made them even more impressive. I imagine that such work would be done by two very different sorts of women — those privileged and with infinite leisure time, and those skilled drudges paid such a pittance that the endless hours could be recouped in the sale. Such disparate origin, yet the beauty of each indistinguishable at the end.

Many of the exhibits and activities, though, are crass and commercial, and loud with self-advertisement. I quickly tired of sitting in the heat to see troupes of animals circling to be judged, or standing to have the purpose and workings of some clacking machine explained in detail. There are the exceptions, but most of what I have seen is clearly of interest mainly to men. The importance and inclinations of women are neglected.

But here Dougie and I have been able to live more the wished-for life. William has his official duties, so Dougie and I spend much time together. At The Camp we have always to consider the servants and guests, in Dunedin and Wellington we meet acquaintances everywhere, and are recognised by many people unknown to us. Here in the hotel, and in the city and the countryside, we experience comparative privacy. We have even remained together on several nights, when William has been away investigating the prospects of Queensland mining companies. Business opportunities are always uppermost in his mind. Gold has not been as plentiful here as in Victoria, but he has hopes for involvement in that as well as other ventures.

Three weeks after our arrival he went to Laidley with a Mr Riddell, who is a leading Brisbane businessman. He was away two nights, and Dougie and I said we preferred to go north of the city to see the banana groves and pineapple plants. We stayed close in a bungalow at Kirri, set in a eucalypt clearing, with an Aboriginal couple as servants. Neither of them was disposed to work, and every task required of them had to be mentioned individually. They made no assumption that because we had needed breakfast yesterday, we would require it today, and even after having been given simple instructions, they would have a long discussion in their own language before the woman did the work.

They came only during part of the day, however, and nothing could spoil the time Dougie and I had together. The privacy of a bedroom, humdrum for a married couple once the honeymoon is over, is bliss for us. It was a substantiation of what we could only dream about at home. Night and day together, free of constraint, able to laugh and tease and touch, to be a man and woman in love.

On the first afternoon we paid a courtesy call to the Noakes family, who owned the property, and came away as soon as we decently could, strolling together along the farm track and through trees. We walked slowly, for it was exceedingly hot despite the shade: even in my lightest clothes I perspired unpleasantly. Dougie took my hand, and for once I could be at ease with that, gently scratch his palm with a finger. There were brightly coloured parakeets with discordant cries, and heat hung heavy in the air. The clouds seemed to move faster than at home, rolling across the sun suddenly and away again.

Such was my pleasure that I had an almost physical pang of regret that the moment could not be indefinitely prolonged, despite the heat: Dougie and I walking happily and close together in a place quite strange to us, and totally unknown to William. My mind seemed to lift from my body, and from a distance I could see the two of us walking side by side, as another quite separate person would do, and see how well matched we were, how intent upon each other, how obviously in love. And yet behind the joy of that realisation was the shimmer of the knowledge that it must pass, that even devotion and completeness cannot hold back time.

We were caught in a cloudburst not far from the bungalow, yet walked calmly through it without caring. When we got back Dougie sent the Aborigines away and they wandered into the downpour just as unconcernedly as we had arrived. The sun was out again even before they were lost to sight among the loose-barked trees, and a soft haze of steam obscured their legs so that they seemed to be walking on their knees.

In the bedroom the shutters were still open and the sunlight made bright oblongs on the matting. We took off our wet clothes quite freely before one another and stood there in the warmth. Dougie picked up my chemise and put it briefly to his face. 'Take off the ring too,' he said. 'I don't want anything of my father about you. Not his house, not wearing clothes he bought you, not within miles and miles of him.'

How easily the wedding ring came from my finger; how readily I put William from my mind. There are moments of such fulfilment that their blaze makes past and future immaterial. We stood for a long time together before going to the bed. Under my hands I could feel the structure of Dougie's body, so much younger than his father's, and more responsive. Even the bumps where the bones have roughly healed after his terrible accident and the succeeding operations. I know the contours of his body better than I know my own, and he is equally familiar with my form. There is a gratefulness in Dougie's embrace that I never feel in his father's, or experienced in Josiah's unsought advances. What relief and release to be able to relax completely: to lie on the bed with Dougie without a part of myself alert for interruption by the servants, or William's unexpected return, even the anxiety that Dougie might leave something in my room that would be noticed. For once there was no hurry to make love and part, no furtiveness. Anticipation could build beneath our quiet talk, and the gentle, companionable aspects of real love could be expressed, as sometimes we had enjoyed them on our buggy rides about the peninsula, or into Dunedin. The days at Kirri will live with me always. Benjamin Disraeli said the traveller sees more than can be remembered, and remembers more than can be seen. Such is my experience here.

'This is the way it should be,' Dougie said. 'How it should be all the time for us.' He bent my leg up at the knee and ran his hand back and forth on the flesh behind the bone. 'We've got to be together somehow. It's the only right thing for all of us. My God it is. Life's unbearable otherwise.' I could see he was close to tears, which is unusual in him. Although he is a man of feeling, his school and family life have accustomed him to affect a bluff, conventional manner as protection.

'Oh, let's just enjoy this while we can,' I said. 'Make the most of what we have, and don't ask for more. '

'But we must have it all — be brave enough to declare what's most important for us. Robert told of me of a saying from his home in Yorkshire: take what you want, and pay for it. He lives by it, and so should we.'

Of course it was as it should be, but Dougie refuses to see that so much in life is not as it should be, and that it cannot be, because of the maze of decisions and happenings from the past that restrict our choices now. There is no socially acceptable way I can leave William and be with Dougie. And although I love him, I know too that there is a feckless quality to his nature, as with Robert's, that will prevent him from succeeding in the world. I am sufficiently his senior, in judgement rather than years, to understand that.

But there in the bungalow I was not going to mar our time together by arguing with him again. It was opportunity to smile, to talk, to be as loud or gentle as we wished in our lovemaking: a rare chance to be as lovers should — focused just on ourselves, with no care or responsibility for any other. Alone and together in the self-regarding heart of shared and complete love. How natural to lie with my breasts free, not exhausted, not tired even, but wonderfully spent. How absolute to talk to a man as honestly and directly as to oneself, to ask for satisfactions never admitted, or expressed, to anyone else. Since Dougie came to me, I know how love and marriage should be, and I rejoice that I have had that experience, whatever cost is demanded.

I have seldom seen Dougie's face when he is asleep, for almost always he must slip back to his own room when we have made love. So even to have him inert beside me was both a novelty and a delight. The face reveals its true contours in sleep, adopting no pose for public scrutiny, attempting no message to accompany words. William's face is heavy and somehow fallen back when he sleeps, Dougie's is youthful and trusting: fine, pale lines fan from his eyes as he lies relaxed, and there is a small, raised scar high on his cheek. He didn't wake when I kissed him and brushed back hair from his forehead. He didn't wake when I repeated his name for my own pleasure, and took his hand in mine. I do love my Dougie.

The time in the bungalow at Kirri, and the few, precious hotel nights in William's absence, so much valued by Dougie, are not the only advantages to our visit. Anywhere he and I can be relaxed together is given a sort of halo by that alone. To share the inner life, to talk in an open and trusting way is equal in importance with physical satisfaction. How happy we are here.

Strange in a way, for otherwise I would not wish to spend much time in Brisbane. It is a thrusting, practical place that still bears much evidence of its origins, and the heat is enervating. The convicts have long gone, but there seems to be a considerable number of German settlers. Material gain is the preoccupation, and there is little evidence of a regard for anything cultural. William has heard terrible stories of the treatment of the Aborigines here. The first free settlers did not recognise land ownership by the local Turrbul people. They were shot, driven away, or died from new diseases. Our servants at Kirri were most unsatisfactory, but people nevertheless, and the indifference to them is callous.

I have grown more detached from William, and critical of his views, but I still admire his toleration and support for other races. His time on the Victorian goldfields among men of so many different backgrounds, races and stations in life shaped his opinions of intrinsic worth, and although he is now accustomed to be with the foremost of the colony, and to be one of them, he has not lost the ability to separate appearance and reality.

Brisbane women are not at all fashionable, and seem unaware that feathers and velvet are the rage in London at present. The dress of many considered society here would be laughed at privately in Dunedin, or Wellington. Mrs Wevets, whose husband is rich and influential, invited me to play at a soirée. She and the other women were overcorseted and wore dresses with bustles far too pronounced to be in fashion. All their buttons were small and dark. The piano was an inferior instrument and out of tune. Mrs Wevets and her dowdy friends talked loudly during my playing, and afterwards could prattle only of servants, food and children with colic. I endeavoured to bring the conversation around to books, mentioning Jane Austen, Charles Dickens and the wonderful Margaret Oliphant, who died only a few weeks ago, but all they were familiar with were the sensational novels of Marie Corelli and Mary Braddon. A distinctly spreading woman with a freckled face told me that *Thelma* was the very best book in the world. I had to bite my tongue and keep to myself the conviction that Corelli's sentimental and false stories will be forgotten, despite the huge present sales, and that Dickens and Oliphant will live on. I came back to the hotel and told Dougie and William that our acquaintance in Dunedin and Wellington had never seemed so congenial.

Both newspapers here are very bad, full of dull commercial facts and figures, and arch, overwritten accounts of European doings. When I said as much to Dougie, he justly reminded me of an article in the Christmas issue of the *Otago Witness*, giving instruction to young ladies to improve their voices. Recommended cures for hoarseness had included preserved apricots, the inhalation of myrrh on a hot shovel and a teaspoon of syrup of squill and marshmallows. There was also the instruction never to read aloud, or try to speak, in a railway carriage. Dougie and I delight in such absurdity.

The Brisbane tradespeople also show to disadvantage in comparison with those of our own colony. Many in the shops demonstrate, by an odd combination of truculence and familiarity, that they resent any implication of inferiority because they serve. There are all sorts of people from all sorts of places, and getting ahead is what matters. On one occasion, when I was returning to the hotel alone, the cabby asked if I would be willing to come with him for pie and a drink. 'I'll show you a good time, lady,' he said, and no doubt had more to offer. No more than thirty, he was strongly built, but gap-toothed, and wore brown boots, a gentleman's cast-off waistcoat and his trouser ends were tied with leather laces. I got down and left him without word, or payment, and he went off discomforted.

When I told Dougie, he said that so many here are coarse and full of cheek. While at one of the livestock exhibitions, he saw a line of men heading behind the tents, and followed in expectation of a refreshment booth, but found instead a small crowd laughing at the spectacle of a donkey that had been sexually excited. 'Where else but here, Conny,' he exclaimed. 'Where else. We say we've freedom and opportunity in the colonies, but my God, there's still so much ignorance, presumption and cruelty. So many loud, poorly mannered people. God knows what sort of a society will come of it all in a hundred years. And the origins of so many people here are of the worst possible kind: criminals and defectives cast out of England.'

I imagine that in time there will be improvement, and even in the old world, I am told, there is plenty that remains barbarous. Not everyone is intolerable, of course, and my impatience of people is increased by my wish to be with Dougie rather than anyone else. At the luncheon William hosted on behalf of our country, on what was thankfully one of the cooler days, I had a long and pleasant conversation with Ida Maslin, the daughter of the magistrate. Not only was she an attractive young woman in crisp blue muslin with puffed sleeves, but she had only recently returned from France and Germany, where she had received excellent instruction in languages and music. We quite neglected others at the table and afterwards sat together under a striped awning. So much did we relax in our talk that before we parted she confided to me she had received a proposal of marriage from the son of her tutor in Bordeaux. How entertaining it is to have young and attractive people talk about their flirtations. We agreed to write to one another, and I invited her to visit us. I suppose I will never see her again, but I will remember her gaiety and intelligence.

Whatever my reservations about the general run of society here, at least I am free from the gossip, and the apprehension of gossip, that I face increasingly at home. Nothing has been said to my face that gives me an opportunity to challenge, but nevertheless the tittle-tattle and scrutiny are real. Shortly before we left Wellington, William and I went to a dinner party at the Plimmers', and after the meal, which had an impressive array of courses, but was marred by the long delays between them, the women went to the drawing rooms and most of the men to the billiards room. In the larger room I enjoyed a lengthy catch-up with Cecilia Higginson, and Violet Enright, then, as courtesy demands, went through to spend time with the other ladies. Mrs Taine, and a Mrs Poole, recently out from Manchester, had their heads together in urgent whisper as I came in, and from Sophia Taine's momentary confusion, it was clear I had been the topic of disclosure.

I could have turned away, but was resolved not to be intimidated. And how much was my own assumption rather than the truth? Maybe they had been taking satisfaction in criticism of my dress, or hair, even the disparity in ages between William and me, rather than any unnatural closeness with Dougie.

'The very person,' said Mrs Taine, quickly recovering her natural boldness. 'We were talking of your success in maintaining households both here and in Dunedin, and your favour with William's children. Not an easy thing to come into a family where the children are already adult.'

'Indeed not,' said her companion.

'Gladys was little more than a child when we married,' I said, 'and we have been close.'

'Yes, of course. The baby of the family. Do come and sit with us,' said Mrs Taine. I did so, and by design disagreed politely with most of what she said. She accepted each correction meekly, and so confirmed that she had indeed been speaking badly of me. After ten minutes of such strained conversation I excused myself and sought other company.

'Such a pleasure to have the opportunity to talk,' said Mrs Poole. 'We were so far apart at dinner and beforehand that we exchanged little more than introductions.' And no matter what we had said to each other since, she would go away with Mrs Taine's opinion of me as her own, such is the fascination of scandal.

William tires more readily now, especially in this unaccustomed heat, and is often happy to go to bed before ten o'clock. I use that as excuse to turn down as many invitations as I can without offence, and Dougie and I wait out his father, then settle to talk. It is a good time of the day, and although Dougie is disappointed we cannot go to the same bedroom, I tell him love expresses itself in many forms. I enjoy these talks, during which we discard superficial topics and convention, talk quite candidly of things close to our hearts. Light commentary, too, which amuses Dougie. William has rather lost his taste for it. My reflections on other women especially intrigue Dougie: often he laughs out loud. He says he had no idea that women, so correct in public, could be so scathing in their confidences. I do not think I flatter myself when I consider that I have been able to open Dougie's eyes to the true feelings of both women and men.

I am aware that Dougie's love entrusts to me a power over him, but the very completeness of his affection is also a reason he might destroy everything. The growing happiness we have in one scale increases the risk and guilt to balance it in the other.

We must both remember that what seems most natural to us is not necessarily so to others. On Tuesday evening the three of us attended one of the better civic dinners put on by the exhibition backers. The tables were mismatched, but with fine enough white and pale blue covers, and the dinner service was of good china, made in England especially for the colony and bearing its own crest. A handsome, dark-haired man, recently arrived from Brussels, had concocted wonderful displays of fruit that were greeted with applause when brought out: pineapples, apples, pears, plums, peaches, melons, apricots, green and black grapes and others I could not recognise. Some were dried or candied, some fresh and cut, some whole and perfect.

The pity was that the speeches lasted longer than the courses, and had less flavour. Dougie drank more claret than was wise, and towards the end of the night, when a man with mutton-chop whiskers was appropriately enough talking about sheep, Dougie leant over to say something to me, and placed his hand on my lap. Just for a moment, and in the familiarity of it, he flexed his thumb and fingers so that I could feel the pressure on my thigh. So slight a thing, and inconspicuous, but I saw that William had noticed, and his gaze remained steady on us when Dougie had removed his hand and finished talking. Trivial, perhaps, but I have told Dougie to be more careful: our time here must not lead to our undoing.

That night in the restricted hotel bed, William insisted that we make love. He was adamant, too, that I take off my nightdress, so that we were naked on the bed, with the window wide, and little relief in the hot, listless air. His breath was heavy with the banquet; the grey hair of his chest was slicked with sweat. He plucked at my nipples with thumb and finger, and didn't answer when I said it hurt. 'Husband and wife. Husband and wife,' he exclaimed several times as he lay on me, until it was almost part of his urgent rhythm. There was a possessive roughness in his taking of me, and we had little to say afterwards. He turned away and fell asleep, snoring loudly. I lay a long time awake. Somewhere in the heat of the night a dog was barking stubbornly, and I felt tears on my face. What sad places our lives lead us to sometimes, even among days of happiness.

Ten

On Tuesday Mr Fox took Father and me to see the electric trams that are this year replacing the horse-drawn ones here. Fox is a member of the Queensland Parliament and a big-wig among Brisbane businessmen. He has considerable civic and personal pride in the switch to electricity, which he sees as a great leap forward. I didn't say that horses are a great love of mine, and to have them dispossessed gives no pleasure. Electricity, steam, internal combustion — for me none of these can compare with the living thing, none of them has the brain that allows a horse to make judgements of terrain and distance. Surely no sense of partnership can be possible with a machine.

As we went about, Fox and Father spent some time attempting to impress each other without wishing to appear too obviously vainglorious. Like two bulls in a paddock, they had to test their strength. I couldn't give a damn about the trams, electric or otherwise, but Conny insisted that I go with them so Father wouldn't notice that I always prefer to be with her. I find little satisfaction in trailing around with him, being introduced to people I'll never see again, and who have as little interest in me as I have in them. Now that I have Conny, I have little patience with other people.

After the tram house, Mr Fox took us close to the river, where he described the '93 Black February floods that devastated the city. From the very spot we stood on, he said, he'd watched whole houses coming down in the rushing water and crashing into the Victoria bridge until it collapsed and was swept away. Dead cattle, sheep, trees and human corpses too. It must have been a terrible time, even allowing for any exaggeration on the part of our guide, but all I could think about was Conny, who had gone into the shops with several ladies of the city. She told me later that she took no more pleasure in the clothes and gossip of her outing, than I did in the trams and stories of the flood.

A few years ago, I would never have believed how completely my life has become centred on one woman. Nothing else is as important to me now. It's almost as Hugo describes his passion for gaming, which has never much interested me. Riding, fishing and races I still much enjoy, working with stock, billiards with friends, but even in the midst of those, I'll abruptly feel a sense of loss and longing: a conviction that happiness is elsewhere. Even when with others at the club, my thoughts are often with dear Conny. These few months here, while Father carries out his light official duties and squirrels for business prospects, are a wonderful opportunity for us to spend time together, and maybe she's right to say we should be thankful for that, and not push things beyond what is propriety as viewed from the outside.

When the trip was first mooted, Father assumed I would remain at The Camp, running it and the telephone office while they were away. Conny and I couldn't reveal to him how important it was that I travel with them, but we worked on the angle that unless I accompanied them to Brisbane, Conny would be left alone too often while Father was working and, even more significantly, taking his trips to mining sites up country.

It was a game of subtle manoeuvre at which Conny is most adept. Father had to fall in with our purpose, while thinking it his own idea. I remember the evening clearly. The three of us were coming back from the curved vinery at The Camp that held the Black Hamburg grapes sent out from Brambletye years ago. Father was complaining of the time he would have to spend away, and the insignificance of his appointment. He'd been one of two New Zealand commissioners to the Paris Exhibition nearly twenty years ago, and said sourly that Brisbane could be nothing but a come down.

'Seddon expects, though, that you'll find many opportunities to do business,' said Conny. 'People from all over Australia and New Zealand will be there, and from Britain as well.'

'What a focus for trade,' I put in. 'And even more to your liking, there'll be the chance to see for yourself if there's money to be made by getting in early on prospects up country.' Nothing interests Father more than the thought that, as in his younger days, he might be in at the beginning of some rich enterprise. And rough country has a fascination for him too, as he showed during his extraordinary and extended expeditions when minister of mines. 'You'll be Johnny on the spot,' I said.

'You won't want me tagging along all the time, or relying on strangers,' Conny said.

He stopped by the dairy, peered in to take satisfaction from his own produce, then walked farther to look beyond the windbreak trees of The Camp towards the sea. He stood quietly for a moment, puffing air through the characteristic droop of his thick, soft moustache, as was his habit when making a decision. He knew Conny couldn't be expected to take part in rough and ready trips, despite her vigour and fortitude.

'It would be best for us all if you came, Dougie,' he said. 'Then Conny won't be dependent on people she doesn't know. With three of us we have more choice, more alternatives, for each,' and he lifted his head, a problem solved.

'It's the best idea,' said Conny, as if surprised by it. 'Yes, quite right.' She took Father's arm, not such a common gesture as formerly, and they walked together across the gravel sweep towards the lion steps. It wasn't that she or I took any pleasure in the deception, but that it was a necessity in both our lives, and no hurt to Father.

How important that decision was. And I've reminded myself, during the many boring and trivial events of this trip, that they are merely intervals in the real life that is time with Conny. While looking at the river and listening to the prattling Mr Fox, while sweating in shirtsleeves to watch the exhibition cattle circle, or listening to some pomposity with a chain across his paunch, I know these are the price of admission to days and nights with my Conny.

Here in Brisbane we move about without arousing comment, whether with father or not. Only when we accompany him to official events is it marked out that Conny is his wife, and I his son. Conny and I have greater freedom than ever before, and that's an enormous boon. She thinks it a fortuitous sojourn, but I'm determined that somehow we make the break from father and have a life together even more complete than we experience here. It's the honest way, and the only way we'll be happy. Father will be hurt I know, and society enjoy the scandal, but it must be done, and I must persuade Conny of that. We belong together and only a certain boldness will achieve it. As the man, it's a decision I must soon make, or live with a sense of cowardice as well as guilt. I'm more convinced than ever after the time Conny and I had at Kirri: nights and days when we could live as those who love each other should live.

I wish we were still there, even though the black servants were ignorant and lazy, Mr and Mrs Noakes poor company and the heat oppressive. How wonderful to come into the bungalow after riding, walk up to Conny and embrace her quite openly. At night to talk in more than whispers and draw out our lovemaking without fear of discovery. Conny's never been more relaxed, never more willing to indulge me as a man, never more open about her own pleasure and feelings. Even the casual signs of her presence are a satisfaction for me. I remember going into the bathroom on the second morning at Kirri, and seeing on the bare boards a scatter of powder left by her after she had bathed and towelled.

And in the fine, pale grains was a single imprint of her foot, small and curved. Behind me I could hear the soft sounds as she dressed in the simple bedroom. I've never loved her more, and felt in the moment a sort of protective anguish.

I remember how we undressed after we were caught in the cloudburst, the languorous anticipation finally beyond either of us to sustain. Never before, or since, have I seen a woman standing completely naked. Everything of her was natural, everything of her own growth and body, with not one hair clip, ribbon or piece of jewellery to mark her as belonging to any time, any family or any man. Ellen would remove only necessary garments, and the casual girls would have their dress hems under their chins like eiderdowns. How neatly formed Conny is, so slim yet womanly and with no ravages of childbirth. How much fuller her breasts are when free from the constriction of clothing, and how the nipples stiffened when mouthed and fingered. She stood in my gaze and smiled, as if she knew precisely the power of such a moment, and its rarity. No doubt old Roper, that zealous Christian and classicist, would decry such revelation as a challenge to the fates, but then he never possessed such a woman as Conny.

My determination for change is not entirely selfish. Increasingly I see how marriage restricts Conny's life and denies her the choices she's entitled to. It's not just that Father's so much older, and in the foreseeable future she'll be tied to a decrepit man, but that he doesn't understand her need for intellectual challenge and cultural opportunity. Father sees music purely as a social accomplishment, and he has no comprehension of the true place of music in Conny's life. It's taken me several years, and the interpreters of my close affection and her confidences, to come to that recognition. Conny needs space and light and Father crowds those things out. All his life he has seized centre stage as his right. I don't pretend to be her equal in sensitivity, but I truly support her talents.

For some days Conny has been cast down somewhat because a Scottish woman novelist she admires has just died. Conny is like that, emotionally tied to eminent musicians and writers as if they were close friends. For myself I feel a bond only with those people I can see, talk to and touch, or have done so in the past — Mother, Kate, my cousins and Jeremy Pointer. Conny is tolerant of my talk of Mother, and of Mary. She feels sympathy for Mary as Father's practical and inadequate replacement for the first wife he loved. Mary, the half-sister, her place in the household depending on my parents' kindness. Mary, the wife of convenience and recognised as such even by the household staff, who thwarted her when they could. Mary, the unhappy tippler of wine and chlorodyne, with the pious silver cross around her neck when in society. Mother had her children as a recognised domain, Conny insists on intellectual independence, but Mary had nothing strong enough to withstand Father's natural dominance, and was completely subjugated to it. Yet she and Mother had been true companions and sisters, and I remember the happiness with which they would take baskets and hats before setting off to gather mushrooms together while there was still dew on the ground.

I surprised Mary tipsy once in the late evening when I'd returned unexpectedly from Dunedin. She'd come down from her room and was standing at the base of the stairs talking to herself. She came very close to me and looked up into my face. 'Am I really part of this family?' she asked.

'Of course,' I said. She took no comfort from it, and her hands trembled.

'I'm just Eliza's shadow,' she said.

'No, no, not at all,' I said falsely.

'I know you all laugh at me among yourselves, when I'm not there. I don't matter to anyone, not even William. I'm not in anybody's heart, you see,' and she put her hand to her mouth, before abruptly turning back up the stairs.

She must have realised that, apart from the need for someone to look after little Gladys, her former brother-in-law saw the marriage as an economic advantage, even a necessity. Not that Mary had money of her own at all, but Father needed to be married so that he could make over much of his property to her and so protect himself from possible bankruptcy if Guthrie & Larnach failed as financial troubles grew.

Only in recent years, with Conny's place in the family so important to me, have I realised the full sadness of Mary's lot. At the time of my return from England, not yet twenty, I was too preoccupied with my own grievances and prospects to give much thought to my first stepmother. She'd always been with the family, and always subordinate — the unwed sister in Eliza's household. Marriage brought no real change, and I must admit to making little effort to become close to her. She was devoted to Gladys, but the rest of us were too old to transfer our affection.

She suffered greatly from headaches and congestions and, she said, took fortified wines for medicinal purposes. Her persistent perfume after any length of time alone was alcohol, and Alice, who would not call her Mother, delighted in aping her vagueness and occasional unsteadiness. Often she needed to rest in her room, and all of us knew the reason. We showed little sympathy. 'Poor Mary,' Conny says when we talk of her, and is resolved to be a different sort of wife and woman. She's independent and will determine her life by her own decisions.

From the outside we must seem an oddly complex and entwined family, but we find ourselves where we are because of a chain of apparently unrelated decisions and varied personalities. Donny says we've all allowed ourselves to be swept along by Father's vigour and ambition, yet he's been more dependent on Father's largesse than any of us. At Oxford he assumed a life he couldn't sustain without Father's backing, and everything since has been a disappointment.

All of the Larnach past seems a long way from Queensland. There are no ghosts for Conny and me here, just opportunity. Even shopping, normally tiresome, I find a pleasure with Conny. She's so quick with her comment that ordinary things are transformed, and here in Brisbane we have no need of pretence when out together.

On Wednesday I carried parcels for her and afterwards we sat together in a tea shop, close to the wide and open doors to catch what stir there was in the air. There were starving, stiff-legged dogs in the street, and a brewery dray delivering barrels of ale. An overdressed, thin man two tables away cleared his nose by honking like a goose, while his wife looked away and repressed disgust.

Nothing around us was memorable, but we talked and laughed incognito and her foot rested against mine beneath the table. We must have glowed, I think, among all that was so ordinary.

'What is it?' she said, breaking off from raillery.

'It's just so damn special, that's all.'

'What?'

'You and me. Just being here.'

'We are special,' she said. 'Life's special.'

After such freedom I find it more difficult to accept the façade we must maintain when there are three of us. Despite Conny and Father being legally husband and wife, more and more it seems unnatural to me, and I'm almost rigid sometimes with the effort to restrain myself in his presence. His constant assumption of superior knowledge and entitlement, his lack of sensitivity, awareness even, to those things of greatest importance to Conny, his increasing conservatism, even his appearance as an old man, though I know that's no fault of his.

I still have love for Father, remember his generosity and affection to me over many years. I'm the favourite son who often took his part when Donny, Colleen or Alice rebelled against him. But now it's hard to see him as anything but an obstacle to my happiness with Conny and I'm determined he won't drag down Conny's life with his own.

Queensland is a huge colony, unspoilt and with some areas still virtually unknown. Father and I have taken trips well out of Brisbane, but I haven't enjoyed them as much as I surmised, and not just because Conny wasn't with us. The heat is terrible. I thought it might be good for the aches and pains of my old injury, but it isn't. Even on horseback I'm uncomfortable, and think fondly of riding my own Tarquin on the tracks of the Otago peninsula in the bracing air, or trotting the buggy into Dunedin.

Last month all three of us went to Caboolture by train to see the sugar cane and cotton on the flats. Father talked with people there on behalf of Wellington business friends, but wasn't impressed by what he was told. We had planned to stay the night, but the heat was unpleasant, even though it's not the hottest time of the year, so we returned on the same day, with Conny fretful and bored as night fell. The distances are immense: God knows what lies in the great heart of Australia.

I think often of the time Conny and I had in the bungalow. I did some longish walks along the ridges and Conny came with me on a shorter one along the creek. The bush was quite open, the bird noise so much louder and more discordant than at home. Each place has its own chorus, doesn't it? The soft call of doves and harsher derision of crows are Brambletye so clearly for me, and at The Camp the swishing flight of heavy wood pigeons, and the clear, pure notes of tuis and bellbirds. The garish colours of the birds and sunsets, and the bursts of mocking laughter from the kookaburras, are the strange fairground of it all at Kirri.

Ewert Noakes said that farther north there are sea-going crocodiles bigger than canoes, whole beaches covered with giant turtles, and lizards that run on their hind legs and attack horses. He knew a prospector who went far up the coast, close to Townsville, with a partner, and in the night a crocodile came from the river to the tent and dragged out his friend to the water. In the darkness he could hear the croc turning over and over, and for a while the shouts of the man, but there was nothing he could do. Conny won't go near the water after hearing the story. Camels, too, Noakes said. People use them in the desert. Surely they must have been brought here from Arab lands. I think Noakes something of a gabber, and he's a little hairy round the fetlocks, as cousin James would say.

Father says it's a very different country from the Victoria he knows, and he doesn't take much to it. If it wasn't for the heat, and Conny being all that really matters to me, I'd spend more time out of Brisbane. But a few hours with Conny alone are worth more than several days' travel in new country. At Kirri, and the times free in Brisbane, I've realised what it is to be completely happy, and focused on the present. Almost all my life, wherever I've been, some other place, time, some other company, has seemed to offer more. In the St Leonard's dormitories, or the Top Field there, in the closed shop of Dunedin business chums, or the casual acquaintance of fellow bachelors, on the fringe of those more important people enjoying my father's hospitality, I longed for some place and some person dear to me alone.

Conny doesn't like to talk about our lovemaking, though she's usually eager in her response. I think she feels the pleasure of intimacy is cheapened when expressed in words. Maybe there's suppressed guilt as well. After we are spent, she likes to lie quietly, sometimes with her eyes closed, and when she does speak, often it'll be of music, or something of her day, perhaps some observation of a friend.

Last night I had a dream of school — the first for some time to drag me back there. It was as much a suppressed recollection as a dream, but all too long ago to be sure now, and maybe the slight eroticism of it has been released by my time with Conny here in Queensland. Not much to it really, just Shillitoe's mother taking him and me to the cake shop on the esplanade of St Leonard's on Sea. Shillitoe was an unpopular junior in my house who attached himself to me in my last term, because, although equally unpopular, I was a senior. I imagine his mother thought the treat might buy whatever protection I could provide. I was aware she was a young mother, anxious for even my approval. When she leant over the table with cake her bosom pressed on my shoulder. In the dream I felt, even through her street clothes, the soft give of her flesh, and was aware of the downy hair at the nape of her neck, the fragrance she wore, and I woke aroused.

I've grown up with companions who think that sex is something women possess, and somehow you have to get it from them. Conny's revealed to me the wonder of lovemaking as a mutual gift. At the best of times with Conny I feel we are in a kind of trance, our actions quite open and deliberate as in the slow movement of one of her favourite symphonies, and quite as inevitable. All else falls away.

Eleven

I am now riding the tiger. Since our return from Queensland late last year, Dougie is insistent that he will not be parted from me for any length of time. He was distraught when William and I came up to Wellington for the '98 parliamentary sessions, and says that a way must be found for us to be together. Our time in Brisbane, so precious, may now become the reason that everything topples into chaos. I have always known that risk, but have taken it for the sake of love and fulfilment. Now I am fairly caught in the conflicting obligations to William, Dougie and myself. Dougie and William argue increasingly, and Dougie's erratic moods before we parted must arouse suspicion. Both he and I returned from Queensland with a terrible cough, and even that was an unwelcome indication to others of our closeness, though perhaps I am overly sensitive to the situation and no one else thought anything of it.

William has asked me nothing directly, and made no open accusation to Dougie, but increasingly he criticises him before me, as if daring me to take his part. I have tried to be especially supportive of William, even dutiful, not from guilt, but because I don't wish to bring on the heartache and scandal that separation in these circumstances entails. He has become more distant, rather than demanding, and his health problems continue. He has persistent catarrh and hacks phlegm in a most unpleasant manner. After New Year he had another long bout of influenza, and has lost weight and energy. His pride, I think, prevents him from facing the situation the three of us are in, and the fear too, of what confrontation may reveal. His formality is interrupted by outbursts of anger at trivial things.

A few days ago a bird flew into his study while he was at Parliament, and he returned to find his chair and desk soiled, and the bird in fluttering agitation. He scolded Molly until she was in tears, yet had previously insisted that the room be kept aired, and when I intervened, he said he would express himself as he saw fit within his own home. 'She was just doing what she thought right,' I said.

'Don't get me started on what a woman considers right,' he said. 'I might have truth to say that you'll regret.'

'I beg your pardon?' I said.

'You heard me.' It was as if he had slapped my face, and for a moment everything was unnaturally still. The customary small noises of the household and the street must have continued, but I was unaware of them. William's face was a confused study of defiance and anguish, but Molly was still standing with us, and neither of us took it further. 'It's all right, Molly,' he said, striving for control. 'I'm damnably tired from the chamber. The imbecilic clamour is becoming unbearable for me,' and he went out abruptly. Molly scurried away, embarrassed at the brief animosity between master and mistress, and I was left, sickened, in the darkening study.

On Saturday evening the Seddons and Wards came for dinner. It was the first time for weeks that William has had any inclination for company. I spent a good deal of time beforehand with Cook to ensure the right dishes, and that they were served on time. The premier takes his food seriously, and in considerable quantity. He once mentioned to me that a lukewarm dish could spoil a meal for him. Mrs Charteris lent me her Bridget, who is something of a wizard with pastry. I think he was pleased with all that was put before him: at least he said so, but William ate little and with no comment, and for once made little attempt to compete with his old friend in reminiscence or anecdote. It made me sad, although I could not show it. I have never had any intention to do him harm, only exercised the right to happiness myself. And surely William's state of mind is not entirely on my account. His financial affairs continue precarious; his health is failing, as is his political ambition.

Richard Seddon is not completely immune to the years himself. His beard is now grey and strangely at odds with the colour of his hair. Louisa has told me privately that he has a heart condition, yet continues to work long hours. If he would agree to get rid of the incompetents among his ministers, the load would be lessened, but he is suspicious of talent and has entrenched loyalty towards old supporters. Unlike William, however, he continues to feel much satisfaction in his life, and is undisputed as leader despite his notorious pomp and verbosity. But he can play to the ordinary people as a larger version of themselves, and they love him for it. Among them he is known as King Dick, and the papers and cartoonists make play with it.

As usual, after the meal I went to the piano and the others gathered to sing. Theresa Ward has a pleasant contralto voice, without the exaggerated vibrato that so many women singers affect. Seddon was enthusiastically loud, quite overpowering the other two men in one of his favourites, 'Bringing in the Sheaves'. He is not especially religious, but the tune delights him. Later, when he and I talked a little apart from the rest, he asked me how William had been feeling. He and other friends were worried about him, he said. It was on the tip of my tongue to say that a knighthood would make all fair, but thankfully I did not. Seddon said William didn't appear himself, was unusually subdued in the House and often sat quite through a full meeting of the Parliamentary Goldfields Committee, or other formal duties, without saying a word.

'I tried to persuade him to have a full medical examination with Dr Langley in Dunedin,' I said. 'But you know how stubborn he can be.'

'There's something not right,' said Seddon. 'He mustn't neglect himself. These aren't easy times for any man of enterprise, but he has an admirable Scottish endurance. Why not ask Thomas Cahill to give him a good checking over?'

'It's not always a good thing to have your best friend as your doctor, and I doubt Dr Langley would see it as professional etiquette. Thomas finds William resistant in any discussion of his health.'

'To hell with etiquette,' he said. 'What's best for him is all that matters.'

William came over with a decanter. 'We agree you need to take more care of yourself,' I said. I was aware as the two men stood close, how much smaller William was. The discrepancy seemed greater than in the past.

'Another jaunt to Queensland, do you think?' he said. 'More long nights and heat?' Was there some special meaning intended in that, or is my anxiety now colouring everything we say? His gaze slid from mine, the droop of his moustache gave that small, characteristic puff, and with one hand he smoothed what thin hair remained on his head.

'Politics exacts a cost from us all,' said Seddon. 'A day in government is more demanding than two on the diggings, eh?'

'But we were young then,' said William.

'You, me and Julius. Who would have thought that we'd be together here so many years later, and that each of us would have done considerable things for our new country? Damn, but it's a story, old friend.'

When William and the premier reminisce it sometimes seems that the political leadership of New Zealand was decided on the goldfields of Victoria. They are entitled to satisfaction in what talent and energy has brought them, but the element of self-congratulation becomes more obvious each time the tales are heard, and Dougie and I know them almost as well as our own lives. Eventually Seddon began on some other mutual acquaintance who had turned up after many years looking for favours. Normally William would enter fully into such memories, and with sufficient humorous exaggeration to hold his own against his friend, but the bounce and confidence he had when I first met him have gone.

Now he is quick to take offence, impatient and dismissive of others, subject to moods of abstraction or sudden anger. At my suggestion he had asked Basil Sievwright's daughter, Ella, to paint a portrait of him, and sent her a photograph to aid her accomplishment of it. Ella is a fine girl, if a little flighty, and with a definite talent that William Hodgkins and I have encouraged. She is studying at London's Slade School of Art, and her father receives good reports of her there. But William was dismayed by the portrait, which arrived yesterday. He claimed it showed him an old man, said he didn't want it hung, and was reluctant to pay for it. My defence of the painting on the basis of Ella's skill made him cross, and despite my best efforts I could not dissuade him from expressing his disappointment in a letter to her. In his own wounded vanity he cared little for Ella's feelings. I will, however, write to her myself, offering the excuse of his poor health and the cares of business and political life.

Thomas Hocken has decided that he will leave his great collection of books and papers to Dunedin. I thought William would be interested to talk about the decision, but he made a brusque reply that Thomas was no doubt wise, because families do not value what is bequeathed to them, and that he would have been better to husband his money earlier in life.

The outward semblance of our lives is often false. My near neighbour Charlotte Charteris was openly admiring and curious that the premier had dined with us, a not unusual occurrence, and the Wards too, who are considered among the best society to be had. The Honourable William Larnach CMG and his wife entertaining the highest in the land. Yet even as she and I talked of it, I felt the emptiness of the evening, the shadow play between husband and wife when real affection is absent. There had seemed a sardonic mockery in the gaslight gleam on the best silverware, the white and yellow flowers given by Annie and Mrs Dallow, the finest claret and champagne from the cellar, the jewels that we three ladies wore, campaign medals from our marriages. I had rather been with Dougie at The Camp, talking of some innocent triviality, while our eyes and hearts met with quite another message. Knowing the truth of my own situation increasingly makes me suspect sham in the carapace that others present. How urgently we work to create an appearance to impress our fellows, while suffering a desperation at the heart of things.

Yet I felt a sad envy of Joseph and Theresa — both younger than the rest of us, he handsome, dapper and charming, and she tall and beautiful. I like her, but in her presence I am aware of my own lack of height. None of that matters, of course: the real cause of my envy is the happiness of their marriage. Neither of them speaks of it, yet it is evident in their easy comradeship, their unaffected smiles and the consideration they show each other.

Towards the end of our evening William and Seddon had a disagreement over the latter's appointment of Harold Beauchamp to the board of the ailing Bank of New Zealand. William felt that he was being supplanted as Seddon's adviser by Beauchamp, who is connected to the premier by marriage and is also a personal friend. William had known Harold's father on the Ararat goldfields, thought him feckless, and considers Harold himself presumptuous. The exchange was smoothed over before Seddon left, but the hackles of both men had been raised. I think Seddon drew back a little because of his concern for William's state of mind.

Thomas Cahill came yesterday afternoon. The wind was so strong that a gust caught the door as Molly was admitting him and it broke a wall mirror, one of the few remaining possessions of Father's first wife, and a gift to me from Mother. 'Ah, seven years bad luck I'm afraid, Conny,' said Thomas, when I came through after Molly's shriek. William was not yet back, and we talked of Alfred Hill's violin concert and the *Sydney Bulletin* that Thomas always passes on to us. He has recently given a public talk on Irish poet Thomas Davis, and was keen for me to read him. All of this would normally have my full concentration, but most of the time now I am anxious and apprehensive.

I cannot tell if Thomas knows about Dougie and me, if William has said anything of us, but I told him I was concerned for William's health and disposition. 'I've asked him several times to come to me for examination but he keeps putting it off,' he said.

'Insist on it as a physician as well as friend,' I said. 'He's in the dumps most of the time and I can't seem to rouse him. Something's amiss. You know him best of all his friends. He needs you more than ever now — needs reassurance from both of us.'

'Money's the bugbear, I think. Money, money, how it holds so many in thrall. Worry if without it, worry to get it, worry about losing it,' he said, and then more firmly, as if making the resolution an impulse, 'I'll talk to him this evening when he comes. I was going to urge him again anyway.'

'He's sick in some way, but won't speak of it,' I said.

'You're right. I'll tackle him again. Something appears to have run down, doesn't it? Does he sleep soundly?'

'No. All snores and gasps that wake him up.'

'And you too, I imagine,' he said. 'You need to look after yourself as well.' I could have told him I lie awake each night longer than William.

'I don't know how best to help him,' I said, aware of Thomas's steady gaze.

'Stand by him as you do, I'm sure. That's best. That's what he wants from you.'

What Thomas's urging might draw from William, who knows. Maybe he will say things to his old friend that he cannot bring himself to say to me. Surely anything, though, is better than the sad tension that is between us. I am doing my best to support William in what ways I can. Rather than spending time in the shops, or with teacup chatter, as so many wives do, or with my music that is my real pleasure and centre, I have more regularly attended the parliamentary debates, sitting in the small gallery reserved for ministers' wives. He likes me to be there, and it is a public affirmation that I accept my role as wife.

Unspoken between us, I think, is the knowledge that Dougie

holds the threat of public calamity. William and I want at all costs to avoid that, even if part of that cost is a sterility at the core of our marriage. Dougie wishes to defy everything and everyone else, in a gamble for our personal happiness. He doesn't realise that love alone cannot provide all that is necessary.

When in the private gallery I spend more time reading, or with my own thoughts, than listening to the members, or talking to other wives. Most parliamentary speeches are undistinguished, and many tedious. Richard Seddon and his chief backers make the decisions in Cabinet and at private meetings well away from the floor of the House and the sessions there are often just customary exchanges, as dogs yap at each other in passing. William has never been especially noted for oratory in Parliament; he speaks seldom now. John McKenzie is rough but direct. Seddon's speech in the House has grafted and false flourishes, but on the hustings he exhibits a plebeian forcefulness and element of theatre. Timaru's William Hall-Jones, minister of justice and public works, is one I pay attention to, and not merely because he supports women's rights. Such an excellent, concise speaker, and he avoids the personal attacks so often indulged in by others. Seddon considers him the best administrator in the present Cabinet. Alfred says he would have made an excellent judge had he entered the legal profession.

There have been hundreds of bad speeches recently as some in the House attempt to stonewall the Old Age Pensions Bill introduced by the government. Seddon knows he will win in the end, and sleeps through the worst of them, a possum-skin rug over his lap and his head resting on a crimson cushion.

When I'm in the gallery I often think of my father, and how he would come home fatigued from a long sitting, yet still entertain us with tales of the most silly members and their fatuous behaviour. He was a fine, kind man and father, and I wish I had told him so more often. Perhaps, however, it is better that he is not with me. I could tell him nothing of what closes on me now, despite the trust and love we had. Like those who presently hold his place in the affairs of the colony, he will no doubt be forgotten soon enough, but I miss him hugely, especially now that all is so close to disaster. When I recall him, tears come easily. Partly they are from love of him, partly for my present predicament. When he died, it was as if a primary colour was lost to my world, and vividness did not return until I fell in love with Dougie. Annie once said she thought I married William partly to replace our father, but motivations are far more complex than that — often unclear even to ourselves.

William spends a lot of time alone now when he is home, but not in the cheerful industry that marked his time in the crowded library at The Camp, or in the Molesworth study, several years ago. It is instead a sad withdrawal. He will sit with a book, or his papers, before him, but pay them no attention. He talks mainly of the past when he does seek conversation, and I think he goes there in his mind while sitting by himself for hours. He rebuffs me if I show concern, and will no longer share with me the closest things.

The generosity of spirit he once had has largely left him and he takes others' achievements as a reflection on his own misfortunes.

Edward Cargill is a most popular choice of Dunedin mayor for this, its jubilee year, not just because his father helped to found the colony, but also because of the contribution he himself has made and the esteem in which he is held. William, who measures himself against all other men of note, begrudges him the success and claims it is due to the family name rather than talent or any conspicuous service.

The memory of Kate seems very strong in William again, almost as affecting as when we took her casket home seven years ago. He talks of her, and to her as well. One evening as I passed the study I heard him repeating her name and when I stopped at the partly open doorway, I saw him standing at the mantelpiece. He had taken her photograph down and held it close to his face, as if to kiss it, and he spoke her name over and over in the gentle voice I have not heard for a long time. The voice he used when we were first married: a voice of trust and love and promise. I did not feel able to go in to him, for that would have been hypocrisy. This is where my love for Dougie has taken me — a marriage in which my husband pours out his heart to a daughter in the grave while I stand mute and unobserved in the hall.

Even when we are together in society, William now withdraws the small attentions that used to mark his affection for me. At the John McGlashan Caledonian Concert he managed an animated voice for those of his acquaintances we met, but had in his brief replies to me only a flat, offhand tone, and when we met Cecilia he barely listened to what she and I were saying, looking past us to watch others. His marked indifference spoiled the whole evening for me, though it was largely for his pleasure that we attended. McGlashan, whom we have visited in Wellington Terrace, is originally from Elgin, and enthusiastic for Scottish music and songs, as is William. His songs, 'The Lad that Comes at E'en' and 'Ken ye the Glen', are popular here, but William was not roused by them.

In one's unhappiness the least attractive aspects of any scene, or experience, crowd to the fore, and I was conscious of the unpleasant compound smell from gas lights, face powder and the stale air of the large, insufficiently ventilated building. The potted palms in the foyer were sickly, the carpet threadbare on the stair cusps, and there seemed a vacuous silliness to people's laughter. As we were coming out of the theatre, I asked William if he had enjoyed the evening. 'No better and no worse than most I've sat through,' he said. 'At least you'll have the satisfaction of being seen to support the thing that gives you the greatest pleasure.'

'I hoped you would enjoy it. It's more your taste than mine,' I said.

'Well, it's kind of you to consider my feelings, but maybe a little late in the piece, don't you think.' The sarcasm was marked and he fidgeted with the brim of his hat.

'But I do consider you.'

'Oh, don't put yourself out. We'll rub along as well as most, I dare say,' and he went off after a cab.

His place was taken almost immediately by the clergyman who had once been my suitor. He wrinkled his face in an awkward smile, asked my opinion of the evening's entertainment and introduced me to his fiancée, a gauche, large-nosed woman obviously older than either of us. Perhaps he wished me to see that, despite my refusal of him, he had achieved someone's love. He was not to know how little feeling of superiority I feel towards anyone at this time. I was close to tears and gave way to them when later by myself at home.

My music is increasingly a refuge. Even my reading at present has that bent: a book on the life of Mendelssohn. While the colony's legislators argue about introducing a pension for the destitute, and Kruger's insolence in the Transvaal, I sit in the wives' gallery, but inhabit the halls of Leipzig and hear the string section of that orchestra.

Young Fanny Neubridge is to give private and public concerts in Auckland next month and asked me to be her accompanist. I said I could not be away for so long, but I have been playing for her in practice until she finds a suitable pianist to travel and perform with her. She sings lighter songs, rather in the manner of French soprano Antoinette Trebelli, who visited here two years ago, and whose 'Penso' from Tosti, and 'Song of Solveig' by Greig, were wonderfully rendered. Fanny has given recitals in Melbourne and Sydney as well as here. Her soprano is true, but she will benefit from further tuition if the right teacher can be found. It is to her advantage, also, that she is an attractive woman not yet thirty, and married to a husband of means who is quite easy that their small son is given over to the nursemaid.

Because Fanny knows little of my circumstances, I find her company a relief from politics and family concerns. Her confidences are so free and innocent, her life so lacking in complication, her marriage so straightforward and her interest so centred on herself that I find myself almost relaxed during the two mornings each week she comes to sing.

I hear little except formalities from my Dunedin friends. Bessie allows long interludes before she answers my letters, and when she does reply there is scant of the old warmth and humour. She must know the situation, and is silently alarmed and disapproving. I miss our closeness a great deal, for I have few such friends, but I understand the cause. Ethel Morley continues to correspond in her typically flippant and wry manner. As her own marriage is unhappy, perhaps she has a greater feeling for what has happened to me, but I cannot broach it with her, or even Annie.

William Hodgkins died just a few months ago, and that has added to the gloom I feel. I am unhappy here, yet strangely not eager to return to The Camp, even to my own dearest Dougie. Nowhere is there solace, or escape.

Two days ago I received a letter postmarked from the south. It was a most unpleasant shock to read, as it damned me for things that are true, and for incest and unnaturalness that are not. 'God will not be mocked,' it said. 'Wanton pleasures of the flesh lead to a moral pigsty, no matter how grand and superior you like to think yourself.' It was signed, 'An honest Presbyterian', and must have been written by someone known to me, because there was mention of two functions we attended, and the hotel in Palmerston where Dougie and I once met was also named. I must face now the realisation that rumour and slander are abroad concerning us. Almost as painful is the self-righteous glee apparent in those who have found us out. Such people will never be persuaded of the purity of our feelings. I burnt the letter immediately after reading it, and will say nothing of it to Dougie, but the taint of it seems with me still.

Twice before leaving Dunedin, I told Dougie that it must stop, but could not maintain my conviction. His misery and mine were insupportable, and surely love denied becomes a sort of poison for the soul. Yet the tension is palpable, and the agony is growing for all of us. A commitment to love, I now realise, means giving up control of one's life in so many ways. The prize is the greatest a man or woman can hope for, but the price for some is everything they have. In the night I lie awake and wonder how it has come to this. How I, accustomed to comment on the foolishness of other women, find myself caught in a situation that would delight a gothic novelist. When I do sleep, it is to wake with only the briefest serenity before the persistent anxiety returns. How will it end, how will it all end, is the growing pulse behind all my thoughts. Sometimes I wish I had Dougie's dreams, no matter what their content.

Last night a memory returned that was almost a vision. Months ago Dougie and I were coming back to The Camp after I had been to the dressmaker's, and he to a birthday lunch for Hugo Isaac, who was shortly to be married. Hugo is pleasant company, but I fear somewhat for his bride. He is younger than Dougie, very selfish and drinks a good deal. He affects superiority, and, like Robert, talks of his wish to go 'home' to England, although he has never lived there.

There was a sea fog through Macandrew Bay that grew so thick we soon could not see the road at all, and Dougie got down and led the horse forward. The fog seemed to turn our own voices and the noise of horse and buggy back on ourselves. Dougie held the horse's bridle close to its head and walked on, turning occasionally to grin, or make light of the situation. Even his smile was difficult to make out, but in a way the fog was a comfort. It made a world of our own: just Dougie and me with all the rest of life blocked out. The strange privacy and intimacy of it on a public road, Dougie guiding us home and the fog conjuring moving walls around us. Something half realised brought me close to tears then, and did so completely in recollection last night. I so love my Dougie, despite all.

Twelve

Conny's gone and it's not to be borne. Life is hellish without her. She feels she must be in Wellington while Father's there and Parliament's in session. I tell her that the wives of many other representatives aren't always in the capital with their husbands, but I think she sees her presence with him as a way of avoiding resolution. Father's realised that Conny and I have an attachment that goes beyond family friendship, although he's perhaps not aware of its full nature. He's made no open challenge to either of us, not even made mention of any incident, or suspicion, from our time in Queensland, but Conny fears what she terms exposure, and has become determined to maintain appearances at all costs, to play the dutiful wife. Father takes increasing satisfaction in scathing comments on my inability to work financial miracles at The Camp, and the frustration I feel at being so much tied to the telephone office.

He and I seem barely able to stand each other's company. We argue, we ignore, or avoid, each other. The disagreements are apparently trivial enough but they represent something sadly wrong between us. I understand that his financial affairs continue to go very badly, that political life disappoints him and that he's uncertain of his wife, but still I find myself unable to bear his comments and manner without retaliation. Even the billiard room has become a place of ill grace and sour competition, rather than companionship and frank conversation. We seldom play, and if we do it's with constraint between us and bare civility. His habit of standing close beside me when I'm lining up a shot is an irritation now. I see in it an unpleasant element of gamesmanship.

We no longer ride together, and go separately with our own friends to the Taieri races. We used to seek out tobaccos on our travels to bring back to each other: unusual brands and aromas that we would talk about. Often he brought back a pipe for me from his trips: most of unusual shape, or odd material. It was an insignificant enough connection, but in itself spoke of affection we left unsaid. That's over also now.

One evening at dinner, in Conny's presence, and shortly before they went north, he reprimanded me for leaving young Walter in charge of the telephone office for much of the day. 'Gallivanting around when there's a job to be done,' he said, 'as if we don't employ enough people as it is.' Conny tried to divert the conversation by talking of Walter's scholastic abilities, but I wasn't going to be unfairly put down, and in front of her.

'Most of the morning I was working on farm accounts with

Patrick,' I said, 'and in the afternoon I looked over the yearling bulls, sorting for the sale. You said you'd come, remember, but you obviously forgot. However, the job's as good as done now.'

'I had papers from Wellington,' said Father, 'and anyway, I'll go down when I've time and check for the sale.'

'Then I've wasted my time if you follow and go over every decision I make here.'

'You'd have done better to stay in the office. Boylan said you went off riding in the afternoon.'

'So I did,' I said, 'but only after I'd seen to the cattle. I'm not going to spend all my days sitting in the damned telephone office taking calls at threepence a time. A monkey could do it.'

'Perhaps I had that in mind,' he said with humourless smile.

And so it went on, until Conny broke in and said she'd leave the table unless the argument stopped. The bitterness continued, however, and later that evening he and I continued to slash at each other in the library. 'Dougie,' he said, 'if you don't like what I provide for you here, out of my resources, then you're welcome to strike out on your own. Go on and show us all what a clever chap you are, so superior to the rest of us that working is beneath you. Go and stay with Alice in Naseby. Skip to Argentina with your flash Harry friends.'

'It'd be a damn sight happier anywhere but here, that's for certain. Do you ever bother to think why none of the others come here unless they have to? Even Gladys prefers to be with Alice, or her friends. This bloody great stone pile on the hill has more ghosts than living family in it. You've driven us out and it will end up an empty and lonely place. Donny says . . .'

But Father raised a hand as if shooing away disagreement. 'Donny says. Donny says. A lot of rubbish is what Donny says, and all of you still come with your hand out, though, don't you. You're not too proud for that. You're full of talk,' he said. 'I've done too much for you all and you'll never amount to anything. Had it too easy too long. You and Donny have lived in a namby-pamby world. You'd have been eaten alive in Ararat.'

'I could've struck out on my own, but you asked me to run things here when you went back into politics, and promised me the place in the end.'

'Things change though, see, and they're often not as we would have them. Don't look to me for a soft life any more. It's every man for himself now, you must understand that. Anyway, leave me alone, I've work to do.' He turned away deliberately to give attention to his desk, just as he would when dismissing someone in his employ, and I almost smacked his silly head.

All that keeps me at The Camp is Conny, yet she is the fundamental, unspoken thing in our dispute. As we argued I looked at his flushed face with its ugly twitches and felt a sort of loathing. This petulant old man is no longer my father.

Anger, love, despair are all jumbled now, and have made me restless. I can't concentrate on anything for long apart from Conny and our predicament, and find myself roaming, driven to any movement as if to escape the stalemate. I look forward to meals as a distraction, but when I'm at the table I can't wait to be finished; I begin conversations, and wish them over before the other person has fully replied. I drink eagerly and find no consolation in it. Alone at night I think of her, picture us making love, she wide-eyed and with her face flushed as when she's sitting astride me. When I'm about the properties with Patrick, I feel disconnected from the farms and people once so vital to me, so much in my thoughts and plans. Patrick has noticed it, I'm sure. He's made no complaint, but we're not as familiar with each other as before, and he goes ahead and makes most day-to-day decisions without bothering me.

At night I go up to the tower, or out into the grounds where there are shadows set firm by the moon, or flitting because of the wind, and sometimes all is dark and only the trees talk in the night, and the morepork. I know the grounds so well I can walk them in the least light, and often go far down the track towards the sea. The knowledge that I will meet no one at such an hour is a safeguard, and the physical act of walking a relief. I talk to myself, and to Conny as if she were with me, and hear myself make noises that aren't words, strange expressions wrung from the tortured mind.

On other nights I stand outside the big house and look up at Conny's room. I haven't been so miserable since my school days at St Leonard's. Conny and I have had such times, such love, and now she is gone again. Until now, I never understood that two people can so grow into each other that it's a sort of death to part.

All my other friendships have suffered, even that with Robert. Less than a week ago he rode out to The Camp, appearing without warning at the telephone office. I hadn't seen him, except briefly at the club, for a long time. He wore his riding clothes and a bowler hat. 'I'm supposed to be working too,' he said, slumped in his typical way in the only other chair, 'but what the hell. It'll all be the same in a hundred years.' A professed part of Robert's philosophy is that nothing has as much significance in the present as we give it, because it will have none in the future. It's a sort of cynicism that prevents him from achieving what he could with his considerable abilities, yet part of what makes him entertaining company — sometimes frivolous and other times piercingly perceptive. Had Conny and I not come together, Robert would have continued my closest friend. In his own way I know he's concerned for me.

He made a knee with his left leg and put his hat on it, drumming his fingers on the taut fabric. 'So what's going on,?' he said. 'You've gone away to some odd place in your head, and you won't let anyone in.'

'It's Conny.' It came out before I made a conscious decision to be honest. Came out because I felt so alone, and knew Robert cared above mere curiosity.

'Of course it's Conny. But it's been Conny, Conny, Conny for a long time now, so what's different?'

'This time I can't bear her being in Wellington.'

'You should've married one of the Cargill girls,' said Robert, 'then the combined dynasty would have controlled Dunedin's business almost totally, and had all of society nodding respectfully before it. Those daughters weren't so rigidly Presbyterian that their knees couldn't be parted. Margaret even married a Catholic, and that put the cat among the pigeons. I would've loved to have heard old Edward's prayers before he sanctioned that.'

'It's not funny,' I said.

'But it is funny in a way, watching what a fellow will do when he's really hooked, hard hooked and nothing else matters.'

'You've known for a while, I guess.'

Robert looked at me levelly, then gave a brief, tight smile. 'Don't feel sorry for yourself, boyo,' he said. 'You'll bear it because there's no other way. No other way for you, or Conny. It's always a woman, isn't it, and you find yourself in the damn jaws of something. You'll bear it because you must, and if you're lucky, and hold your nerve, it'll all blow over with nothing more than gossip and rumour left — nothing to permanently harm any of you. Get your horse, for Christ's sake, man, and let's have a ride. Let's get out of this place and into the fresh air, and when we come back we'll find some good stuff of your old man's to drink.'

We did ride, and we drank, played billiards and talked. I enjoyed all, and he stayed the night, but even that could provide only a temporary distraction. Whatever Robert says, there must be another way. The situation is both intolerable and dishonest. Conny's been physically sick sometimes because of it, and Father's by turns cold, irritable and cutting. I must be with Conny yet she can't be here and Father resists my visits to Wellington. I'll have it out with the old man whatever the consequences. I won't give her up.

Conny and I had a frightful argument two days before they left for Wellington. All three of us had gone down to the Stars and Stripes field late in the afternoon. Father and I had decided to sell two of the carriage horses and a young Clydesdale, and Mr Simmond from Dunedin, who deals in them, had come out. He's a canny man and someone to be watched. Once he tried to chisel extra payment by claiming for feed before he sold on, but I stood up to him. I know a first-class heavy draught can fetch thirty pounds or more, good hacks and carriage horses between fifteen and twenty, and spring-cart sorts somewhat less. We stood beneath the archway of whalebones at the entrance while Boylan brought the horses up. The great bleached bones were strangely pitted and porous, and the heavy wire through the bored holes at the apex much rusted.

I remember the excitement when the bones were erected all those years ago, Donny and I eager to help, and Father and the men using the wagon as a work station. What enthusiasm Father had for the venture then, but on this much later day he stood hunched by the bones, showing little interest in anything around him. Once we had many horses of all sorts, and Father knew them all, but there are fewer now, and he spends little time with them.

Conny was cold and soon eager to return to The Camp. Father and Mr Simmond went into the field to inspect the animals and as we waited for a price to be settled, I told Conny I couldn't stand the thought of her leaving for Wellington, and that we had to plan for a future together, no matter what that entailed. She flinched visibly; her face became even more pale. I put my hand out to her but she turned away slightly. 'Be quiet. How can you think of starting to talk about that here,' she said, 'with William only a few yards away. You aren't the only one with feelings, the only one suffering, or with so much at stake.' I told her that it seemed she'd been avoiding any opportunity for us to talk before she travelled north and that we mustn't part without reaching some decision for our future. 'After the meal then,' she said. 'We can talk in the drawing room when he goes to his study. Not here in this cold, open place. Not like this. Not with him standing there.'

A stiff wind from the inlet sea, over the dark bush and fluffing the long grasses. Conny and I have often been happy at the Stars and Stripes field, but not then. She was a slight figure despite her full outdoor dress and long green coat, and she hugged herself and lifted her shoulders to create warmth. I wondered if she wished we'd never come together, but what's done has to be accepted, and the true unhappiness is to let go of love.

Father and Simmond finished haggling. In earlier years Father would happily have sought my opinion, but now we do nothing together. If he's been bettered by the dealer that's his lookout. They walked back to the gate and Simmond made some polite comments to Conny before beginning his ride back to Dunedin. The three of us had no conversation once he left, except for Father saying Conny would've been better not to have come. For the first time the great arching whalebones seemed to me a folly rather than a sign of optimism and allegiance to the place.

At the table that evening Father grumbled about Gladys's reluctance to spend time at home, her giddy friends and his disappointment at the progress she'd made at the convent. He'd several times written to the mother prioress to point out deficiencies in the teaching, and his disappointed expectations. It's all in the past, and Gladys now almost twenty, but it's become a habit with him to worry at old bait. We had to listen yet again as he wondered bitterly who had poisoned his two favourite Newfoundlands, Stella and Shelly, when he'd had them with him during a stay at Windsor, near Melbourne, more than a decade ago. Who cares about such things so far in the past? What possible use in brooding on them now? So much of what he says is just drivel.

Quite soon Father did go to the study. He was to have a meeting with Basil Sievwright the next morning to discuss business here before leaving for Wellington. I asked if he wanted me to be there as well, but he said I'd have plenty to do when he was away, with running the property and the telephone office. Father knows I despise my menial function there, and often mentions it as a way of gaining perverse satisfaction.

Conny went to the music room, not the drawing room, and I followed. We sat far from the door so that no one standing behind it could possibly overhear our conversation. Such precautions have become almost second nature for us. She knew what my insistence was to be, and would've turned it aside if she could, but I was determined to be heard.

'So you just go to Wellington then, after all we shared and did in Brisbane?' I said. 'We've little enough time here, and apart we have nothing. Fear and guilt are going to spoil everything. For Christ's sake, we've got to tell him and get it over with.'

'How as his wife can I not go? He already knows how much we want to be together, suspects more probably, and this is surely a sort of test. If I stay here when he wants me with him in Wellington, it's an admission of what he senses, and we'll all be caught up in a tumult of blame and shame.'

'I don't care,' I said. 'In fact I want him to realise the truth, that the marriage is a sham, that you and I are going to leave together.

That he's never deserved you anyway.'

'Oh, Dougie, Dougie. You've no idea of all that would follow: the heartache, the difficulties, the guilt. You don't realise, do you? So much in our lives would be disconnected at a stroke. Our families have given us position and comfort we take for granted. Everything would let go, and we'd be pariahs. Can't you see that, for goodness' sake?'

'I don't care. It must be done. Come on, come on, admit it.'

'It's rash and stupid not to care,' she said, 'and it's not your decision alone anyway. Everything depends on care, enormous care. One mistake and everything will be carried away helter skelter.'

I do care. More than anything else I want us to be happy. The bond between Conny and me will be even stronger because of the sacrifice we've made to achieve it. Separation from Conny will bring Father temporary pain, but they've already drawn apart in private. Continuing the marriage won't bring them any closer, and will mean lifelong agony for us.

As I spoke, Conny sat very upright, hands folded in her lap with conscious calm. How trim, lovely and resolute she was, even in the midst of argument, and not afraid to meet my gaze. Other women grow heavy, but Conny remains youthful. 'It has to be done,' I told her. 'My God, it just does.'

'Destroy him publicly, and we'll bring everything down,' she said. 'Even what's between you and me.'

'He's a tough old man. He's survived the loss of two wives already, and he'll cope with the separation from you. He needs only himself as the centre of the world.'

'You don't really think that, Dougie. He's not well. You know that. He's not well, and he's worried about money, and he's disappointed about almost everything in his life.'

'Nothing's going to change that.'

'Maybe not for the better, but it can for the worse. Anyway,' she said, 'if you really want to be honest, let's admit we need him. How in heaven can we get by in any bearable way if we leave The Camp? What money or prospects have we got without him? Some horrid life in a dreary town with you working for some inferior man in business, and I teaching music to schoolgirls. I get sick thinking about it.'

'It won't come to that, and anyway we'd be together.'

'I'm his wife and you're his son.'

I was angry with her then. She sees me as dependent on Father, fails to understand that it's only her presence that keeps me tied to The Camp. I could make my own way in the world, and will, if only she'll come with me. 'You're afraid,' I told her. 'With all your high talk of the rights of women to have an equal education, votes and lives of their own, you're scared. You won't give up the advantages of being the wife to a husband you don't love. You're afraid, and that makes a coward of me too.'

'I'm afraid because I know more. It's so much more difficult for a woman — so much harder to recover any position, or respectability, once it's lost. Better for us to take happiness when we can and not threaten what we have.'

'It's not enough. He's got to be told.'

'Don't you dare,' she said. 'Not now. Nothing's to be said to him,' and when I kept arguing, she moved to the piano stool and began playing. Sullivan it was, and when I came and put my hand on her arm to prevent her playing, she shrugged me off and continued. Had we been alone in the house I may well have shouted at her, or forced her to stop, but I had to stand apart a little, angry and bewildered. Conny's so clever at controlling a situation, so accustomed to starting or finishing a conversation when she wishes, or deciding what will be talked about.

We love each other, without a doubt, but we can't agree on how we live with that love. The pain of our disagreement is all the greater because we're so close, and I recognise that my anger is more despair and longing than any wish to hurt her. I leant towards her. 'We mustn't fight,' I said. 'Not you and me. Dear Jesus, we've only got each other.'

'We must accept what's possible,' she said, ceasing to play, but leaving her hands on the keys, fingers moving slightly in agitation. 'You can be such a fool about some things.'

'And that's all I am to you. A fool?'

'I love you, but you're not always right. That's what I mean.'

'You just don't want to see it.'

'I don't ever want to see what it leads to, and that's clear to me in a dreadful way.'

'There must be some way out,' I said. 'Somehow we must be together.'

'But just not now. Not now when William has put me to the test.'

I could see she was on the point of tears and said no more.

So we parted that evening, and again two days later when she and Father took the steamer to Wellington, with things not right between us. Our kiss to the cheek was formal, and her eyes were down. She can't quite bring herself to let go of one life and seize the other. Despite all her intelligence and independence she still can't do that, so I must make it inevitable for both our sakes.

The night she and the old man went north, I had a dream — a release from the turmoil I experience. I was a boy again, before we all left for England in '78, before Brambletye and St Leonard's, before I grew up and realised that Father has his share of very human failings, before I had any understanding, or fear, of the power of death and love in one's life.

He and I were standing on the cobbles of the stable yard while a groom took the saddles from our horses. The sky was clear blue and the wind from the sea was cool on my sweaty riding trousers. The boy was about my own age, with long, straw hair and thin, bare arms, the skin of which seemed laid directly to the bone. He looked like a Lefroy, though I don't recall we ever employed one of that family in the stables. He was clumsy with the girth strap of my horse, causing it to shy, but Father said nothing until we had walked beyond earshot, and the boy had led the horses away. He held one hand as a shade for his eyes in the slant sun of evening.

'You could've been him,' he said, 'living a life of trivial service. Birth for you and me has been a happy accident, an opportunity to show our mettle to the world. A good start, what a lucky thing it is, but then again a man can do almost anything with pluck and endeavour. Remember that.'

In the dream I had no reply, for he was suddenly my father

of old. He stood looking at me with a smile that bushed out his moustache. The blue of the sky and the green of the trees were presences, not merely colours, and leaves scuttled on the cobbles. 'Eh?' he said, but I still had no answer, just the powerful sense of him. His hand was still raised, resembling a salute, and then he reached out with it and gave me the slight squeeze above my elbow that was his typical sign of affection. 'Never mind, Dougie boy, never mind,' he said finally. 'All's well.' And I woke with tears on my face.

Thirteen

Wednesday the 12th of October 1898 was the day hell burst upon me. William has killed himself. Things rage in my mind and I struggle to survive. Everything is sucked into the whirlpool. I cry out against what has happened, but cannot change it, and know I must bear some responsibility for the agony that drove him to this. I grieve for the husband I once admired and was close to, and feel anger that he has taken the weak man's way out.

It was just another evening in the lives of most people, but the end for William, and for me too in a real way. Every day marks some cataclysm for people somewhere in the world, yet presents a benign countenance to all the others.

In my mind's eye I see the coloured window on the staircase of The Camp, with the cat and the motto that William chose for the Larnachs — Sans Peur, without fear. What irony and sadness that he did not have the courage to face what life has brought the three of us, and now lies dead with a bullet in his brain.

There were signs, of course, and I did my best to show William I would not desert him. He had forbidden Dougie to come to Wellington, claiming that The Camp and Otago business matters were being neglected, although he allowed only limited collaboration between Dougie and Basil Sievwright. There was a desolation in the struggle between father and son, and no solution that could fit us all. Several times over the weekend before, I thought William was about to accuse me directly of being in love with Dougie. He asked me if I'd received any letters from him that might have interesting news, and on the Sunday morning he twice wandered into the room I was in, seemed as if he was about to say something of consequence and then went away without doing so. I learnt later that on the same day he asked John Costall at the parliamentary library if there were any suspicions that his mail was being tampered with. It was surely the letter from Dougie he was expecting.

When we were changing for the evening meal, he stood behind me at the mirror for a time and watched our reflections as I brushed my hair. In the last few months he had become much thinner, and the spark so typical of him quite gone. Even his voice was unusually subdued and hollow with disillusion. 'We should have travelled more,' he said. 'Instead of just Parliament and The Camp, we should have gone to places fresh for both of us. We needed more that was just between ourselves. I realise that now.'

'Maybe, but there's never time,' I said. 'Politics and business matters always crowd each other in your life.' And had they not, would it have made any difference? Would Dougie and I not have found each other anyway?

'Business has tides that go out and in. If you hold your nerve you'll be all right, but if others panic then everyone can be dragged down. I haven't been treated well, even by Seddon, but my value's less to him now. Anyway, family is more important. I know you understand that.' He waited a while, as if hoping for a reply, but what answer could I make that was sincere? Then he left without saying more, and at the table spoke only briefly about blocked guttering at the front of the house, said that we had forgotten to send birthday greetings to his sister and that Thomas might be with us later that night.

On Tuesday he was particularly despondent and I told him I would put off the practice arrangements I had made with Fanny and sit in the gallery. 'You'll see and hear nothing that you haven't experienced before,' he said flatly.

'But we'll be aware of each other,' I said.

'Which one of us will gain most from that?' William was looking at me with a strange intentness, and I was unsure of his meaning.

'Don't you want me to come then?'

'If you think it your place to be there, and want to be there,' he said.

He didn't return home for lunch, or dinner, and Molly said he had left no message. In the evening I sat in the gallery until long after they had returned from supper. William looked up only occasionally. He took no part in the debate.

He didn't come home that night, and again there was no message. There had been occasional times before when he had slept at the club — if he had been particularly busy, or needed to attend some late-night haggle to be ready for a political foray the next day. But I knew, this time, that something was wrong, some dipping down of spirits that was both immensely sad and impossible for either of us to prevent. I hardly slept at all and spent the time in the blue velvet chair by the window, wrapped in a rug and watching the leaping shadows of the shrubs in the windy darkness of the garden. My own voice seemed to be in the skirl of the wind. Everything was being hurried on and unravelled: nothing could be retrieved, and I was sad and helpless.

When William did not appear on Wednesday for lunch or dinner, I sent a message to Alfred asking him to go to Parliament and find him. I had not the courage to go myself. What he had to tell me on his eventual return I would have given my life to undo. The shock was great, but it was not altogether a surprise. After being away for a long time, Alfred returned hatless and agitated to tell me William had been found dead in one of the committee rooms. 'He's shot himself in the head, Conny. My God, what a thing it is.' I told him I couldn't bear to hear the details. 'No, no, I understand. It's beyond belief. I've sent someone to tell Annie and she'll be here soon to be with you. Seddon himself wishes to come and see you tonight. As soon as Annie arrives, I'll go back to Parliament. Seddon was called out at 9 p.m. and given the news. He's gone back to the debating chamber to inform the House and ask the Speaker for an immediate adjournment. What an awful public business it will all become, but we'll protect you.'

He gave me a quick, tight hug, then guided me to the sofa and sat down beside me.

'The Otago family need to be told as soon as possible,' I said.

'Of course, yes, but best everything be done with despatch: the inquest and the funeral, all the farewells. The sooner it's over the less gossip will be encouraged. William wasn't well — that's really all people need to understand. Overwork and that damned business with the banks. There's no doubt in my mind that's behind it. Anything else is unhelpful speculation.'

'Can something so terrible be so clear?'

'Be careful, Conny,' he said. 'All William has left now is reputation. Everything else is private to us in the family.'

'Meaning?' I said, but he wouldn't meet my eye.

'That it's our grief, that's all. Nothing to do with an inquisitive public. God, what an awful thing. To be driven so hard beyond endurance that there's no other way.'

I was unable to reply. Anything I might say seemed inadequate and false. How sad and desperate poor William must have been, and with no one he could turn to. Even as we lived together over the last few days, this terrible decision must have been on his mind. As he looked at me across the table, perhaps he imagined lifting the pistol to his forehead.

When Alfred and Richard Seddon later came back to the house, Thomas Cahill was with them, and Annie met them and brought them through to me. With awkward gallantry the premier put his arm around my shoulders, before a word was spoken, and kissed my cheek. His sorrow and shock were manifestly genuine, and I was surprised at the pleasure I took in that, even in my own turmoil. The pleasure was not for myself, but for William, who would never feel it. Increasingly he had considered himself inadequately appreciated by his friend, but Seddon's sincere affection was clearly evident that night. Several times even his robust voice shook as we talked quietly in the room where so often William had laughed with us all. 'My resources are available to you,' he said. 'It's the least we can do. I've been talking with Alfred, and we've agreed the inquest will be held as quickly as possible, probably tomorrow. Nothing is achieved by a long police investigation in such a sad case. In the House tomorrow I shall speak of William's contribution to the country and our close friendship for many years. Some members have already said they wish the opportunity to record their appreciation.'

I imagine I thanked him. I do remember for some reason how his beard rustled on his waistcoat as he spoke, and the discomforted face of my brother over his shoulder. I would have liked the opportunity to talk to Thomas alone — he was closest to William and most likely to know the truth of his death — but Seddon was to the fore as ever. Thomas did give a word of real comfort as they were leaving. 'There was no suffering whatsoever, I can swear to that,' and he took my hand with a brief pressure. Often he had enthralled us with stories of the macabre deaths he had been called to, and now William himself was added to the list. Yet I cling to Thomas's assurance that William's death was instantaneous. He was the closest of William's friends, and very much shaken despite his professional experience with such tragedies.

Grief's immediate effect is often a deadening of response, I think. I experienced that when Father died, and now again I find myself sad and shocked, but also oddly distanced, so that in the midst of company my attention will be momentarily caught by an ornament askew, the flight of a bird, or scuff marks on my shoes. My vision has been affected: things alter suddenly in perspective, so that objects near to me suddenly recede and those at a distance rear up for a moment.

Annie is closest to me of all my sisters, and being unmarried she is able to stay with me, even sleeping with me when I'm at my lowest. Not that I have been able to sleep much. In the night more than the day I have sudden fits of vomiting, and even when there is no food to come up the paroxysm causes considerable pain. I find when lying, or sitting, that suddenly my legs will start an involuntary twitching. Now that William has gone, the things I most admired in him are fresh in my mind, and the grievances and disappointments of more recent times fade somewhat. I meant him no harm. No harm. I can swear to that.

Dougie left The Camp as soon as he had news, and is with us here, but we manage little time together. He is involved with the arrangements to take William home to Dunedin on the *Hinemoa*, just as we took poor Kate's casket some years ago. Alfred dislikes us being in public together. Dougie did come to see me as soon as he arrived in Wellington. Naturally he was agitated and upset, yet still trying to give me support. There was a strange reserve between us, even though we were alone in the drawing room, almost as if

William still stood between us. Dougie kept asking about his father's personal papers at the time of his death and the whereabouts of his attaché case. When I told him that Alfred had brought it back to the house, he insisted on being allowed to see it.

I knew then that Dougie had written the letter to his father that I had feared and vehemently opposed. I brought the case from the study: worn, brown leather and brass catches speckled with age. Dougie rummaged through it, half turned away, but took nothing. 'Is there anything else?' he asked. 'No envelopes in his pockets?'

'You told him,' I said. 'After all you promised, you told him.'

Dougie was shaking, but he didn't reply for a time, then tried to take my hands in his. 'All I wanted was to act in an honourable way and to be able to be with you. By Christ, I swear to that,' he said finally.

The pendulum of one's life must sometime pass the lowest point, and in that moment, with dear, foolish Dougie weeping silently beside me, I knew I had reached the nadir. Despite the sunlight through the large window and quietness in the house, there seemed a wind roar in the distance and a grimace on the outlines of the furniture. My stomach knotted, but would not allow the relief of regurgitation. This awful time is where love and life have led us. It must be faced, not denied. The buggy rides Dougie and I took to and from Dunedin and about the new roads of the peninsula, the times together at the piano, the glances exchanged when in tiresome company, the assignations in the big house and more occasionally here, the wonderful naked freedom in Kirri, the support and loyalty one to another, were all steps on the way to William's death, though in none of it was there intention to do harm. What responsibility does one have for the decisions of others? Dougie need not have written to his father as a challenge to the marriage: William's response was not in character if he had been in full health and financially secure.

But reason is as yet no consolation: everything shakes about me. My mind veers from a crushing guilt that induces suicidal thoughts of my own, to the conviction that all I have done is fall in love, and love is the best of human emotions. The nights are the worst. My thoughts are most accusing then, and most irrational. That dreadful feeling that there is no light anywhere, no way out, and all is down, down, down, into the pit. Sometimes Annie, sleeping beside me, seems to take on the larger, inert form of William, and sometimes that of Dougie. Sometimes they talk to me, and my refusal to reply is the only denial I can make to their apparition. Dougie is the dreamer, and I rarely so, but now worse things appear.

All this is the swirling, emotional consequence of grief, I tell myself, and will pass with acceptance of William's death. Now that he is gone, it is his earlier self that I remember best: William as he was when first he came to our house as friend of my father's, his openness and admiration in courtship of me, the pleasure he took in my companionship when we were first married, especially in society. 'I am the envy of every man I meet,' he would say gallantly. I remember his generosity, his optimism, his great love for his children. I remember that when the carriage overturned in the river during our return from Lawrence, his only concern was to ensure my safety. I remember the gifts he would bring me and, even more, the pleasure he took in my singing and playing. I remember the confidences early in our marriage, in which I glimpsed the natural man. That is the William Larnach to be upheld, and the man eulogised in the debating chamber by his colleagues.

Alfred said the premier was greatly affected, and asked the members not to judge their brother, as all had seen his health was failing. He called William genial and imperious — the man with a master mind, and Captain Russell, leader of the Opposition, said he was ever kindly, courageous and cheery. Alfred, who greatly fears a scandal, was relieved by how it all went off.

Those members too, however, were speaking of a William Larnach glossed with the attributes of his prime, while we who were closest to him know what sad decline there had been. Our home, our marriage, had not been happy for many months, and there were more causes of that than just Dougie and me. I believe now that the greatest mistake I made was not loving Dougie, but agreeing to wed William nearly eight years ago. I married him because I admired his achievement and was flattered by his attention. I married him to get away from a house of a widowed mother and spinster sisters, and because I had pretensions to live on a larger scale, and ambitions to be useful in the wider world.

I understand at last that it may be a perfectly sensible thing for a woman to marry without love, but not before she has experienced it. The realisation is of no value to me now. William is dead. Without him I cannot live in the same house as Dougie, and for the sake of appearances Alfred is pressing me to leave the colony immediately the funeral is over. It is a grim irony that the letter sent by Dougie with the intent to allow us to be together has made the very thing impossible.

So I lie here, Annie innocent by my side, and watch the dim shadows of the long bedroom drapes, and pale moonlight strips where they don't quite meet, like unlit candles. William is dead by his own hand, and Dougie and I must live with that.

Fourteen

I was called to the telephone office early. It was Alfred, ringing to tell me that Father had shot himself at Parliament the evening before. Instantaneous death, he said, and Seddon had asked for an immediate adjournment of the House. The inquest was to be held that afternoon in the Metropolitan Hotel. Delay would only add to speculation and gossip, Alfred said, and Mr Ashcroft, the coroner, was a long-time friend of Father's who would ensure that proceedings were discreet. Everyone knew Father had been in failing health, Alfred insisted, and the whole thing was a terrible tragedy that no one could have foreseen. I felt Alfred was coaching me for my reaction, but all I cared for was the chance to speak to Conny. She was too overcome to talk to me, Alfred said, and anyway she was not with him. He warned me that both families would be under scrutiny because of the event, and that our behaviour and demeanour must be appropriate. I told him I would pass the awful news to Donny and my sisters, and leave for Wellington that day if possible.

Alfred and I have never been friends, and he resents the closeness between his sister and me. He's full of his profession and public awareness as a former mayor of the city, and proud of the de Bathe Brandon name. As his father was, he's a director of the Australian Mutual Provident Society, and he enjoys to strut in uniform as captain of the Wellington Rifle Volunteers. In his opinion I'm of little account and have achieved nothing of significance by my own efforts or talent. I know he'll do his utmost to prevent Conny and me being together.

At first, however, I was too bowled over to think of any of that. Father's always occupied a huge part in our lives, while we struggled somewhat for breathing space, and now suddenly he's gone. I left the telephone office and walked into the trees he had planted on the south side. Boylan was exercising three of the carriage horses on the track, and we talked briefly of an order for dry feed, and other trivialities, while I tried to keep my emotions to myself. He seemed not to notice the tears I could feel on my face, and went off with the animals, cheerfully enquiring after Father and Conny and saying that a small whale had been washed up at Broad Bay.

I gave the news to those who had to be told, but requested no one come to The Camp, then prepared to catch the steamer. I asked our people to gather before midday and told them of Father's death, with as little as possible of the circumstances. Jane was the most obviously affected. She put her hands to her hair, shook her head as if assailed by a swarm of bees, and sobbed. Of all the servants she is the longest serving, and remembers Father so genial and generous in happier times. The Camp fell silent after the news was known. It seemed I was the only person in the big house: the staff avoided the family rooms as if afraid they might meet me and have no adequate response.

I found myself drawn to the library and the master bedroom: the two places that most strongly summon Father's presence. So much that was personal to him was in those rooms, and like poor Jane, I felt tears start. The incidental and trivial things were the hardest to bear: a photograph of Father and Professor Black taken by a rough stream when he was touring mining sites. Although not included in it, I was there, pulling a face that accounted for their smiles. 'The wind will change,' the professor had said. How strong the memory of Father alive, how difficult and painful to realise him dead. His tobacco bowl stood within hand's reach of his favourite chair, darkest wood with a band of carved leaves around its middle. How often when we talked there did I see his hand rest on it, or quest within, seeking fodder for his pipe. How often after dinner would I go with him and male guests to the library and see him settle with pleasure in his chair, ready for the chinwag in which he'd be supreme.

In his bedroom the matching double-barrelled pistols always on the side table to remind him of the swashbuckling goldfields days he loved to talk about, when he slept with the bank's money, and firearms, by his side. And also there in Father's bedroom a photograph of Conny on her wedding day. Such things are now both mockery and accusation. His high, old-fashioned bed close to the big windows, through which he could see his beloved panorama of sea and hills when he awoke, and his property all around.

After a hurried and careless packing, I went up to the tower and stood there alone, looking over the gardens, trees and beyond to the shifting shimmer of the sea. There was little wind, but the air was cool and carried clearly the coughing of sheep and the challenge of one of the Alderney bulls. I felt as alone and forlorn as often I had at St Leonard's. Everything surrounding me was utterly familiar, yet how indifferent and unchanging it seemed. All that had happened there over the years — the building of the house and setting out of the grounds, François's homeland songs, Donny and I setting ambushes amid the trees, the weekend parties and visits by people of note, or presumption, Mother's walks with us when we small, and mine with Conny years later when we were in love — washed off, and Father dead in Wellington and lost to everything.

Thankfully much of the boat trip was in darkness. I locked my cabin and talked to no one. I lay in my bunk partly dressed and swayed with the motion of the swell, drifting sometimes into a fitful sleep from which I woke myself with jolts of realisation and half-sobs. How trite is the saying that life may become a nightmare, yet I've experienced it. On disembarking, I was amazed and somehow angry that the other passengers could laugh and complain at trivialities, greet those waiting as if nothing in the world had changed.

I know by heart the letter I sent to Father: so many times I'd phrased it in my mind and rewritten it in his study. 'It is the only honest and manly way for us to act in all of this. You and I must give Conny the freedom to choose between us.' When I received the news of his death, my great hope was the letter hadn't arrived and so played no part. Once in Wellington, however, I soon knew that wasn't the case. Alfred and Richard Seddon had made close enquiries and Alfred took some satisfaction in telling me what they knew. Even before I had a chance to see Conny, he insisted we talk alone.

On the day he died, Father had collected the afternoon mail at Parliament and the librarian observed how agitated he was about one of the letters. He wrote an immediate reply and asked the librarian to ensure it would catch the next mail to Dunedin.

I asked Alfred what had happened to the letter Father received. 'None was found as far as I know,' he said, 'and what point would be served by speculating? William was desperately unwell and his finances a shambles, as you know.'

'But to shoot himself?'

'Who knows the level of anyone's endurance,' he said. 'Bankruptcy can't have been far off, and he was ill besides. Everyone says so, even the premier. Nothing's to be gained by poking and prying. My advice is to say as little as possible, especially to the newspapers.'

Alfred is a cool customer and difficult to read. It's impossible for me to confide in him. I think he may have the letter, keeping it as a weapon to use against Conny and me if he needs to. Maybe I do him an injustice; maybe Father destroyed my letter as soon as read. Whether it still exists or not, whether it will do me harm in the future, I must live with the understanding that he received it only hours before his suicide. I have given instructions in The Camp that any letter to me in my father's handwriting should on no account be given to any other person, and I've asked Basil Sievwright to ensure the same for correspondence that may come through him.

Had I fully realised Father's frame of mind at the time, I wouldn't have sent the letter. I still believe it was the right thing to do, but not just then. Had we been living in the same city, no doubt I would have seen how low he had become. My guilt and remorse is at the timing, not the nature, of what I told him.

The inquest returned a verdict of suicide while temporarily insane. I'm told the jury did not even retire to deliberate. Thomas Cahill said he'd noticed a considerable deterioration in Father's health in recent months, and had been pressing him to have an examination, but he refused. Thomas suspected heart disease and depression, he told the inquiry. If he had, then as both friend and doctor he should have done a damn sight more than he did.

I loved Father greatly when I was a boy, and never ceased to love him, despite the deterioration he suffered and the circumstances between us. We were all happiest when Mother was alive: things went downhill after that. When I packed for Wellington, I took a photograph from Father's room. It was taken in San Francisco in 1878 when he was colonial treasurer and we were on our way to London, all of us, including Aunt Mary, except that Donny was already at Oxford and Gladys unborn. Now Mother, Mary, dear Kate and Father, too, are dead. In the photograph he leans easily on the striped back of Mother's chair, with his fob watch and chain across his waistcoat. Pater familias. All then was confidence and optimism and generosity. To the young, tubby photographer, whose manner Father later aped before us, he talked enthusiastically of the Californian goldfields he'd heard so much about when he was young. And he went to those Californian places and talked to me of his own years on the goldfields as he explored the old sites. 'All manner of men follow gold, Dougie,' he told me. 'Every human behaviour is to be seen on the diggings.'

I can't believe he's dead, although since Mother's passing he seemed to become accident prone, always getting knocked about one way or another, but expecting the strength and resilience he had as a young man to last for ever. The times moved against him too. Financial speculation has not worn well over the last decade or so, but Father couldn't give up the practices that made him one of the colony's richest men by the end of the seventies. In the end I think he realised there was no going back. If he couldn't maintain the life he had striven for and attained, he refused to continue a lesser one.

The letter, though, was sent and received. I must live with that. I should have come up to Wellington and told him face to face, for maybe that way we could have got through without this awfulness, but it's no use thinking of such things now, and Conny would've been there to persuade me to let things lie — and lie it was.

Everything's a sad muddle, and I have little opportunity to spend time alone with Conny: Alfred or Annie seem always to be with her, and acquaintances with pining condolences often call. The premier has been helpful in organising for Father's body to travel back by steamer to Dunedin and I've been trying to settle the arrangements for the funeral there. It will be an occasion for pomp and ceremony, with ostentatious attendance by many of those who disputed with Father during his life.

I see better now how great was Mother's influence within our family, though overshadowed at the time by Father's exuberant confidence. Since her death a centre has been lost and all of us pursue our selfish interests. Father's marriages to Aunt Mary and Conny served to make the dissolution more marked, more painful. Conny, though blameless, has suffered much because of that. Maybe she and I can come out of it all into the light. That chance is what I cling to.

It was the day after my arrival in Wellington before I was able to talk to Conny alone for any length of time. Annie had gone home to see her family and I said Conny and I needed to talk about the funeral arrangements. It was a warm, bright afternoon, and she and I sat on the wisteria seat in the garden, she in mourning dress and I also in sober clothes. Her brown eyes seemed larger than ever, her face thinner. At a little distance she could pass for a schoolgirl, so slight is her figure. I especially noticed the smallness of her hands, the pale wrists barely thicker than the ivory shaft of a riding crop.

Despite everything between us, we couldn't at first venture onto the most important concerns, but talked of events and planning and people who'd sent condolences, or come in person, and all the time, although even to hold hands was denied us, we yearned for the comfort of an embrace. Only we two fully understand; only we have all our happiness at risk. Our real world is a small universe of two, although so often forced apart, and other people move like mannequins around us.

'Will you be able to keep The Camp?' Conny asked.

'The lawyers can't find anything in writing. When we get back home I'll make a thorough search for a will.'

'Alfred found nothing here, but I'm willing to testify to William's intention that the place be yours. Alfred says that if he died intestate then a third of everything will go to me, and the rest be divided among you all.'

'It's not that simple. The others will come against us, I'm afraid,' I told her. 'Donny won't arrive from Australia in time for the funeral, but soon after that he, Colleen and Alice will set the legal dogs on us, I'm sure.'

'I'm not sure I understand,' said Conny. I could see she found it distasteful to be picking over the family inheritance so soon after Father's death.

'When he married Mary, he made over his estate to her to protect himself in case of bankruptcy, and when she died so unexpectedly he found himself without control over his own affairs, because Mary, in turn, had made us children her beneficiaries.'

'Well, you're family so surely you'll benefit from that.'

But nothing of Father's affairs is ever simple, as Conny should know. 'Soon after Mary's death he had us each sign a deed relinquishing our interest. He never explained the true significance of it, just that it gave him back the right to collect rents. I never questioned him. Donny told me that Father went up to Auckland with a copy of the deed for him to sign, and gave his word of honour that it contained nothing to his disadvantage, so Donny signed it without reading. Now they'll contest the deed to keep you from getting anything at all.'

'And did he deliberately hoodwink you all?' A small, blue butterfly was jiggling between us and Conny waved it away vigorously. I wanted to reach out and clasp her wrist, and kiss it.

'I suppose he saw it as merely reclaiming what was his, but yes, there was something underhand about it. God knows he was desperate about money by then. I only care that you get what you're entitled to.'

'I hate it all,' Conny said, shaking her head fiercely. 'It feels so sordid to talk about possessions before William is buried. He has no debt to me, and I won't pretend otherwise. I can't bear to think of the manner of his death, and it's all there, the blood and the agony, for everyone to gloat over in the papers.'

'It's not our fault,' I said, more to give her reassurance than from conviction. 'Not at all your fault, and you must believe that absolutely. Everyone knows how sick and unhappy he was, and how distraught about his affairs. And if it is somebody's fault then it's mine. You never wanted to tell him. In the end, though, it would all have come out just the same. I'm convinced of that. None of us could have carried on much longer as it was.'

Conny didn't reply. She made a small fist around a lace hand-kerchief but didn't cry. It was warm in the garden and the walls gave privacy from the street. Molly, who was always about the house, or other servants, could have seen us from the windows, but there was no impropriety. A widow and her stepson talking on a garden seat, and nothing to show there was agony of love greater than the agony of grief. 'Whatever happens,' I said, 'we'll find a way to be together.'

'I don't think there is a way. Not for us to ever live together here in this country. Maybe nowhere.'

'Don't say it. Don't think it. Later we can go some place where no one has heard of William Larnach, or us, and we can be just two people together.'

'It's your dream, isn't it.'

'I hope to God it's yours too,' I said.

'But so much stands in the way of dreams. Just being in love doesn't solve everything that comes against one in life. Being in love isn't always a justification, or a reprieve.'

I'm not sure what Conny meant by that, but I wasn't going to spoil what few minutes we managed together by argument. That quiet meeting in the garden is the best we've had since Father died. She's right that, until he's buried, he should be given the prime place one last time. We sat silently together for a little, but with sympathy for each other, and she reached out and touched the silver cufflinks set with blue stones that were her birthday gift to me. 'You do wear them always,' she said.

'Ever to remind me of you,' I said. 'I still feel the same.'

Conny remained quiet for a time, then she took my hand for a moment. 'And so do I,' she said.

Conny and I haven't slept together since Father's death, and not because of the difficulty in finding opportunity. I miss the closeness, the fierce pleasure, the reassurance, but she has a fastidious sense of appropriateness. When everything has become calm, I'll find a way for us to be together as it should be. I know that as I know nothing else. We have been through too much not to finally have some benefit of Father's terrible act.

He was in despair concerning his finances, whatever else troubled him. My conscience may not be entirely clear, but I, too, can sincerely grieve.

At present I can't settle to anything. I find myself rising from bed or chair, or excusing myself from casual company, to walk the Wellington streets as if that allows me to escape the sudden waves of despair that threaten to overwhelm me. I'm in the pit: slaughtered, as Father would say. Grief, and guilt too perhaps, have caused despondency, and also a strange anger that has no immediate object or release. I swear aloud when by myself, or burst into tears. Last night I heard Mother's voice. 'It's not true. It's not true,' she said. There was no image in the dream, if that's what it was, but her voice as I knew it, and I woke in agony of longing and recognition. Where in the mind is the voice of a lost mother held, and what truth can it speak?

Fifteen

Despite spring it is cold here at The Camp, as it has been so often during the time I have spent on the peninsula. I am looking from the high observation window across the lawns and gardens towards the harbour, and mist is blurring the native bush beyond The Camp. Strange that it might be almost the last time I have this vista. The day after tomorrow Annie and I leave to begin our trip to England, as Alfred has insisted. It is difficult not to feel I leave in some disgrace, at least as far as the two families are concerned, though Dougie and Annie, the best of both, remain totally supportive. Alfred, with his maidenish fear of gossip, wants Dougie and me as far apart as possible in the aftermath of William's death.. That led first to a raging disagreement between them, and then an almost total lack of communication. Although I have no wish to go, I do see the benefit of a temporary separation and have tried to convince

Dougie that restraint now might work to our advantage in the end.

The wind is quickening and the mist also, some seeming snagged in the treetops and shredding away. It is quite certain and natural that the same wind will always return, and I shall not be here, not in the end be anywhere. Quite certain, but unimaginable all the same. Whatever the mass of evidence against it, we all secretly believe the world begins and ends with us.

The last few days have been an appalling strain for us both. I have suffered vomiting bouts again and cannot sleep. In a sense I have endured two funerals. The first was in Wellington, where Seddon and the entire ministry, and many members of both legislative houses besides, accompanied the coffin procession from the Metropolitan Hotel to the railway wharf where the *Hinemoa* was moored. Annie kept close to me, and Doris too, until we boarded. Both were of my bridal party on that day of gaiety and promise, and it has all come to this. We sailed at three in the afternoon and were a small, sad group for the long hours of the voyage, during which Dougie and I were never alone.

When the *Hinemoa* arrived in Dunedin with William's body, there were crowds at the wharf. No doubt, for many people, the funeral was a spectacle and entertainment to fill their day. Seamen carried the coffin to the hearse, which was drawn by William's own carriage horses, and the procession made its dreary way to the Northern Cemetery. Dougie, Alfred and Walter Inder led those walking behind the hearse; Alice, Colleen and Gladys were with me in the mourning coach. Donald had not then arrived from Melbourne. Alice and Colleen remain hostile to me, but Gladys has been kind. She is not greatly forthcoming, but I sense sympathy, and we have at times been able to give each other more than just public comfort. Only twenty years old, and already she has lost both mother and father. Almost as unfortunate, she has grown up in a family of increasing unhappiness. She is the only one of Dougie's immediate family who shows any support for us and will, I think, take his side in the looming squabble for inheritance. Never has she questioned me about the relationship with her brother, though I have no doubt her sisters have done their best to turn her against me. I wish she had spent more time with us during my marriage with William, whatever extra scrutiny that may have meant, and I sincerely hope the future is good to her.

All the leading Otago families were represented at the funeral, even those who had withdrawn invitations from me in recent years, and selected men from among William's peninsula tenants and workers were the pall bearers. Basil Sievwright was especially sensitive in his behaviour. He had close dealings with William for many years, and knew how difficult he had become towards the end of his life; had indeed suffered, like us, his unjustified criticism and impatience. Bessie Hocken and Ethel Morley also proved true friends: Bessie came and stood with me as the coffin was carried from the hearse to the ostentatious family mausoleum where Eliza, Mary and Kate already lie. Then and there I made a pledge to myself that I would never join his women in that place. Bessie has withdrawn intimacy over recent times, disapproving of my closeness to Dougie, but she was generous with comfort then, realising my desolation. And Ethel, a picture as ever, stood close and gave me a cluster of daffodils from her garden, where we have often sat and shared views on everything from colonial goose to the poetry of Tennyson.

William would have approved of the pomp and circumstance of his funeral: he would have regarded it as a sign of the respect people had for him, and his place in the history of the colony. And to an extent it was. The Reverend Hewitson took the service, yet I thought how much I would have preferred dear dead Dr Stuart, and Edward Cargill, the mayor, laid a special wreath from the miners of Kumara and spoke generously of William's contribution, while white clouds tumbled in the sky and people shifted about at the back of the crowd to obtain a better view. I experienced again that odd sense of disengagement that is a safety mechanism of the emotions. The sight of the coffin reminded me of the discussion Dougie and I had had concerning its composition. He said his father would have wanted kauri, because of the importance of that timber when William was in business as a partner in Guthrie & Larnach. He had insisted on heart kauri for the splendid main gates of The Camp. High above the cemetery, with wings unmoving, was an albatross, as if an envoy from the peninsula. I distinctly heard Mrs Reginald Preece complain to the woman alongside that she had stood on her hem. No doubt that will be her lasting impression of the occasion.

Dougie told me later that sadder for him than any eulogy was the sight of old Traveller, William's favourite buggy horse, in the hearse team. The animal seemed downcast, he said, as if realising the loss of his master. Since William's death, Dougie has not criticised his father, despite the difficulties between them. He talks mainly of how things were years ago, when the family were together and all seemed set fair.

I am going away because it is prudent and Alfred demands it, but I will come back, and I know Dougie will be waiting. I am not afraid to stay, but I shall be pleased not to be here when the ugly competition for William's diminished assets begins. I seek nothing from William now. Both the Wellington house and The Camp have been well searched and no will found, and none is held by solicitors. Nor has there been any sign of the letter William gave the librarian for the southern post on the day he died. Dougie has cause to conceal it, but he has told me he has received no mail from his father. My intuition, and hope, is that Basil Sievwright intercepted it and destroyed it unopened. I find him a caring man, as well as prudent. My prayer is that I will never know what William wrote about the three of us before he went into the committee room and locked the door.

By leaving I also avoid the continuing heaped detail in the newspapers concerning William's death. Columns overflow with accounts of the inquest, the witness reports, the observations of friends and associates, the speculation of those who pander to the morbid pleasure of their readers. Nothing, it seems, is to be reserved for private knowledge and grief: there are accounts of William's agitation on receiving the southern mail on the day of his death, even a description, from those who found him, of the blood that had dripped from his head onto his collar.

I have received a great many comforting letters expressing

sympathy and praising William. A few vile ones too, referring to me, that I read no more of once I perceived their drift. People of all stations have come to The Camp to tell me of the part William played in their lives, and I see through their eyes those attributes that drew me to him first of all — the vigour, unselfishness and sense of fair play; the intelligence and resolution. An elderly stonemason appeared just days ago and wished to pay his respects. He wouldn't enter the house, even by the servants' door, but stood outside with his cap off, fingering his bushy eyebrows, to tell me how, during the construction of The Camp, William gave the workmen a whisky each morning, and on the completion of the building presented each of them with a patent lever watch and chain. He held his out to me with pride. On it was inscribed 'A souvenir for good and faithful work at The Camp for W.J.M. Larnach 1876'.

Two days and I will be gone for many months. I have a premonition I will not return to The Camp: not again ascend the lion steps as mistress, welcome guests to the gracious drawing room and imposing dining room, never look down on the magnificent hanging staircase spiralling into the depths of floors beneath — a polished whirlpool of art and craft. No longer sit by myself playing the grand piano while dusk gathers in flounces among the gardens and trees outside. Never again relax in one of the verandah cane chairs and watch the rainbow hues stream in through the coloured glass panels as Dougie tells me of a dream.

I have not yet begun to pack, and have even less enthusiasm than usual for the task. Most of my dresses will have to be left, and I will gather and secure all my personal things so that they are not pawed over in my rooms while I am away. Donald, Colleen and Alice will all unite against poor Dougie, I can see, and despite William's promises he will be driven from The Camp. He will face their hatred, and the satisfied gossip of all those who take an interest in the fall of the Larnachs. And I will not be with him for support and consolation.

Mrs Oswald Harman, who has a square dinner set as her claim to fame, inflicted her company on me yesterday, a presumption arising because she chances to be taking the same ship to England. Her husband is a lawyer, but is better known for adultery than professional diligence. She rattled on about the oddity in William's failure to make a testament and offered platitudes. Things always happen for a reason, she said, and God's plan is revealed in time. There is no God, but what she says is half true. There is a reason for everything, but it lies in the past, not the future.

I shall be a nobody in England, and happy to be so. The name Larnach will create no interest whatsoever. Dear Annie will be with me for company. We will live quite decorously, I imagine, and be patronised by our relatives as colonials. My financial dependence on Alfred, at least in the short term, will be almost complete, yet to escape that was one of the reasons for my marriage. Little turns out the way we wish, or expect. I am determined to advance my music in England, taking advantage of the opportunity to hear first-rate artists, and I am equally determined to take some part in the suffragette movement there. In that respect New Zealand shows the way splendidly to the home country and I have knowledge of the manner in which the franchise was won here. As long as I have access to a piano in tune, I am not entirely alone. Unlike Annie I am not religious; unlike Dougie I feel no sustaining closeness to nature and animals: music is my faith and consolation, and I must be true to it.

And Dougie will wait for my return. I have no doubt of that. His devotion, which has driven us to the place in which we find ourselves, will be constant. What form of contact, what continuance of love, we will have I cannot tell, but he will be there, and we will have time together.

I doubt, however, that we will ever be together again here. I will always have special memories of The Camp. This is where I fell in love for the first time, and Dougie also, I believe, but there are too many ghosts in the big house now. It will always be William's house: Dougie and I must find a place outside his shadow.

Gladys and I cleared William's wardrobes yesterday. It was a painful task, but not one I could leave to any of the servants, even Jane, out of respect for him. Many of his clothes evoked memories for me, some I had chosen in his presence, all carried to greater or lesser degree his own smell. Had Gladys not been with me to keep up a brave conversation, I would have been in tears. What could be more personal than a man's smell, which lingers even after death. None of the clothes will be given away, and when they are burnt, that last natural taint of the body will be gone also. How sad it is, how many mixed emotions well up. Gladys and I remember the same man in different ways: such is the distinction between wife and daughter.

When even his clothes are gone, William's presence at The

Camp will be strong, however, for he shaped it so much with his vision and personality. It doesn't matter who else may own it, or live in it, what use it may be put to, it is William Larnach's house. Only the grand piano I hope to have made my own, so that the keys will always remember my touch, and the dark, burnished wood hold a faint image of my face to intrigue someone a hundred years from now.

There will be places in the gardens though, and on the quiet peninsula roads, where Dougie and I will always be present, and happy together. At the lookout turn he told me the original meaning of his Christian name — black water. It is unlike him to make such a study, and whenever I pass there I think of that conversation, and the particular way the breeze played in his hair as he talked, his intentness on my response. The derivation of my own name has something of irony in it now.

At the old jetty in Broad Bay he gave me a gift of pearl drop earrings as we stood looking over the water. When I asked him what was the occasion, he said the pearls were just because he loved me. The perfect answer, and it comes to me every time I pass by. He held my hand and we stood close. There was moving cloud, the strong smell of the sea, and the swell was jostling in the clusters of small, dark mussels on the piles.

The coachman's house has a confined, dark scullery, and one wet winter day Dougie suddenly drew me in there and kissed me hard against a wall. The rain was insistent on the low roof, and Dougie's face was cold, but how he wanted me. That memory too has permanence.

Once, after an unusually heavy snowfall had blanketed the lawns, Dougie and I went out before others were about and, starting from opposite sides, walked through the snow to meet in the middle. Afterwards we went to the observation room and looked down at the shadowed tracks in the otherwise unblemished white. I like to think that after future such snowfalls our prints might reappear, showing each of us coming from a different direction, meeting, and then walking away together.

Such times and places belong to us as surely as the big house does to William. Perhaps something of that happiness will remain when we have gone, to be felt by couples there who know nothing of us, but share love nevertheless.

Yesterday in the afternoon I spent hours at the piano, alone in the large music room, drawing around myself that sustaining cloak of glittering notes and spilling cadences. Last of all I played the first movement of the 'Moonlight Sonata', and although there was no critic to substantiate my opinion, I believe I captured the truth of it better than ever before. The sound seemed drifting to the high-beamed ceiling and out into the other rooms and the glassed verandah. I sat until all was quiet, then went up to the observation room, where William liked to sit with a spyglass, and I looked right over the grounds and trees of The Camp to Dunedin, and across the shifting, deep colours of the channel to the dark, bushed hills on the other side. There was beauty to it, but also, it seemed to me, a studied indifference to what people might do within its natural frame.

Wellington is where I will return, I imagine. Everything we have been through, the joys and the suffering, makes it more important that there is an outcome, a continuance, a resolution even, so events have not been in vain. 'For God's sake make sure you come back to me,' Dougie said when I told him of Alfred's decision.

Sensation and tragedy are superseded by more lurid versions of the same. All that has happened to us will be forgotten absolutely, buried in the rush of time and the fall of others' lives. Dougie's story and mine is not told in the history of William Larnach. It is our private journey, and only we understand how it came about; only we know the fitness and the wonder of it. It doesn't matter what people say, it matters only that you live fully and yet not wholly selfishly. Love is a world free of morality. No one else can judge it — or us. All of it for love. That is what I cling to, Dougie. All of it for love.

The Larnach Estate

Judgement against Douglas J. Larnach

His Honor Mr Justice Williams yesterday morning delivered judgment in the case Douglas John Larnach v. Basil Sievwright and others, which was heard in Dunedin in December last.

The plaintiff's statement that his father all along intended The Camp property to ultimately belong to him, I see no reason to doubt; but it was not his assigning his interest under the settlement to his father which prevented his father giving effect to that intention. Indeed, in order to enable Mr Larnach to give the property to the plaintiff it would have been a necessary preliminary that the children interested under the settlement should assign their interests back to their father. Whether the deeds of assignment stood or were set aside, The Camp would not belong to the plaintiff, because, whatever Mr Larnach's intentions may have been, he did not give effect to them by making a will, but died intestate . . .

It appears that until a fortnight after Mr Larnach's funeral, in October, 1898, all members of the family were on friendly terms. Then a breach took place, owing, as the plaintiff says, to Mr Solomon, who came out to The Camp with the girls, having demanded the keys. This was about Sunday, the 28th October. Then, the plaintiff says, 'I heard the next day, for the first time, they were going to try to set aside the deed . . .

'I was indignant with them for setting aside the deed. I might, before the trial, have discussed the matter with my stepmother. I went with her to Mr Woodhouse's office several times. Every time she went to see him. I knew she was interested in the defence of the actions brought by the three. I knew the law that the widow got one third if no will. I went into Mr Woodhouse's office to assist her in her defence. I had not then heard the story set up by my sisters and brother that they had been deceived by my father. I only knew they were trying to do my stepmother out of every farthing they could, and I stood by her.'

Otago Witness, *8 February 1900*

Epilogue

Conny and Dougie never again lived together at The Camp, or openly anywhere else. Conny returned from England to live with Annie at 15 Hobson Street, Wellington, next door to Alfred, who supported them financially. Dougie moved to the capital and for some years lived close to Conny at 3 Pipitea Street. All of that, however, is another story.